A Kiss So Deadly

By: Mary Reason Theriot

Dedication

A very special thank you to my parents, Don and Charlene Reason, for taking the time to go over our family history and to help in great detail with this particular book.

I also could not leave out my in-laws for taking time to help me as well. They helped me with the research of the Acadians and their travels from Nova Scotia to America, in particular to Louisiana.

Without the love and support of my family and friends, I would not have pursued this new path in life. I would especially like to thank those that have proofread copy after copy, to give me their honest opinion of the books.

Theresa, thank you so much for your continued encouragement. Without you, some of the characters would not have "come to life."

To my wonderful husband Malwen, your continued love and support mean the world to me. I do not know what I would do without you in my life. One of these nights I am sure you will be able to sleep with both eyes closed. Eventually, I should run out of ideas... or maybe not. These books would not be what they are without you pushing me forward.

To Don Reason and Malcolm "Phil" Theriot for sharing your knowledge and experience of Law Enforcement protocol.

To my fans, I would like to offer a special thank you for your continued support.

Professionally Edited by Little House of Edits and Proofed by Proofreading by Katie

ISBN-10: 1-945393-14-9
ISBN-13: 978-1-945393-14-3

Also Available by Mary Reason Theriot:

The Hideaway

The Traveler

Dr. Frankenstein

Above Suspicion

Horror in the Night

Deadly Seduction

Echoes on the Bayou

Seven Deadly Sins

A Deadly Combination

www.maryreasontheriot.com

Prologue

The Haunting of Marquette Plantation

Everything Genevieve knew and loved was here, but just out of her grasp. This was where she died, and where she would spend all eternity. However, this was not a bad place to spend eternity. Nothing compared to the beauty of Marquette Plantation, especially at night, when the moonlight rippled along the bayou.

She considered herself fortunate to watch her family prosper over the years. Despite the ravages of war, storms, and hard times, this plantation had maintained many of their traditions as well as their French language. She beamed with pride as Bridgette strived to educate people of their unique cultural identity, forged by some four centuries of turbulent history.

After all these years, it has remained a breathtaking place. Marquette Plantation was the image of everything graceful and lovely in the Deep South. Spanish moss dripped from the ancient oak trees, reminiscent of the lace curtains she had purchased so long ago.

In the serene moonlight, ground fog swirled as a light breeze rolled off the bayou. She heard the moans of the poor lost souls trapped in the silver mist as it curled its way around the courtyard. The moon had a ring around it, promising rain soon. The misty halo created an eerie glow across the grounds, bathing the area in a pale light.

Like her life, the beauty of the night had been stolen from her. All that remained was death and evil. If only she knew where the evil lurked, she could warn someone. But she only sensed its presence, heard its raspy breath, and smelled the fetid odor that came from its flesh and blood.

She sat in the courtyard, looked toward the fields, and tried to find where this evil lurked tonight.

The farmland was still just as rich and fertile. There were rows and rows of rice sprouting up. She shook her head; no, it was no longer rice but sugarcane now.

When she looked out over the land, she no longer saw its beauty, peace, and perfection. Instead, she saw the land drenched in blood. They had been fortunate during the war; their plantation had been spared. They had managed to frighten off the weary soldiers, but this was different. Whatever had found a new life here was ugly and brutal, and she was unable to scare it off. The lost souls walked around aimlessly, crying out for help. She must try to find them, to learn what happened to them.

In her vision, she saw the area strewn with dead or dying women. They did not speak; they only let out unearthly wails.

Genevieve never wanted for a thing, except not to die at such an early age. Her heart broke when Pierre married her younger sister so soon after her death. Why the sudden marriage? She understood that he could not take care of their two rowdy sons and lively daughter without help, but he swore to love her until the end of time. Still, she had a hard time forgiving him for his marriage to Amanda, and now she forever wandered the plantation in hopes of finding him in death. She had yet to find him, and she no longer knew how long she had walked these grounds. Had he moved on without her? Did he not know she was bound to this earth in search of him?

Chapter 1

The Life of Pierre and Genevieve Marquette

Pierre looked over his property with overwhelming sorrow. It was not until recently that he understood the anguish his parents must have felt when they fled their beloved home in the northwest province of France.

His family, as well as others, moved to Acadia – what is now known as Nova Scotia - and desperately tried to make a life for themselves.

Now he has found himself in their same plight. Should he stay and hope that he can keep his family safe from the mounting tensions festering here in Acadia?

England was at odds with the Acadians. The British authorities wanted to expel the Acadians to prevent any alliance with the French. A war seemed imminent between the British and the French in North America.

Late one night, Pierre and several other men met to discuss what was happening. Pierre looked at the men, "We should flee before it is too late. There is talk of our fellow Frenchmen settling in a place called Louisiana. This may be our only chance."

Jean Paul shook his head, "Non. It will be a dangerous journey, and I have a wife with child."

Henri scowled, "We may be facing far worse if we remain here."

Etienne stated, "What about the rumors that the Acadians will be exiled by the British authorities?"

Pierre feared the rumors might be true; he had money

saved, but what about their household goods?

Henri reinforced one rumor he had heard, "It has been said that everything we own must be turned over to the British. We will only be allowed to keep what we can carry on a ship. Worse, it has been said that we will not be paid for anything the British confiscate."

Jean Paul said angrily, "It is mere rumors. This cannot be true! It has to be just tongues wagging."

Pierre stated fearfully, "What will the English do once we are exiled? I do not trust them. They may deport us and send us back to France."

Late one night, Pierre woke Genevieve. "Genevieve, we must hurry." Pierre gently shook his wife awake, "There is no time to dawdle."

Genevieve groggily asked him, "What is wrong? Has something happened?"

"I will explain later, but there is no time now." Pierre handed her the clothes he had picked for her to wear, "You must get dressed so that we can go."

Genevieve shook her head in protest, "No, Pierre. It would be scandalous of me to wear britches."

"You must. Your dress and petticoats are too cumbersome for the trip we will be taking."

Knowing it would be both unwise, and futile to argue with her husband, Genevieve did as he said.

So they left with nothing but the clothes on their backs and the light of the moon to guide them. Once they knew they were safe, they made makeshift lanterns to help light their way. They waited until they were certain no one was tracking them before they traveled during the day.

When Pierre and Genevieve made it to New Orleans, Pierre learned that in other parishes, land was available for the taking.

Pierre purchased two thousand acres of untamed land to become their home.

Over the years, Marquette Plantation grew into its own small Cajun village, just like they had back in Acadia.

Chapter 2

Marquette Plantation – Present Day

Fred and Joyce Marquette were listening to an "oldies but goodies station" as they drove home from dinner. They had dropped off Bill and Judy Mayon at home already. She turned to her husband of forty-eight years, "Supper was delicious and I enjoyed our visit with Bill and Judy, but I regret not having a Mardi Gras party this year."

Fred shook his head, "We will make it up at Easter this year. Besides, it really isn't Mardi Gras without Bridgette. Perhaps we should have driven to see her this year."

"We can still do that. We can leave early in the morning and surprise her."

"Let's do it then. I've missed my baby girl."

The driver of the eighteen-wheeler did not see the oil slick on the road and lost control. As the massive vehicle lost traction, the driver honked his horn as a warning, but it was too late for anyone in his path.

The truck driver clutched the steering wheel and pounded on the brakes in an attempt to lessen the effects of the impending accident. He felt the trailer slide to the left before hitting the car. He watched in horror as the car careened through the air. He found his cell phone and called immediately for help, thankful that the road was almost deserted at this hour.

The violent collision created an ear piercing sound of crashing metal and exploding glass. The brief, panic-stricken screams echoed in the night. The immense force had reduced the vehicle involved into twisted metal, almost unrecognizable. Within minutes, the sound of sirens filled the night air.

Chapter 3

Bridgette Marquette had a long drive ahead of her, but was ready to get home. She had missed her parents and was ready to see them.

Besides, there was no way she would miss Mardi Gras in Rexma, Louisiana. Her dad loved the festivities and the promise that Easter would soon be here. While her mom had decided not to throw a Mardi Gras party this year, they could still attend the parade.

Before getting on the interstate, she stopped and purchased a venti white chocolate caramel latte for a caffeine rush and turned up the radio. She was ready for a break and some of her mom's cooking.

When Bridgette drove up to Marquette Plantation, she took in the sight in front of her. A rush of pride moved through her.

The Marquette family had owned the land since 1757. It had withstood the years, and showed the well-earned prosperity of those who worked here.

Pierre had been a determined man who refused to allow anything to come between him and his dream. Bridgette was certain that her dad inherited his stubbornness from Pierre. Her dad refused to allow anyone to tell him that he had to let his dreams die, even after multiple sclerosis attacked his body and left him disabled.

Shaking herself out of her reverie, Bridgette was surprised that her mom had not rushed outside to greet her. Perhaps they had decided to retire early tonight.

Bridgette knocked on the front door and waited. After a couple of minutes passed with no answer, Bridgette called the home phone and was surprised that there was no answer. She tried their cell phone next, but it went to voicemail.

Next, Bridgette called Delores LeBlanc, "Delores, this is Bridgette Marquette. I hate to bother you, but do you know where Mom and Dad are?"

"Oh, my dear, they went to supper with Bill and Judy Mayon."

Bridgette laughed, "Well then, that explains why they did not answer the door."

"Oh, they will be so excited to see you. Your dad has been missing you desperately this week."

"I wanted to surprise them this time, which is why I did not call."

"I don't expect them to stay gone long. But, then again, you know how your dad is when he gets to talking."

"I am going to go inside and wait. At least I can get unpacked and settled before they arrive."

Sheriff Anslum looked at the twisted metal and despised what he would have to do next. He would have to inform Bridgette Marquette that she lost not one, but both of her parents tonight.

Sheriff Anslum took out his phone and called the dispatcher, "Would you please call Delores LeBlanc for me? I need to get Bridgette Marquette's number."

"Yes, sir. I will do that for you right now."

Sheriff Anslum waited a few minutes for the dispatcher to connect the call, "Delores, this is Sheriff Anslum, I hate to bother you at this late hour, but I need Bridgette Marquette's contact information."

He heard Delores draw in a deep breath and with a shaky voice, she stated, "Bridgette called earlier to say that she was at the plantation. She is down for a surprise visit."

"Thank you, ma'am. I appreciate it."

As he drove to Marquette Plantation, he thought about what he was going to say. Bridgette had expected to surprise her parents, and instead, it was her that was going to get the shock of a lifetime.

Now he regretted not asking Delores to meet him at Marquette Plantation. The poor girl was going to need emotional support after his visit.

As he made his way to the front door, he took in the peaceful surroundings. What would become of this place now that Mr. Marquette was dead?

By the time he knocked on the door, it was three o'clock in the morning. He knocked four hard, deliberate knocks before ringing the doorbell.

A woman's voice sounded through the door, "Who is there? Delores is that you?"

He replied, "Ms. Marquette, it's Sheriff Anslum."

He stepped back as he heard the locks being turned. "Is there a problem, Sheriff?"

"I am sorry to bother you at this hour, but I have some news about your parents."

Sheriff Anslum caught a glimpse of fear dance across her eyes. Her voice quivered as she asked, "What... What happened?"

"I regret to inform you that your parents were involved in an automobile accident several hours ago."

The woman in front of him grasped the door for support, "What? What happened? Are they okay? What hospital are they in?"

"I am sorry, but they did not survive."

Bridgette let out a wail as she leaned into him for support. Tears fell from her eyes as the sobs wracked her body. Bridgette let out a sob and then another and then another until a dam of emotion broke and the tears could not be stopped.

"No!" She said, shaking her head, refusing to believe what she was told. It could not be, but it was there in his eyes.

This man that she had known for years, that her parents knew, had become the messenger of death. Horrified, she stated, "It can't be true. Not my parents."

Her knees buckled as her world exploded. She felt his strong arm catch her around the waist. The heartache was overwhelming. "Let me take you inside Bridgette."

She looked up at the sheriff, "This has to be a mistake, a horrible mistake."

Tears burned her eyes as memories of the past charged her, rattling her soul.

Chapter 4

Walking outside, the morning sun greeted Bridgette. She usually loved the colorful sunrise, but not this morning. Today, she was heavy hearted. She never thought she would bury both of her parents at the same time, but as deep as their love was for each other, perhaps it was for the best. She heard that after a loved one passed away, the remaining spouse usually died soon after.

Tears filled Bridgette's eyes as she thought of her parents. She would never be able to forget that dreadful night. A part of her told her that she should be grateful that they died on impact, but it brought her no comfort.

As she drove into Rexma, she looked around and remembered what it had been like growing up here. Rexma was a somewhat rural Louisiana town along Bayou Renee. The main street ran directly in the center of the town, with only one stop light. Tiny little stores lined the downtown; most of the businesses were family owned and operated. There was a barbershop, mechanic's shop, several restaurants, a locksmith, a butcher and meat market that had all withstood the sands of time. Several specialty boutiques opened up here as well. Even the clothing shops, bookstores, and antique stores seemed to be flourishing. The closest chain store was about a half hour drive from here, and Bridgette did not see one moving any closer, especially if the historical society had anything to say about it. At one time, Rexma had been a main hub on the bayou. Rice, sugarcane, cotton, and other agricultural products grown by local farmers for centuries were loaded on the barges and sent off to New Orleans.

This town was founded in 1753 and Bridgette's ancestors, the Marquette's, were among some of the first settlers here. Her family fled Acadia, now called Nova Scotia, and made their way down to Louisiana. Pierre Marquette knew how to farm the land and made his plantation a success; he had a green thumb and succeeded at whatever he did. From the research she did, her family never owned slaves; instead, they built a small Cajun community on the Marquette Plantation where they worked the land and kept to themselves. The plantation was self-contained, not wanting or needing help from the outside world.

Inside the funeral home, Bridgette greeted her parents' friends with a heavy heart. Marlys Landry came over and gave her a hug. "Mo chagren, I am so sorry pauvre ti bête. I still cannot believe they are gone. If you need anything at all, call me. Your parents will be dearly missed."

She squeezed Mrs. Landry's hand, "Merci. You were such a good friend to Mom."

With tears in her eyes, Mrs. Landry said, "Mais, why is it that only the good die young?"

As Bridgette was greeting her parents' friends, a striking blonde haired woman walked through the door. Bridgette's heart skipped a beat as she rushed toward the woman.

Hugging her, Bridgette said, "I can't believe it's you."

"I am so sorry for your loss. I can't believe any of this happened."

"It is all so surreal. I feel as if I am in a dream."

Bridgette took a step back and observed the woman. This woman had been her best friend in high school - her cohort in crime, so to say. "Well, I am certain my dad would be happy that his Barbie girl had come to say her goodbyes."

The corners of Barbara's lips turned upward, "Do you know, even after all this time when he saw me he called me Barbie girl."

"Once dad found something that annoyed you, even just a little, he would use that as a way to joke around with you. But, of course, he said with you it had been easy to come up with that nickname. When he saw you with that blonde hair, tall body, slimness, and the name Barbara Jenkins, it had been a no-brainer. One look at you and it reminded him of one of my Barbie dolls."

"Well, it's no longer Barbara Jenkins, it's Barbara Anderson."

"That's right; I forgot you married Hal Anderson. How's that going?"

"It's going. We have four children who keep me busy. But I love it."

"I can't see you with four children. You are the one who said you would be lucky if you had one child. Something about children, any child, would drive you nuts – that you just did not do kids."

"Yeah, that's true, but when it is your kids you don't mind - sometimes, that is. But, I happened to marry a man who loves kids, and he convinced me that we should have at least one. But after the first, I was in love, and realized that I did want a large family."

"I am so happy for you. I am surprised that you still live in town."

"Hal works offshore as a boat captain, so he works two weeks on, one week off."

"That isn't hard on you, not having him around all the time?"

"Only a person who has never been married would ask that." Laughing, "No, it doesn't bother me. I enjoy our time together, but I also enjoy his time away. I think it makes us cherish our time together more when he's gone so often."

"Well, you look great. Marriage really becomes you."

"I should let you get back to your guests, but we will catch up soon, I promise. Your dad would tell me all about your life whenever I saw him at Tommy's Place."

"Oh my goodness, I completely forgot about Tommy's Place and how that was his favorite place to eat. He used to make these little digs at mom, telling her that Tommy's Place has the best French toast."

Laughing, "That sounds like your dad. He loved to ruffle her feathers."

"Daddy did. I will miss his jokes, his humor, his ability to bring a smile to your face when you felt like your world was coming to an end."

"Well, as I recall, you have a little bit of his humor, but also some of your mom's straightforwardness."

"Yeah, I got a little bit of both of their personalities, which I've been told is a dangerous combination." Remembering back to their childhood, Bridgette stated, "But, as I recall, you can be pretty straightforward and brutally honest when you wanted to be. Even now, I never ask someone if an outfit makes me look big."

Barbie burst into laughter, "Well, it's not my fault you asked such a stupid question."

When they were teenagers, the girls were trying on jeans, trying to decide which pair they liked best. Bridgette innocently asked, "Do these jeans make my butt look big?"

Without hesitation, Barbara replied, "No, your butt makes your butt look big."

It did not matter the occasion, Barbara never held back and said exactly how she felt.

Bridgette saw Father Anthony Rabelais enter the funeral home, "Excuse me, Barbara."

Bridgette gave Barbara another hug and walked over to Father Rabelais. She was ready to put this day behind her.

Father Rabelais walked over to the coffins and asked everyone to join him in The Lord's Prayer. He performed a beautiful service full of respect for her parents. He read the standard funeral Bible verses and reminded all those attending that her parents were in a better place. At the end of the service, he asked that everyone join in the Rosary.

When it was time to move her parents to their final resting place, Bridgette knew that not too many here would be joining them. Few would want to make the three-hour drive to New Orleans. Her parents had made all of their funeral arrangements after her dad had been diagnosed with multiple sclerosis. Her mom had been adamant that she did not want to be buried in the Marquette Family Cemetery located on the plantation grounds, but in her family's mausoleum in New Orleans. Her dad eventually agreed to her requests, as long as he could be buried near her.

Bridgette followed behind the hearse as the funeral procession meandered down the streets of New Orleans. As she drove through the wrought iron gates that separated the cemetery from the rest of New Orleans, she noticed how exquisite their design was. Within this cemetery were buried some of the most famous, and infamous, citizens of New Orleans. Death played no favoritism. In the end, everyone was the same, ashes to ashes and dust to dust.

The family mausoleum was one of the older mausolea in the back of the cemetery. As they neared its location, she noticed that the manager of the cemetery was awaiting their arrival.

After parking her car, she watched as the coffins were wheeled out of the hearses and into the tiny room. Father Rabelais made his way to the front of the mausoleum, and waited to make sure that no other mourners would be joining them.

As Father Rabelais began to speak, his voice resonated in the small room. "Our Father, who art in heaven…"

The drive back to Marquette Plantation was a somber one. Childhood memories flashed through her mind as she made her way back to the plantation. It still amazed her at how time seemed to have stopped here in Rexma, Louisiana. Several houses and businesses kept their landmark status, preserving their history.

Bridgette cherished this town and especially her home. There really was no other choice for her. Without her roots and her family's heritage, she would be lost.

She was a lot more like her dad than she realized. Her Paw Paw Marquette recognized the love her dad had for this land, and left him the house when he died. Now, it would belong to her.

The sheer beauty of the drive did nothing to soothe her soul today. Right now, she craved the solitude of her new home to help console her. A whitetail deer suddenly darted across the road, dashing into the foliage on the other side. She slowed down, in case he had a friend traveling with him; deer tended to run across the road here and drivers had to be careful.

Tomorrow morning she would begin making plans. She needed to explore the plantation to see if anything had to be renovated. The funeral had been lovely, but she was glad to be home and away from the dreariness that had hovered over her since their unexpected deaths.

The tires crunched as she drove over the white oyster shells that lined the circular driveway and she stopped in front of her family home. As she stepped out of her car, a cold breeze cut right through her. Even though Easter would be here soon, there was still a chill in the air. Spring was long overdue; she was ready for winter to come to an end.

Spring was supposed to be a time for new life to come into this world, not to be taken away. Yet here she was, coming back to an empty house after her parents' sudden demise.

Flower blossoms danced in the wind and cascaded to the ground. The distinct smell of spring in the air reminded her of her childhood. The pressures of adulthood seemed like a million years away back then.

She wished the skies were gray, and the weather thunderous to match her gloomy mood. She dreaded returning to an empty house and feared this day would never end. Would she ever come to terms with her parents' death? She would miss seeing her mother run out as soon as Bridgette drove up to greet her with warm kisses and asking about her day. No matter how bad her dad felt, he always had a sparkle in his eyes and a new joke to share with her. It was still such a terrible shock to her system that she lost not one, but both of her parents. If only she could kiss them each one more time, the tears built up inside of her once again as she realized she wouldn't be able to.

During the funeral, it had become hard to keep her erratic thoughts under control. The emotions of all her parents' friends and family began to close in and smother her. It took a great deal of strength on her part not to break down in tears in front of everyone. Throughout the day, she greeted guests from around the parish as they arrived to offer their condolences. Friends, several acquaintances, and what family they had remaining also stopped by. Bridgette vaguely remembered the conversations she had over the course of the day. She had more than likely repeated herself on more than one occasion.

She heard several of the rumors floating around town lately. Not too many people had faith in her capabilities to keep this massive plantation afloat. Throughout the day, several people asked about her plans concerning the plantation. Numerous land developers had been after her dad for years to sell them the property. Her roots were here, though, and she did not foresee selling for any amount of money.

She looked at her childhood home with a forlorn expression. She knew that someday it would be hers, but she never expected it to be this soon or under these circumstances.

As she moved closer to the front door, she noticed the mess. Her heart dropped when she saw that someone had broken the windows on the French doors that lined the front porch. Her resolve weakened as she looked at the disaster. Who would do such a thing, especially today of all days?

She searched through her purse for her phone to call Sheriff Jared Anslum. He would know whom she could call to fix the broken windows.

"Sheriff Anslum, this is Bridgette Marquette. I hate to bother you, but you did say if I need anything, don't hesitate to call you. I just came back from the funeral and the front windows of the house are all broken."

Sheriff Anslum sighed into the phone, "Cher, mo chagren. I am so sorry to hear that. I will call Dwayne at Bayou Glass and have him go over there. Also, I will send Officer Graham Richard out to make a report."

She replied, "There is no reason to send an officer. My mind isn't working today and I wasn't sure who to call to repair the damage."

"Mais non, I am going to send someone out there to check things out. Have you gone inside?"

"No, sir, I have not."

"Well, it would be best to let Officer Richard go in first, just in case."

She let out a sigh, "Mais oui. Yes, sir."

Bridgette could not get over the fact that someone did this to her house. As she was about to get back in her car to wait for Officer Richard, she heard car tires on the gravel driveway. Turning to see who it was, she let out an involuntary groan. She was in no mood to deal with him. The man might be able to turn a lady's head, but something about him made her uneasy.

He was worse than a thorn in your side. Not only did he pester her parents about selling, he had not let up with her. She watched as he stepped out of his Mercedes SL500, being careful not to get dust on his Italian loafers. The man gave her the creeps, just being near him made her skin crawl.

"Ms. Marquette, I wanted to stop by and see how you are doing. I am sorry I did not make it to your parents' funeral, but unfortunately, I had some business that I needed to tend to."

Bridgette looked at the broken glass and wondered if he had something to do with this. She shook her head at the thought. He would not get his hands dirty. Mais non, he was the type of person that paid someone to do his dirty work. Although, she could see him standing on the sidelines to make sure what he paid for was done.

Bridgette took in his appearance and noticed, as always, not a strand of hair was out of place. From the bronze color of his skin, she could tell he stayed in the tanning bed more than in the actual sun. When he smiled, his white teeth were in stark contrast to his skin. Not only did he dress to perfection, but he had a physique that took hours spent in the gym to keep up. However, beneath the lovely exterior was pure ugliness on the inside. Bridgette looked Brett Gibson in the eyes, "Is there something I can do for you, Mr. Gibson?"

Brett noted the disdain that dripped from her voice, "Now Ms. Marquette, that is no way to treat someone who came to offer their condolences for your loss."

"Mr. Gibson I know the real reason you are here, and it is not to offer your condolences. My answer will be the same as my dad's answer. I have no intentions of selling or leasing my land to you so that you can drill for oil. This land is too precious to me to have it destroyed by oil rigs."

He let out an exasperated sigh, "As I explained to your father, technology has come a long way in how we drill for oil. The land won't be destroyed; you can keep the house and open up your bed and breakfast, if that is what you want, and still allow us to drill for oil."

She gave an exacerbated sigh, "No, my father was adamant about not leasing out or selling his land to the likes of you. He may be dead, but I intend to respect his wishes."

Brett Gibson stormed off to his car, slammed the door, and sped away. Officer Richard drove up while Brett drove off in a hurry and waited for the dust to settle before stepping out of his car.

Bridgette gave him a step-by-step account of what happened when she came home, also explaining how Mr. Gibson arrived just as she returned home.

Officer Richard asked, "Did he happen to ask about the broken glass?"

Letting out a long sigh, "Mais non, he never brought it up."

Officer Richard scratched his head and looked at where the retreating car went down the drive. It was strange that he did not ask about all the broken glass and offer to help. Unless, maybe he was the guilty party and wanted to judge that person's reaction to the destruction. Perhaps he should talk with Mr. Gibson and find out what he was really doing here. Ms. Marquette was not the only one he had bothered lately. Several people had filed complaints with the Sheriff's Office regarding his strong-arm tactics.

From his rearview mirror, Brett Gibson watched as Bridgette talked to the young police officer. What were they talking about? Had she somehow figured out what he had been up to behind her back?

He shook his head. No, he had been careful in hiding his tracks. She could not possibly know, could she? Still, he would keep a close eye on her.

Once Bridgette was finally alone in the house, she walked into her bedroom and plopped down on her bed. After a few minutes, she pulled herself up and walked into the bathroom. She looked at her reflection in the mirror. The stress and fatigue of the day showed on her face. Despite her resolution to stay strong, the grief over the loss of her parents became too much. Crumpling to the bathroom floor, she gave in to the tears. She allowed the tears and grief to wash over her. She felt so helpless and alone. As she sat there crying, a calming presence came over her, and she swore she felt arms wrap around her. After the last of the tears flowed, she started the shower and prepared for bed.

Tomorrow was another day, and she had a lot to do if she wanted to open a bed and breakfast soon.

Chapter 5

Bridgette woke up with the sun shining through her bedroom curtains. After yesterday, she was surprised she slept as soundly as she did. She stretched under the covers before getting up.

She peeked out her bedroom window and took in the gorgeous morning. The sky was a brilliant blue and the sun shone brightly with its rays filtering through the ancient oak trees that surrounded the property. It reminded her of delicate lace draped across the grounds. Even the bayou looked calm and peaceful this morning.

Ruefully shaking her head, she walked over to her desk and opened her laptop. She may as well see how many emails she had to answer before starting her day. As she scrolled through the list, a smile formed on her face. Her cohort in crime had sent her an email, or more specifically her best friend, Haley Garrison.

"I did not want to call or text you yesterday. I knew you had enough on your mind, but I did want to check up on you and make sure you are doing okay sweetie. Please remember if you need anything at all, I am here for you.

Don't be a stranger.

Lots of Love,

Haley"

Bridgette replied,

"It was so good to hear from you. I miss you so much, woman. I am doing so-so, but I am hanging in there. I

The email helped lighten the dark mood that hung over Bridgette. She walked into the kitchen to find Delores already busy at work. Delores had worked as the housekeeper here at the plantation for as long as Bridgette could remember.

She poured herself a cup of coffee and took a seat at the bar. "Bonjour. Good morning Delores."

The faint lines around her eyes crinkled at the corners and Delores sighed. "Bonjour, Bridgette. I understand you had a bad day yesterday. You should have called; I would have come over and helped you."

Bridgette shook her head, "You help me out too much as it is and yesterday was just as bad for you as it was for me."

Bridgette saw the tears form in Delores's eyes, "Mais, your parents meant so much to me. I am going to miss them dearly."

"I keep waiting for Mom to pop in any minute, asking me what I am up to now."

Delores wiped her hands on her apron, "This is getting us nowhere. I made you some hot biscuits and sausage gravy to go with it. You are getting too thin pauve ti bête. If you don't take care of yourself, you are going to waste away."

Bridgette let out a laugh as Delores set a piping hot plate of biscuits and gravy in front of her. Her mouth watered just looking at it, "You did not have to cook me anything. I would have been happy with a piece of toast."

"Mais, as if. You need some meat on your bones cher, and I am not the only one who thinks so."

As Bridgette took a bite of the biscuit covered with the sausage gravy, she raised an eyebrow, "What does that mean?"

Delores pointed to the dining room, "Sha bebe, you should see all the food left at your doorstep this morning. Mais, no one must have wanted to wake you this early and left it by the door."

Bridgette looked at all the food and gasped, "Mais, what am I going to do with all this food?"

Delores snickered, "You best start eating."

Chapter 6

Later that night, Bridgette found herself unable to sleep, and wandered aimlessly in the big house. She stepped gingerly across the creaky wood floors in the parlor. The eyes of one of her ancestors in the painting above the fireplace seemed to follow her every move. A noise from the second floor sent her pulse racing. Could it be one of the ghosts? She had often wondered how many spirits resided here. Were they upset at her plans for opening her house to the public?

She hoped the ghosts liked the guests that would be staying here. She knew from experience that some of the ghosts were skittish and would disappear in a flash if they realized you could see them. Others, such as Genevieve, liked to make contact with you. However, Genevieve had been restless lately. She had made her presence known more often, but she appeared almost frantic in her movements. Almost as if she was trying to tell Bridgette something. If only Bridgette could figure out what.

She walked over to the French doors that overlooked the cane fields and watched as the storm moved in. The full moon illuminated the land and created a ghostly haze that hovered over the cane fields.

She loved how the tall green stalks of cane swayed in the wind. Her heart swelled with pride at the fact that the plantation was hers and that no one in her family chose to sell it over the years.

How many times had one of her ancestors stood in this very spot and watched the wind blow? The house had remained well preserved, but with rising costs, she elected to convert it into a bed and breakfast. She did not see how she could keep the plantation running without the extra income. She knew nothing about farming and would let Mr. Robicheaux continue leasing the property. The agreement he and her dad had was a sound one and she saw no reason not to continue with it.

Everyone kept telling her that running a B&B was a monumental challenge, but she was up for it. Besides, she loved this house and would do anything humanly possible to make sure that it stayed in the family. She had such happy memories growing up here and wanted her kids to have those same memories. Of course, she needed a husband first, but she had plenty of time for that.

Marquette Plantation was one of the few plantations in the parish that had survived the civil war with barely any damage. Several other plantations had been burned down to the ground during the war. The plantations that did survive the war became lost over the years to neglect, fire, or flood. The locals were proud of the heritage and had been very generous and offered her as much help as she needed.

Over time, her parents had updated the upstairs and each room now had its own bathroom. Her mother enjoyed entertaining and did not like the fact that her guests would have to share a bathroom. As her dad's multiple sclerosis progressed, her parents renovated the downstairs, turning one section into a massive master bedroom. As renovations on the plantation continued, the electrical and plumbing were brought up to date. Thanks to her mom's love of entertaining, she had the perfect layout for a bed and breakfast. The house was fully furnished, and most of the antique furnishings were from when the house was built. Several of the mattresses upstairs need replacing with newer, more comfortable sets. Plus, the current mattress sets all had a musty smell, possibly from the rooms being closed up for so long.

Back in the day, there were no other plantations near that could equal its grandeur or its farm production. It sat at the end of a long, curvy drive flanked on both sides with ancient oak trees dripping with Spanish moss. The front of the house had three sets of French doors that graced the front porch. Framing each set of French doors were louvered shutters painted a rich ebony black. A horseshoe shaped double stairway graced the entranceway.

On the second floor, she could rent out over fifteen rooms. There was also a coach house, a stable and the old blacksmith shop that were still well preserved. Her family took great pride in making sure over the years nothing fell to neglect.

She wanted to keep the memories of this place alive for years to come. There were a few bed and breakfasts in the area, but none offered an authentic experience of living on a plantation.

Bridgette had already spoken to several people who were willing to help with the tours for a small salary along with room and board. Each of the out-buildings still had rooms attached, but they needed to be brought up to more modern standards before she offered room and board.

She was even considering the addition of a glass

blowing shop here at the plantation. That should bring in the crowds, especially if they sold items made on the plantation.

There was also an old cabin that had been used for bootlegging moonshine on the property years ago. Eventually, she wanted to restore it fully. It was nestled in a corner away from the main house, almost hidden in the swamp. It was in its own little world back there; framed by several large magnolias, cypress, and ancient oak trees shrouded with Spanish moss. Her great, great grand-pere was known as one of the most notorious bootleggers in the parish.

Several silos on the property had to be inspected structurally. When her ancestors began to farm the land, they chose to plant rice and soybeans. Some years, an increase in profits helped them through the tight times. Sugarcane farming did not start here until much later.

When the plantation was built, steamboats traveled along the bayou selling mercantile, as well as picking up the goods to bring up and down the river system. Back then, they even had to wait for the priest to come via boat to perform wedding and baptism ceremonies. The old pier was still in good condition and could be used to fish on or to enjoy the scenery.

Chapter 7

Bridgette was putting away the groceries when her phone rang, the continuous ring danced through her head as she rummaged in the great abyss known as her purse for the phone. It was only after she dumped its contents on the table that she found the blasted phone.

The unknown number made Bridgette hesitate for a moment, "Hello."

"Bridgette, it's Barbara. I was able to get your number from Delores. I hope you don't mind."

"No, not at all. I did not think of even exchanging numbers at the funeral home."

"Well, it's not like you had a lot on your mind." She said, "But, the reason I am calling, is to tell you to get dressed. I am going to come get you, and we are going to go grab some breakfast at Tommy's Place. I think French toast is in order."

Bridgette really did not feel like visiting right now, but perhaps she did need some time away from the house.

"I can meet you there. You don't have to come all the way out here."

"No, you would be saving me; I really need to get out of this house. Hal is home and he is working on some of his manly projects. He is driving me nuts, the kids are driving me crazy, and I just wanted a few hours away from the house. Besides, you need to get out of that house, and take your mind off things, as well."

"All right. All right. I'll be your excuse to break free from that madhouse you call a home then."

"I'll see you soon."

Half an hour later, Bridgette and Barbara were on their way to the little southern café, Tommy's Place.

As they pulled into the parking lot, Barbara said, "We will be lucky if we can find a parking spot, much less one up front."

Bridgette saw an opening between a large SUV and a sporty little car and pointed it out, "Look, there's one. Not exactly a front row parking spot, but it is a parking spot."

"You're making fun of me, aren't you?"

"Guilty."

Barbara shook her head as she parked the car. "Hey, I get excited even over the little things in life. I am just happy to be out of that loony bin of a house. Hal has the kids all worked up this morning about building a swing set out back. Hal, the kids, and power tools are not a good combination."

Over breakfast, the two friends laughed as they ate French toast and caught up on their lives.

Once home, Bridgette had to admit that it felt good to get out of the house and have interaction with another person.

Chapter 8

Her heart pounded in her chest as she strained to hear the noise again. Fear almost paralyzed her. Someone was following her; she was positive she heard the footsteps behind her. They echoed in the soundless night. The streets, generally bursting with life, were devoid of movement, except for the haunting footsteps.

The afternoon had been hot and muggy, but the night air had a chill. It was extremely dark out tonight. Even the moon was hidden. Fog slowly rolled in from the bayou.

She had no real reason to be afraid. Rexma was a safe town, always has been a safe town. Nothing ever happened here. Ever.

However, recently there have been some girls that went missing. **It was reported the girls perhaps fell into the bayou. So there was really no reason to be afraid.**

She looked at the shortcut through the cemetery and considered taking it. Briefly. Shaking her head, she decided it would be safer to stay on the road. It would only take fifteen minutes longer to get home. As she walked home in the dark, she wished she had not lingered so late at the bar.

There was the noise again. Someone was walking behind her. She looked around hoping to see someone else out on the street, but there was not another living soul around. She picked up her pace, hoping that when she rounded the corner there would be some sign of life. As she walked along the old historic area, she took in her surroundings. It amazed her how many times she had walked this area and never once noticed how creepy it was at night.

When she heard the footsteps again, she looked back. For a moment, she thought she saw a man not far from her, but he seemed to have vanished. She heard rumors that on foggy nights, such as this, the restless souls came out to wander the earth. A shiver snaked down her spine; ghost or not she did not like being spooked.

Jackson Street was right around the corner, and she could hear the faint sounds of life from here. Traffic whizzed by and music drifted through the night air. Once she rounded this corner, she was home free. She would not have to worry about the footsteps that seemed to be stalking her every move. She picked up her pace once again, ready to be home.

She heard the noise again. When she turned around once more, a man was standing right behind her. She went to scream, but he acted quickly to muffle any noise she made. He pulled her close to his body, dragging her into the shadows. She tried to fight back, but whatever drug he had on the rag acted fast. Her world quickly went black.

He glided the boat along the bayou and brought his newest prey to the cabin. He had stumbled upon this cabin hunting one day and from the look of the old cabin, it had not been used in years, but had remained structurally sound. Outside, it was almost entirely overgrown and inside was an old bed and an ancient moonshine still. The bayou was not far from the cabin, but hidden enough where you would not find it unless you knew its location.

It was the perfect place to perform his wildest desires. Here he could hide his true nature from the town. No one suspected what he was truly like; he had become quite good at living a double life. As he thought of what was about to come, a rush of excitement built inside of him.

He pushed the door to the cabin closed behind him and bolted the lock. He dropped the unconscious girl onto the bed and quickly restrained her.

Outside the small window, silvery moonlight illuminated the landscape. Shadows danced across the room as the wind blew.

He could pinpoint the day, hour, even the second when he decided to kill. He had done the research, knew the rules, knew what to do, knew what not to do. Fear, rules, and consequences ceased to matter. His long nurtured fantasy had become a reality. He had released the monster within.

He lovingly gazed at the restrained woman. She was still unconscious from the drugs he had administered.

He anxiously waited for her to wake up. To hear her begging. He knew from experience she would beg, cry, and plead. They all did.

Moonlight streamed in through the small windows. Eagerness turned deep inside him. He had gone too long between kills. However, he must maintain some control.

His skin tingled. His stomach clenched. His muscles ached with need. If he did not release the monster soon, he would go insane.

Bailey woke slowly, unable to focus on her surroundings. Darkness surrounded her, and there was a smell of mustiness in the air. She blinked several times, attempting to clear the fog from her mind. She tried to sit up, and panic started to set in when she found her arms and legs restrained.

She heard movement on the side of her. She began to scream when a voice stopped her, "You can scream if you must, but there is no one to hear you."

Tears flowed down her face as a sense of foreboding swept over her. She knew her time on earth had come to an end.

He looked into the young woman's eyes, and a thrill ran through him. Her eyes clearly showed fear and bewilderment. A wicked smile formed on his face. He was so glad he found this place. Here, he did not have to hurry.

Once again, he was sated. The monster lurking inside of him was fed. He followed the moonlit path leading to the cisterns. A small bead of sweat formed across his forehead even though it was cool out tonight.

Over the years, he managed to keep his existence here hidden; he hid his tracks well. Now that the owners were dead, he wondered what plans the daughter had for the old plantation. He may be able to offer her a substantial sum of money and purchase the place from her. That would keep his secret hidden forever.

Once the girl was in the cistern, he walked back to the small cabin to make sure it was secure until his next visit. Tonight went smoothly, the whole adventure effortless.

Before making his way back to the bayou, he decided to check on Bridgette Marquette. Lately, the monster inside of him demanded more of him. However, he must take it slow so that his appetite was not discovered. That would not do at all. In the next few days, he would ask Bridgette Marquette about selling this place to him. Then he could go on, indefinitely, with his plans.

On his way to Marquette Plantation, the rush hit him. Each conquest brought him a high that was better than any drug could give you.

He found the perfect vantage point to watch Bridgette as she prepared for bed. A sinister smile formed across his face as he stared through the windows. She was an extremely attractive woman. Maybe, if he could not convince her to sell the plantation, he could romance her. If he swept her off her feet and married her, then he could live here as well. It would not be hard to continue his hobbies right under her nose. All it would entail was a few sedatives in her drink at bedtime, and she would never know he left.

He strolled leisurely along the bayou as he thought about his options. He was so deep in concentration that the buzzing of the mosquitoes went unnoticed. As he headed back to his vehicle, the streetlight near where he parked his car gave the area an ethereal glow. The orange incandescence of the light reflected off the puddles of rain. He studied the area for a few minutes before unlocking his car. As usual, no one was out at this hour, so once again, his secret was safe.

Chapter 9

"Oh, Bridgette, I hate that you are moving away," wailed Haley as she hugged Bridgette goodbye. "I am afraid we're never going to see each other again."

Bridgette held back the tears, "I promise I'll keep in touch. We can text, we can call, hopefully, we can see each other sometimes." She squeezed her friend's shoulder. "After mom and dad's death, I just did not know what to do. I can't see Marquette Plantation sold to someone else, and if it stays vacant, there's no telling what would happen to it."

"I understand, it's just that I hate losing my best friend. This is such a hard time for you, and I am being the worst friend possible by being selfish. It's not that I mean to, I just don't know what I am going to do without you."

Bridgette sighed, "I feel the same way. It's a good thing we have unlimited data, and text messaging because I will be texting you a lot."

"Well, one good thing came out of this, at least we learned that Rick does have a heart. I am so glad he is going to let you work from home and keep your clients."

Bridgette nodded her head, "I am surprised, but then again Rick always thinks about money and money is something he would lose if I left."

Haley gave her friend another hug, "Enough of this sadness. This is your last weekend here and you need some me time. You have been through a lot and need to take your mind off your troubles. We need to go shopping and have a fabulous meal."

Bridgette grinned, "Shopping sounds nice, but I have so much packing to do."

Haley pushed her friend toward the door, "We can pack later, you need some pampering. First, we play, and then I will help you pack."

Bridgette had to admit a day of fun did sound better than packing. She still did not know what she was going to do with all of her belongings, but at least the condominium manager had understood her dilemma and let her give thirty-day notice. Of course, the main reason he probably let her out of her lease is that he knew he could find a new tenant in no time. This area was in high demand and he would more than likely go up on the next tenant's rent.

They were able to find some great sales and Bridgette bought several pairs of nice slacks, summer dresses, and a gorgeous wrap dress that was in the deep shade of garnet. Bridgette justified her extravagant shopping by telling herself she could wear the clothes when she greeted her guests. Besides, she needed to look good, didn't she?

They decided to eat at Riverside Inn, which overlooked the water. Bridgette's favorite had always been the crab cakes there, and it was going to be a meal she missed.

As they placed their order, Haley flirted shamelessly with the waiter. After he left, she turned her attention back to Bridgette.

"I am sorry, I couldn't help myself. He was too cute not to flirt with."

Bridgette laughed, "I am going to miss your humor most of all. You can always make me laugh, and forget my troubles."

For the rest of their meal, they talked about Haley's dating life, Bridgette's nonexistent dating life, and how bad office life was going to be without Bridgette there.

"I ate too much," Bridgette commented when they finished. "But it was so good. I am going to miss this place."

Haley stopped, "As if you have anything to worry about. I would love to eat what I wanted and not gain a pound." Haley said, giving Bridgette's figure an envious look.

"I have always had a hard time gaining weight, but my mom used to warn me that one day it would catch up to me. For now, though, I am going to enjoy food and not worry about my weight."

"Well, you're lucky, I can gain weight just by looking at food."

Bridgette woke up early, hoping to have everything packed before the moving company arrived. While she did not need her living room or dining room furniture, she did decide to keep her bedroom set. Thankfully, the moving company she hired had great suggestions on where to donate the items she would not bring to Louisiana with her.

The man had agreed to help her load what she wanted to bring with her into the moving van she had rented, and they would donate the rest of the items to a local family who was in need. While her parents' bedroom set was in great condition, Bridgette could not bear the thought of her, or anyone else, sleeping in that bed. Shaking her head, no it was better to donate that as well.

With Delores's help, Bridgette had hired someone to help her rearrange the furniture and unload the moving van when she arrived. If all went as planned, when Bridgette arrived the men should have repainted her parents' room and gotten their furniture removed. Bridgette felt bad, she feared she was taking advantage of Delores and her kindness. But there was no way she could watch her parents' furniture be removed from the house right now. Her emotions were still raw from their death.

When she drove up to the plantation, Delores rushed outside. "I was so worried about you making that drive in this huge vehicle by yourself. But I can see my worries were unnecessary."

Bridgette chuckled, "I was a little worried about driving this vehicle, but it was not that bad. But I am glad to be home."

"Well, I can't wait for you to see the room. The pale yellow gave it a nice, cheery appearance."

"I will have the guys move my furniture into mom and dad's room, but I am not ready to move in there yet. I'll stay in my current room for a little while longer."

"Of course, cher, that is totally understandable. But, at least the room will be ready whenever you are ready to move in."

Delores walked up to the front porch, opened the door, and hollered inside, "Adam and Luke, Bridgette is here with the van."

Two men walked outside and Bridgette scrutinized the men. While she was not in the habit of judging a person by their appearance, one of the men made her uneasy. However, if Delores trusted him, then he must not be all that bad.

As they moved the furniture into the house, Bridgette tried to ascertain what made her uneasy about Luke. There was something off-putting about him, but Bridgette could not pinpoint exactly what. Was it his lack of manners? The clothes he wore or perhaps just the way he stared down at the ground and never looked at anyone directly in the eyes? He was the first handyman, Jack-Of-All-Trades, as he liked to say, that wore khaki slacks and a button-down shirt to work in. Instead of a furniture mover, he looked more like a male model. But to each his own as her dad liked to say. Besides, it was a moot point. He was already here working.

Chapter 10

Bridgette woke completely refreshed in the morning. The sun shone bright and there was not a cloud in the sky. She wanted to go and check on the old cabin today. Besides, it was a perfect day for a ride on her four-wheeler.

Bridgette sat on the front porch, her hands wrapped around a cup of coffee, and watched as a blazing pink and purple painted the morning sky. As much as she enjoyed living here, she missed her parents terribly.

Delores drove up the driveway, stepped out of her car, and walked up to the front porch. "Good morning, cher."

"Morning Delores. I hope you had a good night."

"Any day that I wake up and am greeted by the morning sun, I consider it a good day."

"Would you care to join me for a cup of coffee?"

"I don't want to disturb you; you look like you were enjoying the peacefulness of the morning."

"Nonsense, come have a cup of coffee. It's a lovely morning, and we should enjoy it."

After breakfast, she headed to the barn. Trepidation crawled over her when she saw the lock to the shed cut. *Now, why would someone want to do that?* She opened the shed door, and her heart sank. All four tires on the four-wheeler were slashed. This was the second time someone had destroyed something on her property.

She took out her phone from her jeans pocket and called Officer Richard who had given her his number just in case she had any more trouble.

"Officer Richard this is Bridgette Marquette. I hate to bother you first thing in the morning, but someone broke into the shed out back and slashed all four tires on the four-wheeler."

"I'll be out there in a little bit."

"Thank you so much."

As she walked back to the house, she tried to shake off the disappointment. She had wanted to go riding and find that old cabin. It had been a long six weeks, but everything was almost ready for her to open Marquette Plantation Bed & Breakfast. Should she hold off opening up the bed & breakfast until they figured out who was doing this? She shook her head in disgust. If she did that, then she was letting whoever did this win. It was more than likely someone trying to scare her off.

It was almost an hour later before Officer Richard arrived.

"I am sorry it took so long. I needed to let Sheriff Anslum know what happened, and then we had a morning meeting that I had to attend."

Bridgette waved her hands in the air, "You are fine. There is not much that you can do. I thought you should know, since this is the second time something happened here in a few weeks.”

She escorted Officer Richard back to the shed, “This is how I found it this morning. It was easy to open the door with the lock having been cut.”

He inspected the damage before asking, “Can you think of anyone who may want to scare you off?”

She shook her head ruefully, “Not really. There are several people offering to buy the property since my parents' passing, but my parents had the same offers when they were alive. They never mentioned anything about property damage to me.”

“We have had some complaints about Brett Gibson using strong-arm tactics with some people. He’s trying to buy as much property around here as he can.”

Bridgette replied, “He has made several attempts to purchase or lease the property from me, but he hasn’t tried anything unethical. He badgers me a lot, but even Dad complained about his pestering. But he never mentioned any problems he had with the man.”

“Well, if he starts to give you any problems, let me know. As far as the tires, I will let Cliff over at the Mobile station know that you need some new ones. He can send someone out here to take care of this for you.”

“Thanks, Officer Richard. I appreciate all of your help.”

Officer Richard felt the heat crawl up his neck. Someone thanking him for doing his job was not something he often heard. If his wife saw him now, she would laugh at him. “It’s nothing. I am just doing my job.”

Chapter 11

Sheer exhaustion from today's work took a toll on Bridgette's body. After the day she had had, Bridgette needed a long, hot bath. She poured her favorite scented bubble bath under the steaming water, and lit the candles she had placed around the bathroom. The scent filled the room and she slipped into the water. She took a deep breath and exhaled. She soaked in the tub and let the suds soothe her aching muscles.

No sooner than her head hit the pillow, she drifted off into a deep slumber. Music began to play somewhere in the deep recesses of her mind. It was a slow jazz number, haunting actually. Laughter mixed in with the music as the scent of the magnolia trees drifted in from the open French doors.

She saw herself as a small child peering through spindles on the staircase. The parlor and courtyard were full of men and women dressed exquisitely, and their faces were hidden by masks. It was one of her mom's annual masquerade balls.

Suddenly, a strange sound woke Bridgette up in the middle of her dream. She bolted upright, trying to place what she heard. For a moment, it sounded like someone screaming, but she shook her head at the thought. The ghosts that wandered around the old plantation home never made noises like that. She was just letting her imagination run wild.

She prayed that when the bed and breakfast inn opened in a few short weeks, the ghosts would not rouse any of her guests from their sleep. That would not be good for business.

Tossing back the covers, she left the comfort of her bed. Parting the heavy curtains, she peered into the night. Outside, the night was bathed in an unearthly glow of shimmering moonlight. Fog rolled off the bayou; the heavy mist lingered low to the ground, creating an eerie appearance before her. Then the figure of a woman appeared. Bridgette could not place the face; she did not look familiar at all. The woman standing in the courtyard was tall with flowing blonde-auburn hair, wearing what appeared to be a long sundress of some sort. She looked up to the window and then disappeared as quickly as she appeared.

Suddenly, a chill went through her. She could not explain it, but a bone cold sensation ran through her even though the night air was humid.

Knowing she would not be able to go back to sleep, she went to the kitchen to brew herself a cup of coffee. She wondered why the ghosts had been so restless lately. In all her years of living here, they all seemed to commingle in peace.

She had a few hours before she had to leave for her meeting, so she planned to explore the attic for more treasures. Even as a child, her parents kept the history of Marquette Plantation alive. Over the years, certain pieces were retired to the attic, and she was anxious to find a few more pictures that depicted life during the Civil War.

Growing up, her mom never liked her going up there. She believed the items had been placed up there for a reason, and she did not want to disturb the harmony of the house.

As Bridgette left the attic, she was pleased with her finds. The attic had been a treasure trove of goodies. She also managed to find yet another wonderful old diary.

Later that morning, Bridgette drove into town to grab a bite to eat and attend a meeting with her parents' attorney. She was anxious to return home and read the diary. From the brief inserts she read while in the attic, it appeared to be very fascinating. Genevieve Marquette had written those particular inserts before her unfortunate death. It felt to Bridgette as if she was reliving those days through her words.

After parking her car, Bridgette walked to the restaurant. Suddenly, a feeling of loneliness overcame her. She felt lonelier than she ever felt before in her life. It never bothered her before, but for some unknown reason eating alone this afternoon weighed heavy on her mind. Perhaps she needed to find someone to share her life with after all.

To add to her misery, inside the restaurant the hostess asked her, "Table for one?"

Bridgette ruefully nodded her head, "It's just me for lunch."

The hostess grabbed a menu and showed Bridgette to her table. As Bridgette followed the young woman, she noticed how she made sure her hips swayed, wanting to catch the men's attention. Perhaps if Bridgette dressed differently, she would attract a man. Lord knew what she was doing was not working. She could not remember the last time she had captured a man's attention.

She showed Bridgette to her table and handed her a menu. "Your waitress this afternoon will be Zoe. She will be with you shortly."

Bridgette thanked her and perused the menu while she waited for the waitress. The lunch special, crab cakes with a salad, sounded perfect to her.

Glancing around the dining room, she noticed how busy they were.

A perky young girl in black dress pants and a white cotton button-down shirt made her way to the table with a cheery smile, "Good afternoon. My name is Zoe, and I will be your server today. Can I get you something to drink? Perhaps something from the bar?"

Bridgette shook her head, "Just water, please. I prefer bottled if you have it."

"Yes, ma'am, will do. Can I start you out with an appetizer as well?"

"Actually, I will just have the lunch special."

"The crab cakes here are delicious. I'll be right back with your water."

The waitress returned with her water as well as a basket of bread. She was hungrier than she realized, and the aroma was too tempting to ignore. She took a piece of the hot bread and slathered it with butter. It was a good thing she stuck with crab cakes and a salad, the bread was delicious.

The waitress arrived with her lunch before she could help herself to a second piece of bread. As she cut into one of her crab cakes, a shadow fell across the table. "Good afternoon Ms. Marquette. I saw you sitting here and thought I would drop by to say hello."

He held his hand out and, for a moment, she stared up at him. Breaking her gaze away from him, she shook his hand. An electrical charge danced up her arm from the simple contact. His long fingers reminded her of an artist's hand.

Bridgette looked up to see Marcus DuPont looking down at her. His mesmerizing eyes were framed by dark eyelashes that intensified the rich brown of his eyes. She took in a deep breath and caught a whiff of his cologne. It fit him, spicy with a hint of musk. She licked her lips, wondering if he tasted as good as he smelled.

A friction of awareness tingled along her spine. Damn, the man was good-looking. He had an astonishingly sexy smile. She waved her hand for him to take a seat, "Mr. DuPont, would you care to sit for a moment?"

A lethal grin flashed across his face, showing a hint of a dimple on his left cheek. His smile could melt even the coldest of hearts. "I am meeting clients for lunch, but I wanted to offer my condolences. I would appreciate you keeping me in mind if the plantation turns out to be more than you can handle."

"I appreciate the offer Mr. DuPont, but the plantation has been in my family for generations. It is in my blood. I don't have it in my heart to sell it. Not now, not ever."

Marcus shook her hand before leaving, "The offer stands if you ever do feel like selling."

Bridgette had to give it to the man, he was tenacious. She wondered if he had been this persistent with her parents, or did he just not have faith that she could maintain the property? He was not the only one who did not believe she could keep Marquette Plantation Bed & Breakfast going. She would prove all the non-believers wrong.

She looked at her watch and realized she must hurry if she was going to meet with her parents' attorney in time. The meeting was simply a formality because, thankfully, her parents put everything in writing a long time ago.

After the solemn meeting with the attorney, Bridgette stopped by the local Chamber of Commerce to pick up a few brochures to display for her guests to peruse. Rexma was a historic area, and there were various activities the guests could enjoy. Bridgette believed in helping the local businesses out as much as possible. There were a few swamp tours, various restaurants, and antique stores. She noticed that some of the brochures were very colorful and eye-catching. She needed to look into having a few brochures printed and put on display here as well. There were only a few hotels and a handful of B&B's in the area.

As she drove back home, Bridgette noticed that Mother Nature was showing her wrath this afternoon. A bolt of lightning streaked across the sky, then the earth trembled as the thunder rumbled. Bridgette had hoped to make it inside before the sky opened up, but she was not that lucky. In the short distance from her car to the house, she was drenched and shivering from the rain. A torrential downpour was released from the overly pregnant sky above and cannons of thunder bellowed.

The smell of lemon furniture polish greeted her as she stepped into the house; Delores must be busy cleaning this morning. Bridgette's heels echoed through the house as she made her way inside.

Delores walked out of the dining room, "Mon dieu, you look like a drowned rat, cher."

Bridgette laughed, "The sky opened up before I made it inside."

"You had a visitor while you were gone."

"Please don't tell me someone else wished to offer their condolences and bring by some food. As much as I appreciate the thought, all this food is going to waste."

Delores shook her head, "Mais non. It was Jake Lemoine. He wanted to pass his condolences and drop a hint that he was still interested in buying this place. That man pestered your daddy for years to sell to him."

"That name doesn't sound familiar to me."

"Mais, he is buying up all the land around here. I think he is a business developer of some kind. Your daddy did not want to sell to him. The man swore that he was interested in the house, but your daddy feared he would tear it down and build a subdivision or something else this town did not need."

Bridgette shook her head, "Non, Daddy wouldn't sell this land to someone like him no matter how tight money was or how good the offer would be."

Once Bridgette had changed clothes and dried off, she went into the kitchen to put away the groceries. From the kitchen window, she watched the torrential downpour.

As Bridgette watched the rainfall, she remembered how much her mom despised thunderstorms. Her dad would stand outside and watch the sky during the storm. Her mom would yell at him to come inside, but he always ignored her requests.

While Bridgette was online working, her chat feature buzzed. It was Haley. "I hope I am not bothering you, but I needed someone to talk to. It has been such a bad day. Rick was in an awful mood, and he was just taking it out on everyone."

Bridgette responded, "I am so sorry girl. I don't miss those days."

"There are days when I wish I had your witty comebacks."

"Trust me, you don't want to be like me. My mouth can get me in trouble at times. Sometimes, when someone provokes you, it is better to smile and ignore it instead of hitting them with a sarcastic comment."

"I don't know, sometimes I think it would be better to have a comeback. I hate getting tongue-tied when provoked. My mind goes blank. And afterward, I can't take my mind off of what happened. All I think about is what I should've said or how I handled the matter."

"No, you are better off being yourself. Besides, you will regret saying a sarcastic comment - especially if that person happens to be Rick. Trust me, I know from experience."

"Perhaps you are right. I am so glad we chatted to-night. Don't stay up too late working."

"Hopefully tomorrow goes better for you. Mwah. Love you to pieces."

Chapter 12

Unable to sleep, Bridgette walked into the back courtyard. The dark, velvety night sky was alive with twinkling stars. It was deathly quiet out here tonight as only a faint whisper of a breeze rustled the leaves. A withering fog poured across the area, obliterating everything. The air became thick and tangible. She made her way through the garden, trying to find the fog obscured moon.

For a moment, she did not believe what she was seeing. A blue light seemed to penetrate the fog. Something passed just briefly in front of her. Her eyes narrowed as she peered into the mist, trying to make sense of what she saw.

There, there it was. A female figure was standing in the mist. Her hair was the color of bronze, and she stood at the edge of the courtyard watching her. She blinked and when she looked again the figure had disappeared.

It had to be a trick of her imagination. The mist was playing tricks on her. She continued to stare out into the fog, waiting to see if she caught a glimpse of the figure again, but it did not reappear. There was no one there and, suddenly, she was cold as ice as rivulets of fear raced up her spine. She was being such a sissy; there was nothing to be afraid of. She had lived with these ghosts all of her life.

Lately, there seemed to be strange sights in the darkness and noises that woke her in the middle of the night. The other night she swore she heard a motor in the bayou slowing down near the property. Unearthly screams pierced the night. She heard whispers in the dark that seemed to be eerie and unfathomable. Living along the bayou, she was familiar with all kinds of noises one heard, but this was something different. So far, she was not able to explain the strange occurrences. If only the lady in the mist would talk to her.

Restless, Bridgette pulled out the journals she had found the other day while scouring the attic. Her great grand-mere's diaries had been stored in a trunk, and had managed to remain pretty well preserved. The ink and pages were faded, but still readable. Bridgette made herself comfortable, and began reading.

Dear Diary,
May 1754

Momma taught me how to spin cloth today. She said that I am going to make a good wife one of these days. I can clean house, cook, and now spin cloth.

Dear Diary,
June 1754

I met the man of my dreams - Pierre Marquette. I do not care if he is ten years my senior. No other man can make me feel the way Pierre does. When he speaks, his voice is the only voice I hear. Time stands still when he is near.

At six-foot four, he is one of the tallest men in Acadia. His arms are rippled with muscles; his body lean and tan from hard work. It may be scandalous, but I daydream about what he looks like without a shirt.

When Pierre talks to me, I swear his eyes twinkle. Does he feel the same way about me?

Dear Diary,
August 19, 1754

Today was my wedding day. This has to be the happiest day of my life. I wore an ivory satin dress, and Pierre wore his best suit.

The wedding was magical. The sun shone through the stained glass windows, and sent prisms of color dancing all around the small church. Fragrant fresh flowers from mama's garden filled the church to make this the perfect day.

Dear Diary,
August 1754

Pierre's family helped us build a house. Even in the coldest of winters, it will keep us warm.

Tall pine trees and wildflowers grow in patches around the house. I found several rose bushes growing wild in the woods and transplanted them in the flowerbeds. With the help of Pierre's green thumb, I know they will thrive.

Dear Diary,
September 1754

I am the luckiest woman in Acadia. Whatever Pierre raises, flourishes. Our apple orchard is bountiful, as are the vegetable crop. The most successful crop is potatoes.

Pierre built dykes along the land to protect the crops from the flooding of the fluctuating tides. He is so smart

With the money he earned from his crops, he purchased extra cattle. They are getting so fat and produce enough milk for us to barter with. He is now raising pigs to use for lard and meat.

Dear Diary,
October 1754

We had a couchon da lait tonight. Pierre roasted a whole pig, and it was delicious.

Friends and family came over for a fais-do do. We played music, danced and drank.

Dear Diary,
November 1754

I have been neglectful in my entries of late. Pierre has been busy hunting, trapping, and toiling the land to keep food on our table. We must prepare for the hard winter.

I have stayed home to tend to the household chores. I have kept busy making candles, tending to cheeses, feeding chickens and gathering their eggs.

Dear Diary,
May 1755

My parents gave me a spinning wheel. I will cherish this gift with all my heart. Imagine all the quilts and fine lace I can make.

Dear Diary,
June 1755

I fear my perfect world is on the brink of ruin. Pierre said that England is at odds with the Acadians. The British authorities want to expel the Acadians to prevent any alliance with the French. A war seems imminent between the British and the French in North America.

Dear Diary,
July 1755

Our journey is beginning. The Micmac Indian tribe is helping us hide from the British. They have offered food and shelter. We can never thank them enough for their generosity.

Dear Diary,
October 1755

The chill of wintery air has settled deep into our bones. I am grateful Pierre told me to wear britches. I must confess it may be difficult for me to return to wearing dresses again. I am glad, however, that I was able to bring my writing materials with me. I may have gone mad if I was unable to keep my journal.

Some days the dreary, gray sky matches our mood. There are times when the winds and storms can be unrelenting.

Dear Diary,
November 1755

Is it wrong that I look at this journey as an adventure? At night we make camp, build a fire, and cook a meal. The men hunt for wild game or catch fish along the way.

While the women sleep, the men take turns keeping a lookout. We have run into many dangers. There have been unfriendly Indians, bears, and other dangerous animals.

Dear Diary,
December 25, 1755

I regret that I have not been able to write as often as I want. It has been a long, arduous trip. Several friends have died of illness or exposure along the way.

Unfortunately, it was not much of a Christmas for us this year, but all that matters is that I am with Pierre.

Dear Diary,
February 1756

We are traveling further south. Now we have to watch for deadly snakes and alligators. Along the banks of the Mississippi, there is virtually no civilization. There have been only a few trading posts, villages, and forts.

Thankfully, a few places have welcomed us with open arms. We were given fresh water and a place to rest.

Unfortunately, in some places, we were clearly not welcome.

Dear Diary,
March 1756

We found passage on a ship. Pierre is attempting to keep our spirits high by reminding us that our ancestors forged a new life for themselves in Acadia and we can too.

Dear Diary,
May 1756

We have made it to Louisiana, but our journey is far from over. I long for a place to call home. It is time for us to find somewhere to settle and raise a family.

I am glad that we have met many other Roman Catholics practicing their faith here in Louisiana. We can finally practice our faith without fear of persecution.

Dear Diary,
June 1756

Louisiana is more beautiful than I ever imagined. It is a picturesque sight with its drooping willow trees, rugged oak trees dripping with moss, and the cypress trees growing in the water.

But even better, I can talk to people in my own tongue.

Dear Diary,
August 7, 1756

We are traveling to a place called New Orleans. On either side of the bayou is a curtain of moss-draped swamplands that frame the imposing residences like none I have ever seen. On the banks of the bayous are fields of corn, cotton, sugarcane, and rice.

Dear Diary,
August 22, 1756

As we travel south to New Orleans, I have become fascinated with the tortuous waters of the bayou. They appear glassy. Dusk illuminates the extraordinary splendor. I adore looking into the water and seeing the inverted images of the broad spreading oak trees, and how the cypress trees are reminiscent of long motionless pendants. As the sun descends, it brightens the tops of the trees. That is when the sky turns into beautiful hues of crimson and purples.

I can sit here for hours and watch as the white herons take flight against the hazy sky and how the alligators ripple the water.

As much as I miss our home in Acadia, I know I will be happy here.

Dear Diary,
September 1, 1756

We made it to New Orleans. There is so much activity going on in this city. Ships line the river; their masts bob up and down in the water as they wait to be loaded. With so many people on the docks, it must make it easy for thieves to pilfer here.

I could not help but stare as men unloaded barrels of rum, sacks of sugar, coffee, and a multitude of bales of cotton from ships to the dock. There were hundreds of laborers, roustabouts, and rough looking riverboat men.

Dear Diary,
September 19, 1756

Pierre's fears were confirmed. The Acadians had been forced into exile. Families had been separated, forced to board ships for unknown lands. Some were forced to return to France, while others were sent to prisons in England, and still more were on their way down the coast aboard overcrowded ships. The British then burned their homes to prevent the exiled from returning.

It is disheartening to learn that the rumors were true and that they were forced to forfeit their lands, tenements, livestock, money, and household goods.

How can one government be so cruel to citizens who only wanted to lead a peaceful, yet productive life? The English did not care if families remained together. They merely wanted these Acadians exiled from their land.

Dear Diary,
September 28, 1756

While in New Orleans, Pierre learned that in other parishes, land was available for the taking. We may soon have a place to call home. I am so excited. I am ready to start a family with Pierre. The loss of my unborn child while on this journey had been painful and I fear that I may never carry a child again.

Pierre keeps telling me that he firmly believes if someone owns property, they have power. He wants to own as much land as he can acquire.

Dear Diary,
October 11, 1756

Pierre acquired two thousand acres for a fair price. Pierre is pleased with his purchase. He said he can smell the rich nutrients in the soil.

I am so excited. We will finally have a place to call home. Pierre said that the land has hundreds of acres of pine and cypress trees that need to be cleared. There will be plenty of land to build us a house of our dreams.

Pierre wants to start his own lumber and sawmill business, as well as farming the land. This is going to be a wonderful new adventure in our lives.

Dear Diary,
October 28, 1756

We are starting to clear the land. Our days are long and full of hard work, but as long as I am with Pierre, I am happy.

For now, we are living in a makeshift home with the other Acadians who traveled and settled here with us.

Dear Diary,
November 4, 1756

Pierre is concerned. The waters are rising, and we may have to seek higher ground. We have made such progress here, and I dread leaving again. Pierre has so many worries right now, that I do not have the heart to tell Pierre I am with child. My faith has to stay strong that I will finally give birth to a child for Pierre.

Dear Diary,
November 22, 1756

The high waters have receded. I looked at this as an adventure. We camped out on the levees.

Once I knew we were safe, I told Pierre that he was going to be a father. We celebrated by feasting on the abundance of crawfish, frogs, and catfish left by the recent flood waters.

Dear Diary,
April 1757

These last few months have been difficult. We lost everything in the flood. It took three months for the water to recede in the latest flood.

I felt hopeless, but Pierre looks at this as another challenge to overcome. Sometimes I think he likes these setbacks.

We should soon be welcoming our first child, and I am anxious to see this baby. Pierre has promised when we rebuild this time, it will be the house of my dreams – only he will build it off the ground. I will have my own castle.

Dear Diary,
August 1757

I have not been able to write in my journal as much as I would like, but we have been busy. Pierre is making the untamed land flourish. Marquette Plantation is complete. It is my dream home. Pierre placed the French doors where we can enjoy a breeze that flows through the house from the bayou. Even in the heat of summer, a cool breeze will bring some welcome relief from the oppressive heat. Wraparound porches grace both the first and second floor.

The best news though is that we are now the proud parents of a boy. He looks just like his father.

My favorite time of the day is when Pierre and I sit on the veranda to enjoy a cup of coffee before he heads out to the fields.

Life could not be more perfect. I could not be happier. We have a family and plenty of friends to share the good and bad times with.

Dear Diary,
March 1758

Life is good. The climate is milder here. I no longer miss the snowy winters of Acadia. The waters here are abundant in food, carrying with it shrimp, oysters, crab, and fish. No one will ever go hungry.

Dear Diary,
April 2, 1758

This venture has been profitable. The plantation is now its own small Cajun village, just like we had back in Acadia.

There is a shoemaker and a blacksmith. We make our own cooking vessels, dishes, and silverware. There is a mill to grind the grain into flour where it can be baked into bread. We have found fruits to make jellies and preserves.

We all live well off of the land. I am overjoyed to have such good friends to share the trials and tribulations of the times with.

Dear Diary,
April 1758

Pierre and I will soon be welcoming another child into our family. We have been working hard day in and day out. It is time to harvest the rice. We work in the fields from sun up to sun down. But we won't go hungry. The ducks and geese that flock to the rice fields to eat make the perfect dinner meal for us.

Dear Diary,
February 1763

I am worried once again. Louisiana went from

being under the control of the French government to the Spanish government.

But Pierre said we have nothing to worry about. All he cares about is making a life for us.

Dear Diary,
March 1763

I am married to such a good man. Pierre welcomes any of his fellow brothers with open arms and allows them to build homes here. All he asks in return is help working the crops.

Dear Diary,
April 1763

One of our dear friends has left us. He left his young wife here in our charge, though.

He told the poor woman that he no longer desired to work the land, and wanted to move on. My heart breaks for her. He abandoned her in the middle of the night.

Dear Diary,
May 19, 1763

We had trouble here yesterday. It seems that a young wife fell in love with her husband's best friend. Instead of running off together, they decided to kill the husband so that they could be together.

The wife had previously informed us that her

husband had abandoned her. Unfortunately, the land flooded, and his body was discovered.

Regrettably, she and the best friend had left before justice could be served, more than likely fearing that they would soon be discovered.

Dear Diary,
May 1775

Pierre is not concerned about the American Revolution. He said it is between the American colonies and has nothing to do with Louisiana.

Dear Diary,
June 1779

Spain declared war upon England. With Louisiana being under Spanish control, Louisiana was brought into the war. Some of the Acadians see this as an opportunity to fight back against the tyranny England imposed on them. Thankfully, Pierre has elected to stay here.

Dear Diary,
June 1769

I am so scared. Yellow fever has hit the area with a vengeance. It is taking so many of our friends' lives.

But, I also fear that I am sick. I am not ready to die. I pray that my health is strong enough to overcome this disease.

Dear Diary,
November 1769

It is with a heavy heart that I write Genevieve's final entry. Yellow fever has taken her from us.

I have no choice but to marry Genevieve's spinster sister, Amanda. It is inappropriate for two single adults to live under one roof together, and there is no way I can care for our two rowdy sons and lively daughter without help.

The children are a raucous lot and lost without their dear mother. I can only hope that I will grow to love Amanda.

Bridgette could not stop the tears from flowing as she read Genevieve's journal. It was so touching to read the vicissitudes that she faced in her life.

It was very interesting reading what Genevieve had written. She would love to work on getting those memoirs published since people from this area strove to keep their history alive. Bridgette had a feeling the book would be very popular and could sell copies here to guests. While reading the diaries, she learned how challenging life on the bayou had been for her family. She could just imagine how hot this old house must have been in the summer since it was stifling with humidity. Her ancestors had to live off of the land and had learned how to make do with whatever they found. It was not as if they had a choice back then; they could not simply run to the store and get whatever was needed.

Reading the diary entries reinforced how proud she was to be a Cajun. Their entire culture had evolved into something unique to this region. There was no doubt the *les Cadiens* had a struggle. One of her strongest desires was to teach her guests about that very struggle, and how her ancestors persevered.

Chapter 13

The monster inside of him was hungry once more. The hunger inside of him could not be sated for long; he seemed to always need more. Tonight, he did not have to rush. He had all night to pleasure himself. Perhaps, he would do an encore performance.

He grabbed her from the bateau and placed her on the ground. He used a knife to cut off the restraints on her feet. Grabbing the rope tied around her hands, he dragged her into the woods.

She turned her face up toward the sky. It was pitch black out except for the soft glow of the moon. She felt the rough ground beneath her feet while branches and leaves crunched as she stumbled behind him. She watched as the flashlight flickered up ahead. It looked as if he was taking her deep into the woods, but where was she?

Would this be the end of her life? Did he plan on raping and killing her out in the middle of nowhere? She began to hyperventilate as they entered a clearing in the woods. Up ahead was an old shack that he forced her into.

Pushing her onto the makeshift bed, he pressed his mouth to hers. She tried to keep from gagging as his tongue invaded her mouth. As he pulled away from her, he let out a sinister laugh. She tried to imagine herself anyplace but here.

"Next time, I want you to show more enthusiasm."

He bent down and kissed the tears from her face. Her glazed eyes looked at him with fear. She struggled against the restraints one more time.

She glared at him, "What is wrong with you? Why must you force yourself on a woman?"

His temper flared. He slapped her across the face, warning her, "You don't want to make me mad."

He jumped back on the bed and straddled her. She looked into his eyes and saw the demonic evil glaring back at her.

He tossed the girl down the cistern, allowing her to die a slow, agonizing death. He wondered how long it would take her to succumb to death.

As he left his hiding spot, A flock of buzzards circled overhead. Something dead was near the bayou. He watched as they flew in lazy circles. Did some poor unfortunate woodland creature meet its demise or was it old enough to be at the end of its life? Perhaps it just up and died. That is how life went, sometimes. But then, sometimes death had to be helped along.

Shadows crept along the bank as he glided the bateau through the murky water. Once on land, he hid the small boat. Closing his eyes, he put himself into his other skin. His outer layer. The one the public saw. However, he had to keep the beast that answered to a hungry, sexual creature hidden. That beast was a living thing, living within his body. It was always there, lying in wait.

Chapter 14

Bridgette was pulling weeds in the front flowerbed when she heard, "Hey lady, what are you doing?"

Startled, Bridgette turned to see who was talking to her. She let out a happy cry when she saw Haley walking toward her. Bridgette broke into a run to greet her best friend. "Oh, my…! What are you doing here?"

Giving Bridgette a huge hug, "I felt so bad for missing your parents' funeral, that I had to come see you. I wanted to make sure that you are okay.

Tingling from shock and pleasure, Bridgette stated, "You did not have to come all this way, you could have called." Giving her friend a hug, "But I am so glad to see you. I have missed talking face-to-face with you." Brushing off the dirt from her pants, Bridgette told her friend, "Let's go inside, get something to drink and catch up."

"I can't wait to see the house and talk to you. I want to hear everything that is going on in your life." Giving her another hug, "And, girl, you look beautiful. The fresh air must be doing you a lot of good."

"I look good? You need glasses." Flipping Haley's hair, "But you look gorgeous. I love the new do." Haley was always the fashionista between the friends. It was evident in the clothes she wore, her makeup and the way she carried herself. Where Bridgette did not worry with which designer made her clothes, Haley had her favorite designers.

Blowing her friend a kiss, "Thank you. I was ready for something new."

"Bridgette, are you really doing okay?" Haley asked.

"Some days are harder than others, but overall, yes, I am fine," Bridgette stated. "How long can you stay for?" she asked.

"Unfortunately, not long. Rick has me meeting a new author in New Orleans. But I wanted to check on you beforehand."

In the kitchen, Bridgette poured them each a glass of sweet tea and brought it to the back porch where they could talk and visit. "I am so glad you did, even if it is for a short while."

Laughing, Haley confessed, "Besides, I'm not certain that I am ready to sleep in a haunted house."

Bridgette chuckled, "I would have told the ghosts to leave you alone. After all, we would not want them running you off on your very first night. I usually wait until someone has outstayed their welcome before I ask the ghosts to scare them off."

"Oh, well, I see how it is. You use them for your own manipulative ways."

Shaking her head while giggling, Bridgette confessed, "I wish it was that easy. I never know when the ghosts will make an appearance."

Bridgette and Haley visited for several hours. Haley looked down at her watch and sighed, "Well, if I am going to make it to New Orleans before nightfall, I best get on the road. It was great seeing you again. I promise I will be back and next time I will spend the night."

Bridgette hugged her friend goodbye, and stated, "I have missed you so much. Thank you for stopping by. You made my day."

Chapter 15

Genevieve stared out into the darkness; the evil was here once again. Why must the cruel winds of fate blow when least expected? As she waited for the new soul to appear, she recalled better times.

When she closed her eyes, she saw her children as they were when she died. If only she could have held her infant son for a little while longer. He had been nine months old when she died and looked just like his father.

She died right after Thanksgiving. That had been the last joyous holiday as a family. Everyone who lived on the plantation had gathered for the celebration. Not only did they have turkey with all the trimmings, but Pierre cooked a hog as well. They feasted and then sat on the porch and ate sweet potato pie.

It had been such a happy day. Her daughter wore a new dress that her daddy purchased from the mercantile boat. She would swish the dress to watch it twirl around her. She took after her mother in so many ways. Her long chestnut hair hung in ringlets, and there was a look of excitement always in her dark eyes. She was truly a beautiful little girl, but she could be even more mischievous than her brothers. She was the apple of her daddy's eye. And being the only daughter, Pierre spoiled her rotten.

Chapter 16

Marcus DuPont woke up this morning quite refreshed considering the lack of sleep. Looking around his bedroom, he wondered if this place would ever feel like home. He could not remember the last time he stayed somewhere and truly felt at home. He had moved around so much over the past few years that he no longer knew what it was like to stay grounded for any given period of time.

He was on a mission today, one that he did not plan to fail. Ms. Bridgette Marquette did not know it right now, but he planned on convincing her to sell the plantation to him. He would not accept no for an answer. He did not get where he was by giving up; he was responsible for building the small family real estate business his grandfather started into its current success. Now, they owned several luxury hotels, as well as resorts. Currently, he was turning old plantations into high dollar spas, and Marquette Plantation would be a great addition to his business.

After a quick shower, he stepped into his massive walk-in closet and picked out a white Oxford shirt and a pair of black slacks. He thought about a jacket, but decided to forgo it with the heat.

He pulled his car out of the garage and headed out for his surprise visit with the beautiful Bridgette Marquette.

Chapter 17

"Bridgette... Bridgette..." Bridgette woke up slowly to find Genevieve standing at the edge of her bed. She was still as a statue and completely fixated on her. In all of her years living here, Genevieve seldom came into her room at night, or if she did, she never made her presence known. That had changed recently as she visited her more and more lately.

Bridgette looked at her, waiting to see if she would say something. Instead, she just pointed to the courtyard. Bridgette got out of bed and looked out into the courtyard to see what Genevieve was pointing at. Beyond the courtyard was a blur of images, none seemed to have a face. Bridgette was unsure where these new ghosts came from. She turned to ask Genevieve but watched in dismay as she disappeared once more.

Looking back outside, she saw the slightest hint of orange and pink hues coming over the bayou. Sunrise would soon be here, and the sky would be vibrant with yellows, reds, and purples to greet the morning sun. Bridgette stepped outside to catch a breath of fresh air. The air still carried the lingering scent of gardenias from her mother's garden. Growing up, her mom would place the gardenia blossoms all throughout the house, making the house aromatic.

Knowing she would not be able to go back to bed, Bridgette decided to get her day started. Besides, the day had come. The day that she would remove her parents' belongings from their room, so that she could use their room as her bedroom. It was the only logical choice. Their room was separate from the other bedrooms that her guests could use. The guests could stay upstairs, while she remained downstairs and had some privacy.

With a deep breath, she opened their closet. As she carefully boxed their clothes, she brought her dad's favorite jacket to her nose and inhaled the scent. Tears formed in her eyes as memories rushed forward.

She thought this would be easy, that she had given herself enough time to heal. However, going through their belongings was more difficult than she realized. With a shaky breath, she told herself that she had to get through this. The B&B would be opening soon and she could no longer delay this daunting task.

Straightening her back, she continued to pack their clothes in boxes. The clothes would be donated to the church for their annual yard sale. The clothes were still in good shape, and someone could make good use of them. Special mementos would be kept in the attic.

As Bridgette was going through the items stored on the upper shelf, she came across a box of photos. She carried the box to the bed and slowly started going through them. She smiled when she saw a picture of her dad and her fishing when she was little. As she went through the photos, Delores knocked on the bedroom door before entering. "My dear, I told you I would have helped. This isn't something you need to do by yourself."

"I appreciate the offer Delores, but this is something I wanted to do. Or maybe something I needed to do to put some closure to their death."

"If you need anything, anything at all, I am here to help you."

Walking over to Delores, Bridgette gave her a hug. "I really do appreciate all of your help and everything you have done."

Chapter 18

Having been so busy getting the plantation ready for guests, Bridgette decided to take the afternoon off. Perhaps shopping and a trip to the beauty salon would lift her spirits.

Before leaving Bridgette called the salon to see if they had any openings, "A Cut Above, this is Meghan. How can I help you?"

"I know this is last minute, but do you happen to have any appointments available this afternoon?"

Popping her gum, Meghan responded, "As a matter of fact, my two o'clock just canceled."

Bridgette noticed the time and realized that she would not have time to do any major clothes shopping, but being pampered with a haircut sounded more relaxing than shopping for clothes, "I can make it there for two o'clock."

"Name please."

"Bridgette Marquette."

"See you in a few then, honey."

As Bridgette stepped outside, she enjoyed the humid breeze thick with a sweet fragrance of gardenias. Sunlight filtered through the live oak branches. In the distance, the noise of a busy woodpecker echoed off the trees. It was so peaceful out here.

The beautiful day helped lift her spirits and Bridgette left for town. As she walked into the salon, a young woman got up from a beautician's chair shaking her head. "You must be Bridgette."

Laughing, "I am. I am not sure what I want, just something different."

"Girl, you have beautiful hair. We just need to give it some new life." Patting on the seat, "Now sit, and let me see if your mom was telling the truth when she talked about how thick your hair is."

Tears filled Bridgette's eyes at the mention of her mom, "That's right. I completely forgot that Mom came here weekly."

Taking a tissue out of the box, the beautician wiped the tears forming in her eyes, "Mrs. Marquette was one of my best customers and your dad always made me laugh. He would sit in here and keep us company while your mom had her hair styled."

Smiling, Bridgette stated, "Dad loved to make people laugh. He was known for his jocularity."

"I do miss seeing them. It is such a shame what happened." Wiping her eyes once more, "But enough of this sad talk. Let's get to styling this hair."

Bridgette could not bring herself to look in the mirror until she finished and nervously waited.

After she had finished, she spun her around in the swivel chair, lifted Bridgette's chin, and pointed to the mirror, "Voila! Now, look at yourself."

Bridgette gasped at the image in the mirror. She added long layers that framed her face. The haircut was feminine yet still sophisticated.

"Oh my goodness, it is perfect. I adore it."

Chapter 19

Death lived in the bayou, hiding in the shadows. Death never let its victim know when it would strike. Its movement silent. The only noise heard in the bayou was that of the victim's short scream.

An alligator moved through the dark, moon-dappled water, barely making a ripple. It searched for its prey, and when found would be taken to the deep of the muddy bottom.

A hunter's moon hung high in the sky. Tonight death would be busy. The bayou would gain a few more secrets.

An owl hooted its mournful notes high from its hiding place. A rabbit ran for its life. The owl swooped from its perch, spreading its wings. The rabbit had no chance of survival. While the bayou may be teeming with life, it was also vigorous with death.

Tonight, he proved just how common death could be in the bayou. He walked back to his bateau from the small cabin. The smell of his latest lover, freshly ripened peaches, still lingered in his nose. Nothing compared to preying on a small town girl; they were beautiful and trusting, which made them such easy prey. A quick smile and wave easily lured them into his trap. When alcohol was added to the mix, they became completely pliable. His appetite was once again sated, but for how long?

The air felt cool against his heated skin, and the ground

was damp under his feet. Leaves layered the ground, helping to deaden the sound of his footfalls. Several branches reached out from the trees, slapping at his face. He weaved his way through the dense forest, keenly aware that he was the only person out at this hour. It gave him time to reflect on tonight.

The minutes ticked by as he walked to the bayou. He stopped at the edge of the small clearing to ensure no one was around. Nothing stirred, not even the woodland animals. Stepping into the clearing, the night enveloped him.

A rustling sounded behind him. He stopped and waited to see who was approaching. His heart raced a little faster in anticipation. Who could be out at this hour? He chided himself for panicking. No one was out at this hour. It must be some small woodland creature. He heard the sound again, this time it was closer. He peered into the darkness, but the blackness was all he saw. He moved deeper into the brush and waited. Something or someone was out there. At that moment, a majestic sight appeared, a whitetail deer darted from the trees.

Once he made his way across the bayou, he secured the bateau to an ancient oak tree. The gnarled branches reached out into the water, giving him the perfect camouflage for the bateau. He walked briskly to his parked car. Anyone watching would assume he was working late, as usual. If they only knew what evil lurked behind his eyes.

He took out his keys from his pocket as he neared his car. As he started the automobile, he listened with pleasure as the finely tuned engine purred to life.

Before pulling out of the parking spot, he dropped the hardtop to his convertible. He wanted to feel the humid air on his skin.

He sped toward home, along the bayou he recently traveled, leaving the lights of downtown in his rearview mirror. He turned down the driveway and made his way down the winding road. Before pulling his car into the garage, he remembered to put the top up. He walked across the small breezeway that led from the garage to the main house. A lot of pride and tender loving care had gone into the house before he bought it. Even from here, he could hear the burbling fountain that was the centerpiece of the horseshoe drive in front of the house. As he stepped inside, he caught a whiff of the honeysuckle that grew rampant on the property.

Walking through the house in the dark, he relished the silence of the night. He made his way up the back staircase to the master suite. He quickly disrobed, making sure to place his dirty clothes in the hamper basket to be washed.

The exhilaration of the recent killings was fresh in his mind, making it difficult to sleep. He grabbed a towel from the bathroom and headed back downstairs. Perhaps a quick dip in the pool would help relax him enough to sleep. He walked through the French doors and onto the brick patio.

Placing a towel on a chaise lounge, he dove into the water. He cut through the blue water with effortless efficiency. After swimming several laps, his body finally tired. He flipped over to his back and floated in the pool as he watched the stars twinkle like diamonds against the night sky before retiring inside.

Reluctantly, he pulled himself out of the pool. He would need to get some sleep before his busy day tomorrow. A trip to the Marquette Plantation was in order; he must convince Bridgette Marquette to sell him the house. With the place busy with guests, someone may notice his comings and goings. That would not do at all. He went unnoticed all this time, and he planned to keep it that way.

Bridgette looked up from the desk when she heard a man clear his throat. "You must be Mr. Tim Doucette."

"Yes, ma'am. And I do appreciate you doing this favor for Father Rabelais. It has been hard to find work recently, and I appreciate any opportunity I can get."

"What kind of gardening do you do?" Bridgette asked.

"I do it all. Landscaping, maintenance, you name it." Mr. Doucette smiled. "I am happiest when my hands are in the dirt."

"Would the grounds at Marquette Plantation be too much for you?"

"Oh no, miss. While the landscaping is beautiful, it would not be hard to make these grounds a show-place. The live oaks need to be trimmed to let more light in. I would suggest putting in some blossom trees, perhaps some dogwoods, magnolias and some azalea bushes. A rock garden would be nice, especially with a waterfall. I would suggest planting some St. Augustine grass that can handle the shade. It depends on your budget, but it would be easy to spruce up the grounds."

"Would it be possible to provide an estimate? I would have to start out small, until the plantation starts bringing in more money, but I am certain we can work

something out. That is, of course, if you have any interest in tackling it."

His eyes lit up, "I would be honored. And I am certain
we can work something out. Father Rabelais had mentioned that perhaps I could be paid with room and
board for a while."

Bridgette nodded her head, "He did mention that you
needed a place to live. However, if living on the plantation would be too much of an inconvenience for you,
I am certain we can work something out."

"I just need a roof over my head, until I am financially
stable. Room and board would be perfect, miss."

"Why don't I show you the sharecropper cabin, and
then you can make your decision. It can be renovated
to your taste."

After Mr. Doucette left, Bridgette felt guilty about ne-
glecting the flowerbeds lately. Bridgette went outside
and watered the rose bushes. A chilly breeze whipped
through the air and sent goosebumps up her body.
Even the rose bushes shuddered with the wind.

Bridgette could not explain it, but she felt uncomfortable outside. It was a strange feeling, and an unwelcome one. *"Perhaps it is because it is getting dark."*
She told herself - as if that would explain it.

After watering the roses, she reached for her snippers.
She cut a few rose blossoms to bring inside.

As she walked inside, she still could not shake the uneasy feeling. When she opened the door, the windows rattled and a low creaking noise came from inside the house. The hair on her arms stood on end. She took slow steps and opened the door completely. The house was bathed in darkness. She strained her eyes against the shadows. With shaking fingers, she turned on the lights.

The house stood still, quiet as a grave. Almost as if it were waiting.

"Is that you, Genevieve?" Bridgette asked in a whisper. "Are you mad that I opened the house as a bed-and-breakfast?"

Without warning, the door slammed closed behind her, causing her to jump. A chill swept through the room. A blanket of fog descended the stairs and into the room. The light in the entryway began to burn brighter.

A lady began to take shape in the fog, "You have to help them. There are souls trapped here. They have to be found and released."

"How do I help them? Where are they trapped?"

"You have to help them!" The ghostly vision pleaded as it dissipated.

Chapter 21

Bridgette had found herself awake an hour before her alarm clock was set to go off. She groaned and threw the covers off of her. She may as well start her day; there was no sense in dozing off for an hour. Marquette Plantation Bed & Breakfast had been open for three months now and she had a full house. She needed to make sure there were plenty of breakfast items prepared.

She was glad that she opened the plantation as a B&B. At first, business had been slow, but it was picking up. A few of the locals did not like that the house was open to the public, but she ignored their criticisms. Those that supported her were greater than those criticizing her.

She was planning a luncheon for the Historical Society. If this went well, they were considering having their monthly meetings here, which would help her with advertising. Word of mouth was always the best form of advertising, and the members of the Historical Society loved to gossip.

As she walked into the kitchen, she noticed an unusual blue light coming from the dining room. It made the hallway appear dark and eerie. She walked into the room to see what was going on. The blue light seemed to pass through the French doors and straight outside. Following close behind, the first hints of morning light greeted her. Traces of a light fog clung low to the ground and created a ghostly and suspenseful atmosphere. The blue light hovered just above the courtyard.

Suddenly, a low moan filled the air, and it felt as if ice water washed over her. The air around her grew cold as the blue light took off and headed toward the bayou before the dense forest swallowed it. To date, this was the most bizarre occurrence she had experienced here.

*

As Bridgette arranged the various breakfast pastries for the guests this morning, she heard Delores enter.

"Good morning."

"Morning, cher. Did everything go well last night?"

"Last night was great, but this morning was strange. There seemed to be an eerie blue light hovering in the dining room early this morning. I followed it outside, but it disappeared in the woods."

Delores gave Bridgette a warm hug, "Ah, cher, I am sure it gave you the freesons."

This statement took Bridgette's mind off her worries for a moment, "Freesons?"

"That's what we call goosebumps."

As they talked about the strange occurrence, guests filtered in for their breakfast and coffee. One of her guests from North Carolina came up to her, "I heard that this place was haunted which is the main reason I decided to come here. I am so glad I did. Did you hear the cries this morning?"

Bridgette looked at her surprised, "You heard that?"

The lady could barely contain her excitement, "Oh yes.

It woke me up from a sound sleep.”

“Oh, I am so sorry. I hope that it did not scare you.”

The lady exclaimed, “Oh my, no. I jumped out of bed to see what was going on. I stepped out onto the porch in hopes of seeing something, but, unfortunately, I did not. I am trying to convince my husband into staying another night. That is, if you have a room available for tonight.”

Bridgette wearily shook her head. She did not like that her main guests were the ones who hoped to see a ghost; she wanted them to be interested in the history here. “I will have to check and see. Why don’t you stop by the front desk after you talk to your husband? I am sure something can be arranged.”

She smiled at Bridgette, “Oh my, thank you.”

As the guest walked away, Henry, the local postmaster, walked through the front door. "Good morning, Henry. How are you doing today?"

"I am doing fine. You have a package today."

Bridgette beamed when she saw that it was from Haley. "Thank you Henry.” Waving her hand towards the buffet table, "Help yourself to some goodies and the coffee is nice and strong this morning."

"Thank you Miss Bridgette, you are too kind to me."

After Henry left, Bridgette opened the package Haley sent to her. Bridgette chuckled when she unwrapped the book. Inside the book was a card. Bridgette opened the card and snickered, "Thought you might need this to help you talk to the ghosts."

She sent a text to Haley, "Thank you so much for the book."

"I found it in New Orleans. I immediately thought of you when I saw it in the voodoo shop's window."

"It is perfect. Mwah."

Before Bridgette could put away her gift, there was a knock at the door. When Bridgette opened the door, she grinned at her unexpected guest. "Mr. Hebert, it is so nice to see you."

Allen Hebert, or Tootsie as his friends called him, had been one of her dad's closest friends. He was one of the sweetest men she had ever met - besides her dad, of course.

"I hope you don't mind, cher. I just wanted to see how things were coming along," with the sadness in his voice, he continued, "and I was missing your dad, and thought perhaps coming here would bring me closer to him."

"You are always welcome here Mr. Hebert. I miss dad too. It has been so hard living here and not thinking about them."

"Mais, I have to tell myself that they are in a better place. That your dad is no longer in pain. But some days it is hard."

Bridgette nodded her head, "Yes, sir, it is. But I know they would not want us to stay sad. They would want us to enjoy life."

Mr. Hebert's eyes brimmed with tears, "I know that in my head. Just doesn't feel that way right now."

Bridgette, overwhelmed with empathy, fought back the tears. "We'll help each other through this. It won't always hurt this much."

Delores walked into the room, "I thought I heard your voice, Mr. Hebert. It is so nice to see you today." Leading him into the dining room, she told him, "I fixed some crawfish etouffee for lunch. Won't you please join us?"

Mr. Hebert laughed, "Etoufee sounds perfect." He said in his heavy Cajun accent, "We can eat and re-member our old friends as we talk."

As the three ate and remembered Bridgette's parents, they savored their meal. Mr. Hebert stated after the meal, "Ah, c'est bon." He wiped his mouth and put his napkin on the table. Patting his hand on his stomach, he told Delores, "It was just as good as mamere's cook-ing."

Delores snickered, "You crazy old coot, no one cooks better than your mere did, but I'll take the compli-ment."

Chapter 22

Bridgette soaked in the scenery as she drove into town. While navigating the road, she tried not to think about how much she missed her parents.

The little gift shop was located in the historic section of town. True southern charm emanated from the area. Cobblestone streets, brick sidewalks, ornate black lamp posts with matching planters lined Main Street.

Bridgette was on a mission today, however. She had spotted the little gift shop last time she was in town, and wanted to check it out. She found a parking spot right in front.

A vintage sign dangled from above - an ivory background with the parchment look and calligraphy writing. Bridgette pushed on the old door and stepped inside. The bell chimed, announcing her entrance. The welcoming aroma of apple pie teased her senses.

"Welcome to Maddie Joe's," a sweet southern voice said. A young woman with short brown hair looked up from the newspaper she was reading. "May I help you?"

"I am just browsing. But thank you. You do have a lovely shop." Bridgette stated as she glanced around. Whimsical wind chimes and hand-painted signs with colorful sayings dotted the walls. Candles and knick-knacks lined the many shelves.

The young lady came over to Bridgette and introduced yourself "I am Maddie Joe, and you must be Bridgette Marquette." She said with a huge smile.

Bridgette gave her a confused look, "Yes, I am Bridgette." She said as she scrunched her brow.

Maddie Joe laughed, "You look a lot like your dad. I am sorry for your loss. He was such a kind man. He always made me laugh."

"Dad did have a way of making people laugh. I still miss them so much."

"It was such a terrible accident. How are you holding up? I can't even begin to imagine how you must feel." She paused to catch her breath. "You have to feel awful."

"I am doing all right, some days are worse than others." Bridgette diverted her eyes, looking around the store. She had hoped to lift her mood, and not wallow in misery today.

"Well, I am glad to hear that, and I am also thrilled that you did not sell the plantation, and instead decided to open it as a bed-and-breakfast. Are you looking for something specific?"

"I am not sure. I suppose I will know when I see it. You have so many charming items in here."

"Thank you. We needed something different in this town, someplace to buy cute gifts."

Bridgette asked, "Is that a candle you are burning?"

"Yes, it is. Doesn't it smell divine?"

Bridgette nodded her head, "It does. I may have to buy some for the plantation."

The bell over the door jingled announcing another customer and Maddie Joe turned to see who had entered.

"Well, if it isn't Mrs. Mabry. It is good to see you." Bridgette watched as the elderly woman moved through the store.

Mrs. Mabry stopped when she saw Bridgette, "Well, if it isn't Joyce's daughter. I am so sorry about your loss. It was heartbreaking to hear the news."

Bridgette took the elderly lady's hand in hers and gave it a squeeze, "Thank you."

Mrs. Mabry continued, "I understand you decided to stay in town. I am sure your dad would be thrilled about that. I am not sure how your parents would feel about strangers being in their home, but I know it would have broken your dad's heart to see the plantation sold."

"As much as my mom liked to entertain, I don't think she would be too upset to learn that I opened a bed-and-breakfast."

As Mrs. Mabry chose her candles, Bridgette thought about what she had said. Would her parents be upset that she had opened the plantation?

Bridgette chose a few candles as well, and found a cute gift to send Haley. She told Maddie Joe, "I love the scents of these candles. I am not going to be able to resist coming into your shop."

As Maddie Joe rang up the items, she stated, "Oh, I am so glad you're going to be a regular customer. I like the sound of that." She handed Bridgette a bag that resembled her sign. It had matching tissue paper peeking out from the top. "Stop by anytime you want to have a chat, or buy candles." Her brown eyes twinkled when she smiled.

"I will." Bridgette waved over her shoulder as she left.

The uneasiness of talking about her parents' death lessened as she stepped onto the sidewalk.

The trip into town had been successful. Not only did she have a new, favorite boutique but she had arranged for some of the local artists to display their artwork. The artwork would also be available for purchase, which really excited Bridgette.

Chapter 23

Bridgette was sound asleep when a noise reverberated through the house. She tossed and turned for a little while longer, hoping that the sound would go away. Suddenly, someone whispered in her ear, "You have to wake up now."

She bolted upright in bed, trying to get her bearings. The noise was not in her head, but coming from outside. She jumped out of bed and walked to the French doors. Peering into the darkness, she could barely make anything out. It sounded as if someone was riding a four-wheeler in the sugar cane fields, but who would do something like that? Did a guest take the four-wheeler out for a joy ride? Throwing on a robe, she walked into the kitchen to grab a flashlight and made her way to the shed. The lock was still secure, so she peered through the window and noticed that the four-wheeler was inside.

Come daylight, she would ride out to the cane fields and see what happened. It was too dark to venture that way tonight. Besides, if there was someone out there, she had no desire to meet up with them in the dark unarmed. Unable to sleep, Bridgette prepared a pot of coffee and began proofreading the next manuscript that was due at the end of the month.

Once it was daylight out, she walked back to the shed to retrieve the four-wheeler. When she arrived at the edge of the cane fields, her heart dropped to the pit of her stomach. There was barely a stalk left standing.

Someone had practically destroyed all of this section of the crop.

She tried to hold back the tears as she called Officer Richard, "Officer Richard this is Bridgette Marquette. I hate to bother you again, but we had more trouble on the plantation, sir. This time someone has decided to go joyriding in the sugar cane fields. They destroyed a nice-sized section before taking off."

"I will be there as soon as I can."

"I appreciate that. I still need to let Mr. Robicheaux know, since he leases the land."

As Bridgette returned to the house, she hunched her shoulders and hung her head low. They never had problems before. Who would do something like this? It had to be kids out causing trouble, but why now?

Feeling overwhelmed, and needing some advice, Bridgette sent Haley a text, "Did I make a mistake? Should I have just sold the plantation?"

Haley immediately texted back, "No, you are not going to self-doubt yourself! You would have hated yourself if you had sold the plantation."

"True. But right now, I am wondering about my life. Did I do the right thing?"

"Do not doubt yourself for one minute. You are doing what's right. It will all come together."

"I am so glad I have you in my life. Love you to pieces girl."

As Officer Richard drove out to the plantation, he thought about this whole situation. Something was way off. Sometimes the kids caused mischief, but not to this degree. They always respected the crops that grew around here. They all knew to keep the four-wheelers along the paths and not destroy the crops. This was an attempt to scare Bridgette Marquette, but why?

When he arrived at the plantation, daylight was settling over Rexma. Patches of low-lying fog still hovered over the area, but it was quickly dissipating in the morning sun. Before getting out of his car, he grabbed his camera to take pictures of the damage.

When Bridgette saw his car pull up, she rushed out the door. As she descended the front steps, he could see the fire in her eyes. There was no doubt about it, the lady was furious.

She asked in a raised voice, "Can you believe that someone would do something like this? Mr. Robicheaux is coming over to assess the damage."

He felt the fury radiating from her. She was hotter than a Louisiana summer night right now.

"You still have no idea who could want you off of this land bad enough to try to scare you off of it?"

She gave an exasperated sigh, "There has always been someone wanting this property, but they have never done anything like this before. I am furious right now. If someone thought they could scare me off, they have another thing coming to them."

He saw the rage bubbling underneath the surface. The

whole time she talked her arms flailed, and she furiously tapped her foot.

"I am going to take some pictures and look around."

Bridgette asked, "Do you want me to go with you?"

He replied, "No, I want to look over the area with a fresh set of eyes. I might notice more if I don't have any distractions."

"I will have Mr. Robicheaux wait at the house until you get back."

Before heading off, he asked, "Have you noticed anything else strange happening around here? Possibly received any strange calls or packages?"

She shook her head, "No, nothing. The only person that has pestered me is Mr. Brett Gibson, and I don't see that man getting his hands dirty."

Officer Richard kept his thoughts to himself. The man may not get his actual hands dirty, but he would pay someone to do his dirty work for him.

As Officer Richard headed off to take pictures of the field, Bridgette became even angrier. If she needed to take a proactive stance to protect her house, she would. If it meant that she had to install security cameras around the place, she would, but only as a last resort. She would not permit someone to scare her away. Her life would not come to a screeching halt because someone wanted to do malicious pranks to her property. She would stand up for herself and not let someone drag her down.

Chapter 24

Sheriff Jared Anslum ruefully shook his head as he headed to his car. There were only two days remaining of school, and now they had another missing girl.

Sheriff Anslum was one hundred percent Cajun. He was not a tall man, barely five feet eleven inches, and his dark skin was starting to look weathered from all the sun, but he preferred to be outside as much as possible. His typical outfit for work was a white or khaki button-down shirt and jeans that fit over his alligator boots. He kept his stark black hair cut short and always wore his cowboy hat. He turned fifty this year, and gray was just starting to pepper his hair. He tried to stay fit and trim, but lately, he noticed the beginnings of a beer gut.

His dark brown eyes showed no emotion as he looked over the officers gathered at the location their missing victim was last seen. Sheriff Anslum warned his deputies to be careful of where they stepped; the area near the bayou was nothing but an overgrown marsh. The water could go from shallow to deep without warning.

Currently, they were searching blindly for the missing young woman. Amy Daigle had stumbled out of a party drunk and more than likely stoned, without telling her friends goodbye. She had not been heard from since then. The back of the house where the party occurred ran along the bayou, so her body may be found near the edge of it. Unless she was fortunate enough to receive a ride by a passerby, but so far, no one had come forward.

This was the second report of a local missing girl over the last year, and Sheriff Anslum prayed that the two cases were not connected. Maggie Hargrave was still missing after being reported missing by her boyfriend almost a year ago. She stormed out of his house upset and was never heard from again. Her trail had long grown cold and Sheriff Anslum did not have much hope that she would be found alive. If they did not find these poor young women's bodies, it was harder for their loved ones to find the closure they needed. People needed that closure, it brought them comfort.

He prayed that none of his men were holding out hope to find the young woman alive. There was a chance that she fell in the bayou and drowned. Unfortunately, that sort of thing did happen around here. The searchers were being methodical in their patterns. They used sticks and flashlights to peer into the long marsh grass; a grid had been laid out and each area was thoroughly gone through before moving on. That way, nothing would be overlooked.

By the end of the day, the rain was beating down on them. The bayou waters were starting to pick up, giving those out on the water a hard time. However, so far, no body had been found.

He reached for the radio to make the call, "The weather is getting worse. That's it. C'est tout. C'est fini."

Chapter 25

From the dining room, Bridgette peered outside. It was early, but she needed to make sure everything was ready for her guests. A breeze blew, and a ripple moved across the murky waters of the bayou. The night sky disappeared and was replaced by the morning sun's welcoming presence in the sky. It was such a peaceful morning. The first hints of the sun's rays danced through the cypress trees and tall grass of the marsh. The ghosts seemed restless last night; she could hear them roaming the halls at all hours of the night. At one time, she swore a piercing scream echoed through the night air, but that was impossible. Maybe the distraught young mistress of the house was mourning her loss.

She opened the French doors to let the fresh morning air in. It would not be long before the sweltering heat of south Louisiana took over, but for now, she planned to enjoy the cool, crisp air. When she stepped outside, a mist formed in front of her and pointed toward the bayou. Could it be the spirits were trying to tell her something? Lately, her sleep had been filled with tossing and turning, and she woke up in a cold sweat with a feeling of foreboding.

As the mist cleared, she made her plans for the day. She wanted to fish for a bit this morning. She had an envie, or a craving, for a court bouillon, a spicy tomato based Creole stew. With fish plentiful in the bayou, there was no reason to go to the store. Besides, there was nothing better than freshly caught fish.

She went back to the caretaker's shed to find a fishing

pole. Before casting her line, she surveyed the bright blue skies. The fresh air smelled so sweet and clean, and a light mist still lingered over the water. The cypress knees and moss dangling from the ancient oak trees glittered in the morning sunlight. She closed her eyes and took in the tranquility of the morning.

Bridgette watched as a heron stepped slowly in the shallow water along the bank of the bayou, searching for an unsuspecting minnow. Its blue-gray plumage had a peachy cast that looked iridescent in the sunlight.

A flock of white ibis squawked overhead and landed on the bank. As the heron searched for its supper, the ibis foraged for insects.

Bridgette smiled to herself as she thought about all the times her dad and she would have their talks out here.

Bridgette sat on the pier next to her father and dipped her toes in the water while she kicked her feet in the air occasionally. "Daddy, why doesn't momma like the ghosts?"

"Your mom doesn't care for things she can't see or understand."

"How come I can hear the ghosts, but not see them?"

Her dad patted her on the head, "I tell you what, let's try something. Turn around and look at the house for me."

Bridgette did as she was told, "Now what daddy?"

"I want you just to look, but don't focus on anything."

"So I don't need to look at anything really?" Bridgette asked confused.

Her dad chuckled, "No, I just want you to stare out into the open. Do not focus on anything specific. Just take it all in."

Bridgette stared into the trees and thought she heard a woman humming. Her dad instructed her, "Just listen."

A woman materialized in front of her, "You are getting so big."

Bridgette looked at the lady, "Are you a ghost?"

The lady giggled, "I am Genevieve. I am so happy you can see me now."

An excited Bridgette turned and looked at her dad, "Thank you, daddy. She did not look old or scary at all."

Her dad tousled her hair, "The ghosts here aren't mean. They are all friendly. If you want to see them, you just have to really concentrate."

"Can anyone see the ghosts? Can I bring my friends here to see them?"

Bridgette was exhausted and could not wait to crawl into bed. She fixed herself a nice hot bath to help put her mind at ease. She had never once felt uneasy about being out here alone with her guests, but lately, the house seemed to have a different aura, one that she could not explain. Maybe it was the death of her parents that had her so displaced.

As the hot water began to ease her tired muscles, she felt her body relaxing. After her bath, she turned on the television for some background noise. Tonight she did not want the familiar sounds of the house to put her to sleep. She found a channel playing old sitcoms and listened to that as she fell into a deep slumber.

The dream started out in a haze; she heard someone calling her name. The voice did not sound familiar, and she had a hard time making out where she was.

Suddenly, a figure appeared from the fog. It was Genevieve Marquette, and she seemed to be in tremendous peril as she searched the fog. The light of the full moon did little to help illuminate the area as the dense mist surrounded the courtyard. The wind picked up, carrying with it a low howl. A chill crept down her spine; it almost sounded like crying.

The voices in the mist seemed to call her name. Suddenly, the air became fetid, and darkness took over. Evil invaded her dream, enveloping her.

Bridgette sat up in bed and tried to calm her nerves. She had never had a dream like that before. She looked at the alarm clock and groaned when she saw the time. It was only three o'clock in the morning. She climbed out of bed and looked out her bedroom window. No mist awaited her; no fog rolled in from the bayou. A starry night with a sliver of a moon was all she saw.

Even though ghosts roamed here, she had never experienced a dream like this before. It almost bordered on a nightmare. This house held so much history; so many lives of her ancestors were here. She hoped that her parents were not among the ghosts roaming these grounds. She prayed every night that they had moved on and found peace in their sudden deaths.

Chapter 26

He made sure he had the ether soaked rag ready. As his target moved in closer, no one was near. He struck quickly, dragging her limp body into the van.

After he had her restrained in the cabin, he leered down at her. "You know what I will do to you, don't you?" The deep masculine voice asked. "I am going to do things to you that you won't like."

She whimpered and struggled against the restraints at her wrists and ankles. There was little chance of escaping unless he chose to release her.

"Please let me go," she begged. "I won't tell anyone what happened."

She tried to make out his face, but it was too dark. She pulled against the chains and heard him laugh at her futile attempts to escape.

"Please, I am begging you to let me go," she implored, "I won't tell anyone."

"Please, you don't have to hurt me," she wailed.

"If you must persist with this constant pleading, I will have to gag you. Also, I do not like screaming. It distracts me," he informed her nonchalantly. "I do promise you this though, if you force me to gag you, it won't be a pleasant experience for you at all."

She sensed him walking around the bed.

"You are quite lovely, you know that."

She let out a soft whimper, not sure what he had in store for her. Pulling against the restraints, she sobbed. This man wanted to humiliate and hurt her, but why?

He lifted her body from the bed and stepped outside. He headed to the cistern, not far from the old cabin, and dropped her body in it. She let out a loud howl that was swallowed by the night when her body made contact with the acid that he placed in there. No one would know what became of her. There would be no body to find.

Silence settled around him once more. He turned to leave and felt the euphoria of the night leave his body. The excitement of the chase no longer heated his blood. A smile pulled at the corner of his mouth. He was restful now, until the evil beast that lurked inside of him needed to be fed again.

Chapter 27

As she drifted off to sleep, a voice called to her, *"Bridgette. Bridgette."*

Bridgette tried to find where the voice was coming from, but she could not seem to see through the thick and oppressive fog. In the distance, she heard the water rippling against the pier. Still, she could make out nothing. The voice had grown quiet. Out of nowhere, gray hands reached out from the water. The fingers left deep slashes in the fog.

Suddenly, the hands disappeared and she was swallowed whole by the thick fog. She futilely tried to push through the swirling fog, but could not. It was almost as if she was standing in the middle of a cloud. The world around her became dark and impenetrable.

The hairs on the back of her neck bristled without warning. There was something else in the fog, something menacing. She could sense the danger. She searched, looking for any danger.

Thunder began to rumble somewhere in the distance. The air was charged with kinetic energy. The fog started to shift. Goosebumps rose on her arms and a voice cried out, "Evil is close at hand. Be careful. You can't trust him."

"Who can't I trust?" She cried out.

The fog dissipated a little more. She could make out the bayou and what appeared to be an old cabin. The water in the bayou churned as the wind howled around her, pushing her towards the cabin.

Lightning flashed around her; thunder crackled in the night sky and suddenly, she heard women crying in the wind. They eerily moaned and pleaded for help. She looked down at the water and women's faces stared back up at her, their arms reaching out to her for help. A scream pierced the night, echoing around her. On and on it went, not stopping.

Bridgette bolted upright in bed. She peered into the darkness trying to see if anyone else was in the room. She listened intently, hoping to hear the noise once again. A thin stream of moonlight found its way through a small slit in the curtains and danced across the room.

Throwing the covers off of her, she got out of bed. Walking across the room, she parted the curtains to peer into the night. A full moon and twinkling stars lit up the sky. She gasped at the sight of a young lady walking in the courtyard. Bridgette was frozen in place, spellbound. Her heart caught in her throat. Why did the young woman choose now to show herself? Bridgette did not recall seeing her growing up, this young woman did not look anything like Genevieve Marquette. Who could she be?

Unable to sleep, Bridgette headed toward the kitchen to prepare breakfast. Soon her guests would be waking up, looking for breakfast, and wanting tours of the grounds. As she walked past the dining room, a rock crashed through one of the windows of the French doors and littered the floor with glass shards. She looked over at the rock and noticed a piece of paper securely held by a rubber band. A shiver snaked down her spine. If this continued, she would have to keep extra glass on hand. Without even touching the rock, she called the sheriff's office dispatcher, "My name is Bridgette Marquette. Since it is so early I did not want to call Officer Richard directly, but I need to report another incident at my house. Someone just threw a rock straight through the dining room door."

"Officer Richard is actually on duty tonight. I will radio him and let him know. Do you think the perpetrator is still around?"

Fear washed over Bridgette, "I never thought about that. I was so angry when it came flying through the door, I did not think about anything else."

The dispatcher asked, "Were you passing by when it came through the door? Did you happen to turn on a light to alert the vandal that you were there?"

"Yes, it came through as I passed by. I was walking through the house in the dark, though. I did not want to wake up any of the guests just yet."

"Officer Richard will be there shortly. Please stay away from any of the windows and do not go outside until we know the scene is secure. Also, will you please stay on the line with me until Officer Richard gets there so that we know you are safe?"

"Of course, I am happy to do that." Without hanging up, Bridgette made her way to the kitchen to put on a pot of coffee. She'd done this so many times in the past, she did not need a light. Once the coffee was started, she made sure the dining room doors were definitely closed. She did not want any of the guests walking in there with shards of glass everywhere. Besides, it would be best to keep the crime scene uncontaminated.

As she poured herself a cup of coffee, Officer Richard pulled up. After hanging up with the dispatcher, she walked to the front door to let him in. She whispered to inform him, "My guests are still asleep. I was trying to keep the noise level down so they wouldn't wake up and be in your way."

As he put on his latex gloves, he nodded in acknowledgment. Before picking up anything, he took several shots with his digital camera from different angles. Next, he started to bag the evidence. He informed her in a soft voice, "I already called the glass company. They will be here at daybreak to fix the door. He said that if this keeps up, he will open a small office here."

Bridgette let out a soft laugh, "I was thinking basically the same thing this morning after looking at the shards of glass." He took notice of the note secured to the rock. From what he could see, it simply read, "LEAVE". Then he stepped outside to look for footprints of any kind.

He informed Bridgette, "I don't want to remove the note from the rock while I am here. The lab techs should analyze everything as they see fit. They will get us the results as fast as possible."

Fury built up inside of her. Thankfully, the person who did this destroyed the dining room window instead of throwing the rock in one of the bedrooms a guest was staying in, but it still upset her nonetheless.

Who wanted to run her off of this property and why? As Officer Richard finished his analysis of the crime scene, Bridgette grabbed a broom and started cleaning up the remainder of the mess. How many more busted windows would she replace before the cops found out who was doing this? It's not as if they were not trying, it's just that the perpetrator was being extremely careful in how he did this. He wanted to scare her, but did not want to get caught.

If only she could curl up on the couch and cry, but tears would not do her any good.

After the last guest left, Bridgette decided to go into town for groceries. This may be her only chance for a few days, as the next few nights are busy with guests who are staying more than one night.

Once back home, Bridgette juggled her groceries as she used her foot to prop open the door. The milk was sliding and she was ninety percent certain the eggs would hit the porch and end up a scrambled mess. She should have waited, carried less inside in one haul, but the dark clouds promised a downpour any second.

Her phone rang in her pocket. A vibration that was stubbornly persistent, but there was no way she could answer the call.

After managing to get the doors open, she hit the light with her elbow. They did not turn on. Just darkness. *Wonderful. Fabulous. Just what I need.* She hit the lights again, still nothing.

Had the storm already knocked out the power? Sometimes the high winds could do that in this area. Ha, who was she kidding? Sometimes it took merely a gust of wind to knock out the electricity.

She let out a sigh of relief as her phone stopped ringing. She walked through the dark house into the kitch-
en, dropping her bags onto the counter.

The wind started to howl outside, and the shutters
banged against the side of the house.

It was dark even in the kitchen. She fumbled through
the darkness and tried the light switch in the kitchen.
Her fingers jerked the switch quickly, up and down, up
and down. Nothing. Nothing, but darkness. Yep, no
electricity.

Hopefully, the storm passed and the electricity was
back on before her guests arrived.

As Bridgette was going to check the breaker box, her
phone dinged. The sudden noise scared Bridgette
enough to cause her heart to skip a beat.

It was a text from Haley, "Dylan stopped by the office.
He wanted to see how you are doing since he hasn't
heard from you."

"Ugh, I am such a bad person. I completely forgot
about Dylan lol."

"Ha-ha - well I figured since you haven't mentioned
Dylan he must not be the one for you."

"He is nice, but no he did not make my toes curl when
we kissed."

"Girl, forget toes curling - you need someone who sets your body on fire."

Chapter 28

He sat in the back of the bar, hiding in the shadows. He observed the two friends as they drank and partied on the dance floor of the crowded bar. Both girls were having the time of their life, not a care in the world. After tonight, there would only be one friend left. He had watched them in the past. He knew both girls went their separate ways in the early morning hours.

Both girls were drinking heavily tonight. They would be an easy conquest, either one would be ripe for the picking. He walked over to both girls and offered them a hit of ecstasy, knowing they would greedily accept the free drug.

He watched as they left the bar, hugging each other goodnight before parting ways. One stumbled off down the road while the other headed to her vehicle. He decided to go after the girl who had a hard time opening her car door. Besides, he could not allow her to get on the road and kill some unsuspecting motorist.

As he carried her to the cabin, he breathed in the smell of alcohol emanating from her small body. She went down easily, with no fight at all. He hoped that she would show some spunk when she realized what was about to happen to her, but she would remain unconscious long after he finished with her.

His shoes rustled through the dry leaves that lined the ground. The dank smell of the bayou filled the air and mixed with the pine trees. The night was humid and warm and by the time he made it to the cabin, a light sheen of sweat covered his body.

Chapter 29

Bridgette seemed to be born for this job. Her mom used to tell her she was a natural-born storyteller and that trait came in handy when dealing with the diverse guests who stayed at Marquette Plantation Bed & Breakfast. Several locals even came to take tours of the grounds as well as the house.

A few of the local customers had even asked if they could come for one of the fabulous meals they heard she served out here. She would need another dining area if she wanted to serve meals to the locals as well. As it stood, the guests had no problem sitting down at the massive table and visiting with each other. There was another parlor off the dining room, which she used the room for cheese and crackers at night, but that could be moved into a smaller parlor on the other side of the house.

If she opened up a small restaurant, she would have to hire a chef instead of her and Delores handling the cooking for the guests. With the additional renovations she wanted to make to the property, the extra income would come in handy.

Bridgette noticed Mr. Greg Dawson, her latest guest here at the B&B, walking down the stairs. She could not put her finger on it, but he seemed to stand out from the other guests. He was inordinately tall and she had to crane her neck just to talk to him.

He dressed casually this morning in blue jeans and a polo shirt. His build suggested he worked out daily and had a rugged look about him that caused her heart to skip a beat. He was an extremely good-looking man with a well-defined tan, but for some reason, he wore sunglasses over his eyes no matter where he was, inside or outside. She found it very unsettling. He was one of the few male guests who stayed here without a companion. With his looks, she doubted he had trouble finding an attractive woman to hang adoringly on his arm.

She watched as he stopped in the foyer to examine several of the treasures she found up in the attic. "Good morning Mr. Dawson, I hope you slept well last night."

"I slept very well last night. I thought for sure I would hear a few ghosts moving about, but I guess I was not lucky enough for that." Mr. Dawson stopped and looked around the place once more. "You have a lovely home."

"Thank you so much. I am very proud of it. Unlike other plantations here, Marquette Plantation has been in my family since it was built. We were very blessed."

He nodded his head in agreement, "Have you picked up the breakfast pastries from this morning? I wanted to come downstairs to read the paper outside along with a muffin and a cup of coffee."

When Bridgette handed him a copy of the paper, an article caught her eye. As he headed for the dining room, she grabbed another paper and went to find Delores, "Have you seen the morning paper?"

Delores looked up at her, "I haven't had time to read it yet. Why? What's wrong?"

"There is another missing girl. She was out partying

with some friends and cut out early. She hasn't been seen since."

Delores tsked as she read the article, "That's horrible. Says here that they suspect the poor girl may have stumbled into the bayou while heavily intoxicated. This is the third girl this year that has gone missing under similar circumstances."

Pictures of all three missing girls were included in the article and Bridgette could not help but stare at the picture of the first young woman who went missing. There was something familiar about her. She swore she had seen her somewhere, but she could not seem to place where.

At that moment, she heard Mr. Dawson as he stepped back inside, "The coffee was wonderful, as usual. I feel at home here, this is a very compelling place. The architecture is so striking, your ancestors showed great pride in their work."

Bridgette looked at him curiously. She was used to guests praising the house, but she had a feeling there was something more he wanted to add. "Were there a lot of renovations needed?"

Bridgette shook her head, "My family has taken great pride in the house as the years passed. Only minor renovations needed to be done when I decided to open it as a bed and breakfast."

He hesitated a moment before asking, "Have you considered selling the house? I imagine upkeep is quite expensive for a place this size."

"I wouldn't dream of selling this house. I plan on raising my family here and passing on the history. I couldn't bear to see it torn down."

He asked, "What if the person interested in buying it wanted to purchase it for personal reasons? Such as living here?"

Bridgette shook her head, "No, I could never sell this house. It means way too much to me."

"Well, there was no harm in asking. Thanks again for allowing me the opportunity to stay here."

"You are very welcome."

She watched as he headed up to his room. Why the sudden interest in purchasing the property? Her parents never mentioned this many people interested in the plantation.

Delores let out a small whistle, "If I were a few years younger, I sure would be interested in that one there."

Bridgette looked at her in surprise, "He was just talking to me about the architecture of the house. He hinted around about buying it is all."

"I am just saying, I could find a few other things to talk about besides some old ghosts. That man there is a hunk!"

"You think he is a hunk?"

Delores teased Bridgette, "Oh yeah. He is tall, well-built, and sexy as all get out. Besides, I think he was admiring more than just the house."

That comment alone made Bridgette laugh, "He wanted to know if I was interested in selling this place."

As Delores walked away, Bridgette mused over Mr. Dawson one more time. He was good-looking, but he had an air about him that she could not seem to place. She also remembered her momma's warning about handsome men. Sometimes a man could be too handsome. She always warned Bridgette to be wary of a man when everything came too easy for him.

Bridgette shook her head and placed the newspaper near the buffet for one of her guests to read as well. The picture of the young missing girl caught her eye one more time. She could not remember where she may have seen her, but she swore she saw her before.

Later that afternoon, Mr. Dawson approached Bridgette, "I know you probably don't mix business with pleasure, but would you like to go out for a drink?"

Against her better judgment, "I would love to." For once, she would throw caution to the wind. Delores was right, Mr. Dawson was an attractive man.

"I am sure that you are busy during supper, so how about we leave around eight o'clock?"

Bridgette responded, "I can meet you at the front desk at eight." That gave her enough time to greet her supper guests and make sure everything was going smoothly before leaving. She needed to take a shower and dress before the supper rush.

She asked Delores, "Do you think you can stay late today? I have a date."

Delores was beaming as she responded, "Of course I can, cher. Who is the lucky man?"

"Mr. Dawson asked me out for a drink tonight and, against my better judgment, I accepted."

"Mais, cher, you need to get out and enjoy yourself!"

As Bridgette headed to her room, she began to panic. Maybe accepting Mr. Dawson's offer was not such a good idea after all. It may not be wise to date a guest, but he was only a guest for a short time. He mentioned when he had checked in that he planned to move here. He did business in Rexma quite a bit. Perhaps this was a beautiful start to a long-term relationship? Besides, it's just a drink. She could always call up to his room and cancel by saying that the dinner crowd was busier than usual.

Shaking her head, Delores was right, she needed to get out more. There was nothing wrong with him taking her out and buying her a drink. She would be an old maid before long if she did not start enjoying herself.

Before heading to the dining room, she looked at her reflection. She had a few wrinkles, but, thankfully, no one would ever guess she was almost thirty. She had carefully applied her makeup, but even without makeup, she looked good.

After making sure everything was flowing smoothly for dinner service, Bridgette walked over to the front desk where she saw Greg Dawson already waiting for her, "I hope I haven't kept you waiting long."

He shook his head, "I just walked downstairs." He held out his arm, "Shall we go?"

She slipped her hand into the crook of his arm and

allowed him to escort her outside. After opening the car door for her, he walked around to the driver's side. His car took her by surprise. It was an Audi A5 convertible.

He chuckled, "I did have a hard time finding a convert-ible that I fit into. I must admit though, that I have a thing for speed and as soon as I saw this car on the car lot, I had to have it. It handles the Louisiana roads su-perbly."

Bridgette rested her head back against the headrest and took in the beautiful night. As they drove to downtown Rexma, she asked, "So where are you from?"

Greg looked over at her, "I am from a little town not far from here, Cottonport."

"What brought you to this area?"

"I am looking into some new business ventures this way. I do not have any family left and have lived in various places over the years, but I am tired of not having a place to call home. It's time for me to start putting roots down somewhere."

Bridgette looked at him with sympathy in her eyes, "I know what it's like not to have any family left. That's one of the reasons I cannot sell the plantation. This, and my memories, are all that is left of my immediate family. I just can't let it go."

"My family moved around a lot, so I never lived in one place long. I guess that is why I don't understand how a person can love a piece of land so much."

"I can understand that. Every time I look out a window, I envision one of my ancestors doing the same thing. I found several old diaries I would like to get published so guests can experience what life was like here at one time."

Greg looked over at her, "I think several of the guests would like that. It is hard to imagine life back then. Kids, especially, don't seem to grasp that there was no electricity or televisions back then."

"I know. None of my dad's brothers had any interest in the plantation and could not wait to move. Over the years, he would invite my cousins to come stay, but they never accepted the invitations. They did come for the funeral, but were anxious to leave."

Greg found a parking space outside of Lagniappe, "I figure you don't get out much, and the bar here is nice and low-key. I hear the piano player is quite good."

"I've been here several times for lunch. The food is excellent."

"Well, let's go find us a spot at the bar and enjoy ourselves."

The bar was pleasant, but full, at nighttime. The music coming from the piano was low enough where you could hear yourself talk, but still enjoy the added background atmosphere. They found an empty table near the back corner. Bridgette smiled at Greg, "This is very nice. Thank you so much for asking me out tonight."

He picked up her hand and gently kissed it. She blushed at the romantic gesture, "No, thank you for agreeing to come out with me. I must admit that I have an ulterior motive for asking you out."

Bridgette's heart sank. "Oh? And what is that ulterior motive?"

He let out a small chuckle, "I want you all to myself for a night. At the plantation, the guests would constantly interrupt us. They all seem to love talking to you, and I can't blame them. You have a natural ability about you to tell the story of your family."

The waitress picked that moment to show up, "My name is Pam. What can I get for y'all tonight?"

Bridgette ordered a pomegranate margarita, and Greg ordered a manhattan. Bridgette watched as the waitress walked away to place their orders at the bar.

She focused her attention back on Greg and smiled up at him, "So you never did say what it is that you do."

He let out a laugh, "I find land to lease for oil wells and such. It is quite boring and completely different from what you do."

Bridgette looked over at Greg skeptically. She wondered if his interest in talking to her was about leasing their land out for oil. She never liked the idea of how they come in and tear up the land you worked so hard for. They say that they leave it in better condition than they found it, but she never believed that. She asked, "Are you interested in some land over here?"

"A few pieces of property caught my attention, but I also came to check out the competition. Another competitor is also buying land around here."

Bridgette hated to think of the land around here being

bought for oil drilling. She despised seeing the landscape ruined by derricks all over the place.

Greg saw the worry on her face, "Don't worry. Right now, we are only looking. There are a few more properties that show promise, but I swear if my company does become interested in leasing your land, I will inform them that you aren't interested."

"I appreciate it. I can't see leasing out my land so that it can be lined with oil derricks."

He snickered, "Even if it is more money than you ever dreamed of?"

She shook her head, "No. My family worked too hard for me to harm the land."

Greg decided to change the subject, "So what made you decide to open up the plantation as an inn? You seem to be a natural at it; I love how you make the guests feel welcome; tell them about your family and the history of the place."

Now it was her turn to let out a laugh, "My mom used to tell me I was a born storyteller. I want everyone who comes to the plantation to know about the place they are visiting. It is something special to me, and I want them to understand why."

"What did you do before moving back home?"

"Before my parents passed away, I worked in South Carolina for a small publishing company. I do not write the stories, but I do edit them. I still work there; I just work from home now."

"I am impressed. I did not even realize that you are working two jobs right now."

She shook her head, "It's hardly work. I am doing something I love and it makes it a joy to do. The proofreading and editing I do when the guests have all retired for the night, or if there is a lull in between guests. It provides a steady income."

"I must say, you are a shrewd business woman. I mean you saw the potential in turning the plantation into an inn, as well as keeping your old job to ensure that you had a steady income."

"I must admit that I did consider quitting my job in South Carolina, but my boss did not want to lose me, so we came up with an arrangement that works for us all. I have several clients that did not want to lose their editor. We have had a good working relationship for years and it is sometimes hard to develop a working relationship between an author and editor. I am extremely lucky with my clients. We get along great. I can give them my opinion on what needs to be changed and they listen to my suggestions. I can't guarantee that they listen to all of my suggestions, but they do listen."

Greg admitted, "I must confess that I am not an avid reader. I rarely even read a newspaper."

The waitress returned with their drinks and Bridgette realized that she had talked about herself non-stop. "I am so sorry. I did not mean to talk about myself so much. I have a tendency to talk incessantly. It's a bad habit of mine."

He gave her one of his charming smiles, "Nonsense, I love to listen to you talk. I hope to learn more about you while I am here. As I mentioned earlier, I do plan on moving here. I guess since I can't talk you into selling me your plantation, I will have to look at other properties."

Bridgette took a sip of her drink and looked at him intently, "I can give you the names of several good real estate agents, if you want. But I have no intention of selling.   I am not sure if any of the surrounding plantations are for sale, but the real estate agents would know. The Chamber of Commerce may also be able to help you."

"And when it comes to getting to know you better?"

She looked into his eyes, "I think that is something we can agree on."

He picked up her hand and kissed it one more time, "I am so glad."

On the drive back to the plantation, Bridgette could not remember the last time she had such a pleasant night. She was glad she went against her better judgment and accepted Greg's offer of a drink. As she unlocked the front door, she felt his hand on the small of her back. Her heart fluttered in anticipation. She looked up at him, wondering if he would kiss her good night. She was breathless as he bent down. He gently kissed her on the mouth, "Thank you once again for allowing me the pleasure of your company. I hope we can do it again very soon."

She whispered, "Yes. I would like that very much."

Before they could say anything else, a small potted plant perched on the edge of the porch crashed to the ground. She jumped as the noise startled her. Next, all the white rockers lining the porch began to rock in a furious motion, their legs slamming against the floorboards of the porch.

A shiver crept down Bridgette's back, "That's strange."

Greg looked at the chaos around him knowing that there must be some reasonable explanation, "It is more than likely just the wind."

Bridgette gave him a bewildered look; they both knew there was no wind. The air was suddenly unnaturally still around them; time was held in suspension. Why were the ghosts so restless? What were they trying to tell her?

Chapter 30

A smile formed on his face as he thought about how well tonight went. He was pleased with the outcome of the impromptu date.

He had always been the quiet type, keeping his thoughts hidden. No one knew what went on in his head, which was how he liked it. The gears in his head were always turning, never stopping. This was what made him successful in business. There was something mysterious about him, but nobody was ever privy to his inner thoughts.

Women always found him attractive. He was tall, well-built, and dressed to perfection. They found something alluring about his goatee and wavy hair. Unfortunately, he found it best to remain a loner. He kept an aloofness about him even in business dealings.

He found Bridgette Marquette completely alluring. He never had a woman turn him down for anything. This was an entirely new experience for him; she dismissed the offer without even thinking about it. He thought for sure when he offered to purchase the plantation from her, she would jump at the offer, but the woman was shrewder at business than he anticipated. He did not like being caught off guard.

However, he was not ready to admit defeat. If he could not buy it outright from her, maybe he could charm it from her. Women were such gullible creatures at times and there was no denying the strong physical reaction between the two of them. It would not hurt to mix business with pleasure while trying to convince her to sell the property to him.

As he stepped out of his car and headed into his office, he had to put himself into his other skin. The skin he allowed the public to see. No one could ever know about the monster that lived inside of him, the sexual beast that fed on Marquette Plantation Bed & Breakfast innocent and sometimes not-so-innocent young women. It lurked right under the surface just waiting to pounce at any moment. It had become insatiable lately, never satisfied.

He must control the monster inside of him. He had to. It was too soon to feed it once again. Another woman too soon would not be wise. If he left town right now to find another, it would be noticed. No, he must wait.

Chapter 31

Bridgette stood in front of the dining room's French doors and stared out across the bayou. The setting sun cast an orange glow along the water and a thick clump of cypress trees littered one corner of the bayou. There had not been many changes since her childhood, however lately the house felt different, as if something brooding was looming overhead. She could not pinpoint it, but something did not feel right, almost as if something out there did not belong.

A breeze rolled in off the bayou bringing with it the chirping of the birds nearby. As she breathed in the fresh air, off in the distance she heard an alligator slip into the murky bayou water. This was her home, yet lately, she felt as if she did not know it.

Bridgette was so deep in thought, she did not hear Delores come up behind her.

"Ms. Marquette, I finished cleaning the kitchen. Did you need me to do anything else before I leave?"

Bridgette nearly jumped out of her skin when Delores spoke. "I am so sorry. I did not hear you come into the room."

"You looked miles away."

"I was remembering how Dad and I would go catch fish from the pier. Even after he was diagnosed with multiple sclerosis, fishing was one of our favorite activities."

Being the only child, and a girl, she was extremely close

to her dad, being the classic "Daddy's girl". Growing up, they were almost inseparable. Over the years, she watched as the disabling disease took over her dad's body and became unpredictable and erratic over time. The worst of the disabling manifestations were the blurred vision, numbness in his lower extremities, and debilitating fatigue. Some days, he could not get out of bed. Right before his death, she could tell the MS was accelerating. Her mom noticed that he had dexterity problems and slurred speech. Maybe Bridgette should be glad that her dad was killed before multiple sclerosis did its worst.

Delores shook her head, "Mais, your parents were such good friends. They never once treated me as if I was just a housekeeper. It is such a shame that they were taken from this earth so early in life."

Bridgette walked over and gave Delores a hug, "You are like family. I am so glad you could stay on and help me."

"Mon dieu, you were always like one of my own children." Patting her hand, she informed her, "I put a pot roast in the oven for supper tonight. Are there many guests?"

"There are a few, but it should really pick up next month. The website is up and going, and I started advertising as well. This is just so exciting. I enjoy all the guests here, sharing the regal beauty of the surroundings."

"Mais, I don't like you staying out here by yourself with these people."

Bridgette shook her head, "I am fine, the guests have

all been so polite."

"You should be out having fun, not holed up here. Mais, if you spend all your time here you will never find a man."

Bridgette let out a laugh, "I still have plenty of time to find a man. You worry too much."

Delores shook her head, "There aren't too many single men in Rexma. I do not think your parents planned on you staying and trying to keep this big old place running.   You could sell and start a new life for yourself."

Bridgette just shook her head, "Mais non, I couldn't fathom the thought of selling this place. It is a part of me. I have always loved this place."

Delores sighed and kissed Bridgette's forehead, "I'll let the matter drop for now. You know you can always count on me to help you with anything you may need. I'll see you next week, unless you need me sooner."

Bridgette followed Delores out the door and locked up behind her. Everything was finally starting to fall into place. She enjoyed running Marquette Plantation Bed & Breakfast. There was a lot riding on this new venture, if this did not work out, she would not be able to keep this place. With her parents' sudden death, the limited money in the estate would not be enough to keep the plantation running forever.

Looking outside one more time, she made up her mind to go walking around the property to prove that her imagination was working overtime. Lately, she had felt like she was being watched at night, and she was becoming obsessed with making sure the blinds were closed and the curtains were drawn.

She changed into a pair of tennis shoes and headed out the door. Tonight, she would walk along the bayou. For a moment, her courage wavered as she stared at the dense growth of forest. She heard something rustling out in the woods and her heart caught in her throat for a moment. There was a wall of cypress trees that flanked one area. This part of the bayou always scared her, even as a child she was afraid of it. With dusk fast approaching, she turned around and headed home.

Once back home, Bridgette picked up the mail at the front desk and went outside. The evening air was thick with humidity. A swirl of blazing orange and purple painted the sky. She stood on the porch and savored the evening breeze. She walked over to the porch swing and made herself comfortable while she looked through the day's mail. Electric bill. Water bill. Cell phone bill. More and more bills. Nothing interesting.

Sighing, she went back inside. Bridgette heard the sound of little feet coming down the stairs and her heart skipped a beat. Her smallest guest yet was coming down the stairs with her mom. "Hurry up mommy. I want to get some cookies before they're all gone."

Mrs. Thompson smiled at Bridgette, "Angie wanted to know if she could have some more cookies."

Bridgette bent down so that she could look the little girl in the eye, "Well, of course you can. Take as many cookies as you want."

The little girl tugged on her mom's skirt, "I want this many cookies."

The little girl held up four fingers and giggled. Her mom kissed the top of the child's head. "That's an awful lot of cookies for your little tummy."

The little girl shook her head, "But I wuv cookies!"

Her mom chuckled. "Well, so does your dad. Something tells me he will eat whatever you don't." The little girl shook her head again, "Uh-uh. You have to get daddy his own cookies."

As the mom walked the child back upstairs to their room, Bridgette felt her heart break. Bridgette's parents would never know the joy of loving their grandchildren. The sadness was almost too much.

Bridgette thought about her own grandparents and how lucky she had been to know them. Pawpaw Marquette had been a lively character. When she was little, she would climb up onto his lap so that he could rock her.

"And who's dis petite fille?"

Bridgette giggled, "Pawpaw, it's me!"

Shrugging, "Me?" He would look over to Maw Maw Marquette "Do we know anyone named Me?"

Playing along with the joke, she would respond, "Mais non, it must be a stranger. I don't know a Me."

"Pawpaw, it's me, Bridgette." She giggled and pointed to herself.

"Oh, it's Bridgette." He said as he tapped her on the nose, evoking a belly laugh.

Bridgette enjoyed their little ritual. At night she would watch her dad and Pawpaw play checkers on the porch, which is probably why she has a game of checkers for her guests to play. It brought back fond memories for her.

That night she fell into a deep slumber. The dream started off with her as a child, maybe around eight or nine years of age. She had on a dress her mother bought her to wear to church.

After returning home from Sunday Mass, she was in the dining room setting the table for the pot roast with all the fixings her mom made. She was scuffing her shoes on the wood floor, loving the sound her shoes made. She especially loved the sound her mom's heels made on the stairs. As she stood there setting the table, an image formed in front of her. It was not the man who let her play the piano with him; it was a woman. She looked at the woman, "Hello, my name is Bridgette, do you remember me?"

The lady looked at her and smiled, "Mon cher, but of course, I do. We met while you were fishing with your dad."

Bridgette heard her mom entering the room and watched in disappointment as Genevieve faded away.

Bridgette knew better than to tell her mom about the ghost, her mom did not believe in them so it was a secret that Bridgette and her dad shared. She could not wait to tell him that she saw Genevieve.

By the time her mom served the warm apple dumplings with the homemade vanilla ice cream, she was giddy with excitement. She could not wait to have her dad all to herself. As her parents sat sipping their coffee and talking about the day, the scene faded.

Suddenly, she found herself in a small cabin. She looked around, unsure which cabin this was. It did not resemble the other cabins on the property. She ran out of the cabin and found herself deep in the swamp. She could hear the bayou water to one side, but it was dark all around her.

Someone was near her. Coldness overtook her and it felt as if she was actually frozen. She hugged her arms around herself in an attempt to warm up. She gasped at the realization that she was naked. A whisper came from the dark, urging her to run. She ran frantically through the woods, branches scraped at her face. Images flashed through her mind about what could be at her feet. She swore she felt snakes slithering beneath her.

She looked behind her to see who was chasing her, but saw no one. Up ahead the plantation lights beckoned her to safety and she made a dash for it. If she could just make it inside, she would be safe. Suddenly a dark, menacing figure appeared before her. The night was filled with guttural screams that pierced the air.

She bolted upright in bed, covered in a cold sweat with tears streaming down her face. Her heart was pulsing in fear; this was the most vivid dream she had ever had. It completely overwhelmed her.

Chapter 32

Bridgette was arranging blueberry muffins and cappuccino with chocolate chip muffins on the buffet when Greg Dawson walked into the dining room. He was wearing a pair of jeans that should be illegal, they molded his body sinfully.

"Good morning Ms. Marquette. Did you sleep well last night?"

She smiled up at him, "Yes, I did. What about you? You didn't come back last night."

"I got so tied up at the office that I lost track of the time. I didn't want to call and wake you to unlock the doors."

She let out a soft chuckle, "Well, that's a good thing I guess."

"I was thinking of taking a tour of the grounds. Is there a particular trail I should follow?"

Bridgette looked around the dining room to make sure the guests were content. "Let me check with Delores, but I should be able to get away for a little while. Perhaps if I showed you the grounds, you would see why I love it so much."

Excited about spending some time with Greg, Bridgette went in search of Delores.

"Good morning, Delores." Bridgette walked over and gave Delores a hug.

"Good morning."

"Isn't it a beautiful day?"

"Well, you are in a good mood this morning. I am so glad to see you smiling again."

"My mood is definitely improving. In fact, I was wondering if you would not mind watching over things for a while. I was going to give Mr. Dawson a tour of the grounds."

Delores looked at Bridgette and smiled, "I take it your date with the good-looking Mr. Dawson went well, then, and you want to spend some more time with him."

"Yes, yes it did. It felt good to get out of the house and spend time with someone of the opposite sex. And, as far as the tour, I want him to see for himself why I love this place as much as I do."

Delores asked, "Mm-hmm. Could this be the beginning of a romance?"

Bridgette shrugged her shoulders, "It's too early to tell. But I did enjoy my date with him. And he was the perfect gentleman."

"Hmmm, I was kind of hoping he would show you a little romance and sweep you off your feet. But, perhaps he will do that today."

Bridgette laughed, "Delores, I am surprised at you."

Delores chuckled, "Child, please. I know what goes on between a man and a woman. And it might be time someone reminded you."

Shaking her head, Bridgette replied, "I am not sure Gregory is interested in me that way. We will have to wait and see."

Delores chuckled to herself as Bridgette went to meet Greg.

"Are you ready? Delores is going to man the front desk while we tour the grounds."

When they reached the shed, Bridgette opened the doors and uncovered the four-wheeler.

"Do you want me to drive?"

"*Typical male*," she thought to herself. She shook her head, "I better drive. I know this property like the back of my hand."

With the sugar cane fields freshly cut, she would make good time getting to the back of the property. It had been a while since she was back there and needed to check on things anyway. She slowed down for a moment and turned to him, "Somewhere on the outskirts of the property is an old shack where moonshine was cooked. I eventually want to make the cabin and its history part of the tour."

He asked, "You don't remember where it is?"

Shaking her head, "Not exactly, but I think I remember the general vicinity. That is the one place Dad was adamant about us not visiting."

She picked up some speed as they got further away from the plantation, leaving a trail of dust behind them. She had to pay attention to the scenery around them or she would start to think about how his body felt against hers, and how the heat of his body scorched her.

Once at their destination, she cut the engine to the four-wheeler. She went to move out of his grip when he gently turned her head to look into his eyes. Without warning, he tilted her chin up and kissed her. The kiss was unexpected but entirely welcome. As the kiss deepened, something deep inside of her awakened. Reaching up, she laced her fingers through his wavy hair to bring him closer to her.

A soft sigh escaped her lips as shivers of pleasure danced through her body. Just as abruptly as the kiss began, he pulled back. His eyes looked deep into hers, "I've wanted to do that all morning, but I figured it would be inappropriate in front of the other guests. I don't want anyone to think you give out kisses to the men who stay here."

Laughing, she climbed off of the four-wheeler after him and followed him to the bayou's edge. The kiss left her thoughts jumbled in her mind.

Looking out onto the water, he said, "It is beautiful back here, very serene. I see why you want to keep it to yourself."

"Not entirely to myself. I did open my house to the

public."

He let out a chuckle, "I stand corrected. You did at that."

As they walked along the bayou, she felt Greg take her hand in his. She tried not to notice how her hand tingled from the simple contact or how her stomach felt as if a million butterflies were fluttering about. She cast a sideways glance at Greg; he was entirely too sexy. Did she have time to mix business with pleasure?

He smiled down at her, "A penny for your thoughts."

She giggled, "I was just thinking how nice it is to be out in the fresh air. I feel like I am playing hooky."

"Well, I, for one, am glad that you offered to show me around. Here I was planning on walking along some of the paths; instead, I get a personal tour of the property."

He pulled her closer to him and teased her lips with his before kissing her thoroughly. He felt her lean into him and deepened the kiss. It took everything he had to break the kiss.

He gazed at her seductively, "I don't know where this may be going, but I plan on finding out."

"I want to take it slow. With so much happening, my emotions are in complete turmoil."

He ran his fingers through the silkiness of her hair before cupping her face. He pulled her closer to him one more time; he could not seem to get enough of her. Her arms came up and wrapped around his neck, bringing him even closer. His breath mixed with hers. This time, she reluctantly broke off the kiss.

He watched as the sunlight teased the highlights in her hair when she shook her head. She pulled him to the four-wheeler, "Come on. I have one more spot to take you."

As she took off down the bayou a little more, he enjoyed the scenery that seemed to fly past them. As they rounded the bend where she believed the old cabin was located, her phone went off. She stopped to see who was calling.

"Delores is something wrong?"

"You have a walk in. Do you have a room available?"

"Yes, I have two rooms available for tonight. I'll be right there."

Delores answered, "I can check them in if you like."

"No, I need to get back. I am not far from the house."

She looked back at Greg, "Sorry, work calls."

He replied, "I understand."

Besides, he wanted to go to the old cabin by himself. He was curious to see if anyone from the plantation had traveled that way.

As Bridgette washed the dishes from the dinner service, she heard someone walk up behind her. Greg quietly said, "I wanted to thank you one more time for this morning. I feel privileged that you took the time to show me around."

She told him, "I enjoyed myself as well. It was nice to get away for a bit."

He placed his hands on her shoulders, moving her thick mane of hair out of the way. His fingers flexed around her tightened neck muscles.

She dropped her head as he massaged the back of her neck. She let out a soft sigh, "Mmmm, that feels good. Your hands are like magic."

He chuckled, thinking of the best thing to say in a moment like this. "It is the least I can do for all your hospitality."

She looked outside and watched as the heavens opened up. "It looks as if the rain that was threatening to break free is finally here."

He sighed, "It sure does, and I have to go out tonight."

She tried to hide the disappointment in her voice, "You have to go out in this?"

"Someone I have been trying to meet with is finally available. And before he changes his mind again, I want a chance to talk to him. He has about two hundred acres that he leases out in North Louisiana for hunting. They are starting to strike oil around there and I want to talk to him about surveying his property in case there is oil on it. I need to strike while the iron is hot."

"And these people usually have no problem letting you lease out their land and strip it bare?"

"It's not quite like that. We make sure to write the lease where it says we will leave the land better than how we find it when we are finished."

"Yeah, but what about all the trees that you tear down while drilling for oil?"

"Unfortunately, some trees have to be removed, but we try to be as minimally invasive as possible. There is a fine line between destruction and preservation, but we try not to destroy anything that we don't have to."

Shaking her head, "I don't know. I am still not convinced that there won't be permanent damage to the property."

"Perhaps sometime you will allow me the chance to show you how our operation works."

As another loud clap of thunder shook the house, Bridgette replied, "I would love to spend a little more time in your company, but I don't see you changing my mind with regards to the oil drilling business." As she escorted him to the door, "Please be careful out in this storm. Should I wait up to let you in? After all, you do have a room here."

Gently kissing her on the lips, "No, there isn't any need for that. I will be very late, I'm sure, especially if things go my way. Just hold my room for me. I look forward to seeing you again Ms. Marquette."

Throwing on a robe over her mismatched pajamas, she walked into the kitchen. She fixed herself a glass of ice water and stared out into the night.

Feeling restless, she stepped out onto the back porch. The air was thick with the coming of summer, sweat dampened her skin. The dank smell of the bayou tick-led her senses.

Inexplicably, Bridgette's skin crawled. She felt it again, as if she were being watched - that hidden eyes were assessing her every movement.

"Talking to too many ghosts," she told herself.

She looked at her watch and grimaced, it was nearly one thirty in the morning now. The rain had stopped, and the moonlight cast an eerie glow across the land.

Her body was tired, but her mind still spinning. She checked her emails one last time and hoped sleep would come. However, she knew it would not. *Wretched insomnia.*

Bridgette jumped involuntarily when her cell phone dinged with the text message, "Still up?"

"As usual." She replied

"Anything wrong?"

"Man trouble."

"Wanna talk about it?"

"Gregory kissed me today, but it did not go further than a kiss. I am still worried he may be using me."

"If he does use you, he will have to answer to me."

Before Bridgette could type a response the house creaked overhead, and for a second, Bridgette thought

she heard footsteps. It was probably one of her guests
moving around. But then again, it could be a ghost.

Chapter 33

The rain was relentless as it came down in sheets. The windshield wipers swiped at a frenzied pace, unable to keep up with the onslaught of rain. He safely navigated his car through the dark streets. Power must be out because none of the street lights were on.

He hunched up close to the steering wheel to see where he was driving. The pumps could not keep up with the torrential downpour; ditches overflowed and flooded the road with the rain water. He was immune to the elements when he had a mission. Tonight's mission was to find himself a companion and rain would not deter him from his hunting.

He knew the perfect place to hunt tonight. Rain or shine, electricity or not, people would be at Shooters. Jacque Billiot was one hell of a business man and his was the only bar in town with a generator. He loved money too much to close so he stayed open three hundred sixty-five days a year, regardless of the weather. No one would think twice about a drunk woman who did not make it home in this weather.

He parked his car in a hidden spot and dashed into the bar, trying not to get drenched in the process. He had discovered this bar by accident one night. This was not his typical hangout, yet something about the bar intrigued him.

The music seemed to make the place come alive. People came here for one reason - to forget about their worries. No one paid particular attention to him, which was just the way he wanted it.

He watched his target from a distance. She would make the perfect companion for tonight. The way she moved was highly seductive, just the mere thought of what he planned on doing to her excited him.

It was by pure chance that he discovered the cabin. It had been during the dead of winter when he saw it peeking out from the trees. Any other season and he would have missed it. It made the perfect cover for his hobby since it was normally hidden by a living canopy of trees.

This solitary location had somehow remained private all of these years. At the time, he wondered if the land owners even knew of the place.

Once he saw it, he knew it was the perfect place to bring his companions. When he found the old cisterns not far from the cabin, he was certain. He could dispose of his date as soon as he had his way with her without fear of her ever talking. Before succumbing to temptation, he did his research and found out where those with the same affliction as him went wrong and made sure to learn from their mistakes. He had to dispose of the bodies where they would never be found.

It took quite a few trips out here to fill the cisterns with the acid. He wanted the bodies disposed of fast, not wanting any smells of decomposition wafting through the area. It had worked out perfectly. That was until the current owner decided to open the place up as a bed and breakfast. Now, more and more people were walking about so he had to be extra careful, which he despised.

He traveled the path with his companion over his shoulder. She was heavier than he anticipated. The path was starting to show signs of use. He tried to avoid using the same path leading to the cabin, not wanting anyone to find it too easy. He had been here so many times before he could do it blindfolded and did not need a well-worn path to show him the way.

The ground was starting to get muddy; he needed to be mindful of how he left, not wanting to leave any footprints in the mud.

The sight of the small cabin caused his heart to beat faster in sheer anticipation, and he quickened his pace. With the current change in owners, he was forced to come by bayou, which made the trek a little more complicated, but still well worth the extra bit of exercise.

A rustling through the trees announced his presence. If he were a suspicious person, he would believe it to be the ghosts of those he had loved. He, however, did not believe in that nonsense. It was merely the storm starting to pick up.

He secured her to the bed so that he could strip. He laid his clothes out so they would dry somewhat before he left.

He looked down at his newest companion; she was so lovely lying there completely vulnerable and helpless. As he took his companion by force, the storm outside picked up, as if the rain was trying to keep up with his rhythm.

He ignored the girl's cries and screams. It had been too long since someone satisfied the monster deep inside of him.

By the time he was done and ready to return home, the rain was subsiding. He made his way back to his car, his clothes still damp and uncomfortable. He reached into the trunk and pulled out a towel that he kept handy for just these occasions. He did not want the fine leather of his car to be ruined by wet clothes.

The roads were devoid of life at this hour, so he arrived home in no time. He could not wait for a hot shower and a stiff drink to finish the night off.

Chapter 34

A fine, steamy mist shrouded the oak trees surrounding the plantation. A heavy breeze riffled through the Spanish moss dripping from the ancient branches. The crushed rock shimmered in the moonlight.

Bridgette watched as the rain came down in sheets outside. Lightning streaked across the dusky sky, followed by an ear-splitting crackle. The thunderstorm was right on top of them. Lately, she had despised these ominous thunderstorms.

Unable to calm her nerves, she walked into the kitchen to make herself a cup of hot tea. If she could not sleep, she may as well get some editing work done. She needed something to keep her mind occupied. Back in her room, she made herself comfortable on the settee. She opened up her laptop to work.

The piercing sound of the alarm clock woke her. During the early hours of the morning, she must have finally dozed off. She eased herself from her cramped position and stretched her constricted muscles. Opening the French doors, she stepped outside for a breath of fresh air. The air was crisp with the fragrance of pine and gardenia.

Dressing quickly, she headed off to the kitchen. After the breakfast rush was over, she went to town to run some errands.

While in town, Bridgette decided to stop by Lagniappe before returning home. She found a seat at the bar and was surprised that lunch time was relatively quiet.

The bartender asked, "Can I get you a drink?"

Bridgette replied, "Just a coke please, but can I also see your bar menu?"

"Sure." He reached under the bar top and pulled out a small laminated menu. The bar menu was a lot smaller than the dining room menu, but Bridgette was not in the mood to sit by herself in a crowd of people.

She decided on a basket of fried catfish with a side of crawfish etouffee. As she waited for her food, she sipped her coke and looked around. A few more people came into the bar, not wanting to wait for a table to become available in the dining room.

When the bartender placed the plate of fried catfish and crawfish etouffee in front of her, she was surprised the portion was larger than she would have expected for lunch. The spicy aroma of the etouffee teased her taste buds. She picked up a fork and dug into the spicy dish. She dragged her fried catfish through the accompanying homemade tartar sauce and was in heaven. It's a good thing she did not eat like this too often or her cholesterol levels would be off the charts. She could eat fried catfish every day and never tire of it, that and gumbo were her two favorite comfort foods.

As she enjoyed her lunch, she watched the local news. She was so busy at the plantation that she had only caught bits and pieces of the news lately. The weatherman was discussing the storm that hit the area last night and how it should be several more days before they would experience another storm like that. She could definitely take a few days of no rain. The ground outside was over-saturated with all the rain they had been getting, it did not take long last night for certain areas to flood.

Next, the screen flashed to a residential home where a couple in their fifties were talking to a young female journalist. They appeared to be severely distraught, but Bridgette was not sure about what so she asked the bartender if he could turn it up a little.

At the bottom of the screen flashed pictures of the three girls reported missing. The couple talking to the reporter was holding a photograph of another young girl. A shiver snaked down Bridgette's spine. A fourth young woman had apparently gone missing.

The bartender looked over at Bridgette, "It's a shame about Kelli Jo. She liked to party and could out drink most men in this town."

"What does everyone say about four women going missing over the last year?"

He shook his head, "Not much. All four of those girls liked to party and drink heavily. With that rainstorm last night, I can see how Kelli Jo would have found her way into the bayou without knowing it. She has blacked out on several occasions."

Bridgette felt sorry for anyone who needed to drink to that extent. "You would think since they were from here, they would know to stay away from the bayou."

"I can't explain it, but stranger things have happened around here."

Bridgette could not help but agree with him. As she was leaving the bar, she ran into Greg Dawson. "I am so sorry. I did not notice you there."

He smiled down at her, "That's okay. I was busy focusing on my phone and checking my emails; I was not looking where I was going."

"I've been guilty of that as well."

He asked, "I am guessing you have already eaten lunch?"

"Yes. I had a few errands to run here in town and decided to stop for a quick bite to eat." Bridgette could not explain why she felt the need to babble on incessantly when she was near this man. He probably thought she was a nonstop talker.

"Well, I guess my timing is off today. If I had come a few minutes earlier as I intended, we could have enjoyed our lunch together."

"That would have been very nice since I hate eating by myself. I should be used to it by now, but it can be lonely eating alone."

Greg shook his head, "I guess I have adapted to it, I have been doing it for so long."

Bridgette noticed the rush of feelings that ran through her body as she talked to the man. There was a strong physical attraction, but something about him unsettled her. She just could not place it.

He had her feeling like a schoolgirl with a crush. She adjusted her sunglasses as she took in his rugged good looks one more time. He was dressed more casually than usual, but he was still a very handsome man.

Even with her forebodings, she wanted to go out with him again, "We have to make plans to meet for lunch soon."

He agreed, "Absolutely. I checked out a little earlier. I will be gone for a few weeks on business, but when I return, I would love to stay with you again."

She smiled up at him, "I would love to have you stay with us. Just let me know when you are coming back and I'll have your room ready."

"I prefer to stay at your plantation so I will call you when my schedule is ironed out. It is homier than a hotel."

She thanked him for the warm compliment, "I am so glad to hear that. I want everyone to feel at home there and relax. I am afraid that some guests are scared they will hear something go bump in the night."

He shook his head, "I don't think you have anything to worry about. Honestly, I don't believe in ghosts."

"We have skeptics and believers who stay there, all hoping to find out if ghosts exist. Personally, I do believe ghosts walk among us. But I do not believe they are harmful. They are just lost souls that couldn't find their way into the light."

"When I come back to town, perhaps you can show me one of your ghosts at the plantation."

Bridgette let out a small laugh, "It is all a matter of how we see things. I would be more than happy to stay up with you one night to see what happens around the plantation. I've noticed a few guests stay out late in the courtyard hoping to catch a glimpse of something."

As Bridgette laid in bed that night, the news of the missing girls kept playing repeatedly in her head. She knew she had seen one of those girls somewhere, she just could not place where. For some unknown reason, the news story left her jumpy all day.

She woke with a scream trapped in her throat. The dream was similar to the other dreams, there were figures in the mist calling out, warning her. She flung off the covers and slipped on a robe. Needing some fresh air, she stepped outside. The early morning air helped calm her troubled spirit. It looked like it would be a gorgeous day. The sun was starting to peek through the sky, warm and inviting. Today would be ideal for a barbecue on the pier. Maybe that would shake the feelings from last night.

Lately, she swore something evil was looming overhead. Maybe she was reading more into the missing women than she needed to be, this was Rexma after all; nothing ever happened here. There was nothing evil lurking about. She was letting her imagination work overtime was all.

As she tried to shake off the remnants of the dream, she stepped into the shower, thankful there were only a few guests this morning. Business was doing well, but it was time consuming. She also had several books she needed to edit and send back to the authors.

The warm water helped to wake her. She reached for the bath sponge and lathered the soap over her body. The pulsating water eased her tense back muscles. After a few minutes of pure bliss, she turned off the water so that she could start her day.

Once in the kitchen, she started the coffee maker. While the coffee percolated, she turned on the news and busied herself with putting breakfast out before her guests started making their way downstairs.

Chapter 35

A sinister smile formed on his face. The police had found nothing on the missing girls. They suspected they either drowned or just left town. He managed a great accomplishment. In a town this size, everyone usually knew everything about anything, and yet no one knew anything about him.

He whistled as he walked down the sidewalk. The morning was already hot, but he did not care. He waved nonchalantly to a woman walking her dog as he noticed several people were already out this early in the morning.

The morning was full of life. A soft breeze blew gently through the town.

He must hunt again. Maybe this time he needed to hunt outside of town, perhaps New Orleans. The monster inside of him was moving closer to the surface, wanting to be fed more than usual.

Marla Allen was restless. Her nerves were strung too tight to relax. She had been stuck in the boring seminar her company sent her to all day. Perhaps a jog would help burn off some of this pent up energy. She really wanted to go party, but too many of her colleagues were here. That was not the impression she needed to set.

She changed into her running outfit and pulled her hair up in a ponytail. She found her phone's running playlist, put on her earphones, and headed out.

He knew as soon as he saw her, she would be his next companion. He could already imagine what it would be like to torture her and act out one of his fantasies.

She was a little over five feet tall and wore a Lycra running outfit, which left nothing to the imagination. Her hair was pulled into a ponytail high on her head and her body glistened with sweat. Her skin reminded him of rich caramel, showing him she spent a lot of time outside. If only he could have a taste of her right now, just to see if she tasted as sweet as she looked.

He could not pinpoint exactly what it was that attracted him to her. It's not as if she oozed sexuality, but there was a sensuality to her. She would be his.

It'd been too long since he brought a woman to his private place. The pain he inflicted on the last one excited him too quickly. He would take more time with the next one.

Need coursed through him as he followed her, keeping at a safe distance. He must wait for the opportune moment. Looking around, barely anyone was out. He was anxious to bring her to his little room. He could just imagine the way she would feel, see the fear in her eyes.

As soon as she rounded the bend into the shadows of the trees, he made his move. When he attacked, she struggled to break free from his firm grasp. He brought the ether-soaked rag to her mouth and clamped down on her, forcing her to breathe in the drug.

⸺⸻ ⟫ ∘◯◯∘ ⟪ ⸻⸺

She had a hard time waking. She remembered running and then arms grabbing her, and hands clamping over her mouth. Afraid to open her eyes, she slowly let the room come into focus. She tried to move, but discovered someone had restrained her on what felt like a bed. She looked around and spiraled into terror. The bed was the only furniture in the room.

A figure emerged from the darkness. The man was built like a linebacker, all muscle, and filled the entire doorway. It was too dark at first to make out any distinct features. As he moved closer, she saw that his lips were curled up menacingly, his eyes pierced into the darkness of the room.

When he saw that she was about to scream, he placed his finger on her mouth, "Shh, you don't want to scream. It would just make me mad."

She looked up at him with tears welling up in her eyes. "Please don't hurt me," she cried. "If you let me go, I won't tell a soul."

He bent down and stroked her hair. She tried to pull on her restraints one more time, but her attempts were futile. There was no way to escape. "Please, I just want to go home."

He slapped her hard across the face. She let out a pitiful moan. Fear grew deep inside her as she watched him start to unbutton his shirt. Frantically, she pulled at the restraints hoping beyond hope that she   could   break   free.

She tried to picture herself someplace other than here. She wished she could push what was happening to her out of her mind. She squeezed her eyes shut in pain as he increased his satanic torture.

He reached up and wrapped his hand around her throat, squeezing tightly. Her eyes felt as if they would pop from her head. Her lungs were on fire, desperately needing air to survive. She struggled to breathe when, suddenly, he released her throat.

He slapped her hard across the face, drawing blood. She let out a scream as fear and pain intermingled in her mind. She could not take much more.

Pain radiated through her body. Unable to hold back a scream, she let out a sound of sheer agony.

Chapter 36

He bolted upright in bed in sheer panic to look around, trying to place where he was. His breathing was rapid, and a cold sweat covered his body. All around him was an eerie silence. The only light in the room came from the small alarm clock on the nightstand. A light breeze from the overhead fan skimmed across his body, helping to cool him down even more.

The dream, or maybe nightmare was the better word, had been so real that he half expected to find himself surrounded by the haunting faces that plagued his dream. He walked naked to the bedroom window and peered outside, wanting to make sure there were no ghostly images lurking about.

He chastised himself for believing all the ghost stories he heard. He never took stock in them, and he certainly should not let it play into his mind now. There was no such thing as ghosts.

He walked into the bathroom and splashed some cold water onto his face. As he stared at his reflection in the mirror, the dream slowly resurfaced. The faces of all the women he trapped in the cisterns over the years haunted his mind. In his dream, they were chasing him, luring him back to where he trapped them. They reached for him with their bony fingers, taunting him with their guttural cries as they pleaded desperately not to be left alone in the dark.

The unwelcome dream seemed to linger in his mind. He could not shake the feeling of paranoia, as if something was waiting to happen. He tried to shake the feeling away; he could not afford to feel anything. The monster was rising up inside of him once more. He had been insatiable lately, constantly needing to be fed.

Today was a gloomy day, matching his mood perfectly. The sun refused to break through the heavy gray clouds that loomed overhead.

On the way home, he noticed a car on the side of the road with a flat tire. The driver caught his attention more than the car. He felt a stir deep inside of him just from a glimpse of her. Looking around to make sure no one was coming, he did a quick u-turn and slowly approached the car. She looked down at the car tire all the while shaking her head, clearly unsure of what to do.

The monster inside of him had begged for a playmate all day. A wicked smile formed on his face as he realized this might be just the perfect playmate for him. He would gladly help free her from her current dilemma, but she may not like the price.

Excited about his latest find, he pressed down on the gas pedal anxious to get to the cabin. For the next few minutes, he envisioned everything that he would do tonight. The rush of power flowed through him as he allowed the sensation to swallow him whole.

As he made his way down the bayou to his secret place, he looked down at the sleeping beauty. She was so easy to overcome, so unsuspecting and trusting. Too bad she would not learn from her mistake. Luck was on his side when he saw there was virtually no activity along the bayou.

After securing the bateau, he threw the young woman over his shoulder and made his way to the cabin. He moved along the tree line, making sure he remained hidden. The crunch of dead leaves and branches echoed through the swamp. He forced himself to slow down, not wanting anyone to hear his movements. Now was not the time to be discovered.

Chapter 37

Detective Ryan Boutin was fast asleep when he heard his cell phone ring. He had answered it before it woke his wife who had been up most of the night with their newborn baby.

"This better be good."

The dispatcher apologized, "Sorry detective. I hope I did not wake the baby."

He let out a sigh, "No, it sounds as if she is still asleep. What's wrong?"

"There is an abandoned car on Highway 172. It is registered to a Mindy Stephens from Brighton, Mississippi."

A shiver of apprehension ran down his spine. With four girls already missing, he did not like that there might be another one. "Is there a problem with the car?"

"The responding officer says it has a flat tire, sir. There are tire tracks behind the car, but there was no sign of the woman."

"Maybe someone brought her to find some help."

"Well, yes sir, Officer Richard suspected that too, but he says a spare tire and jack are in the trunk."

"Call Detective Comeaux. We'll check it out."

"Yes, sir."

He laid in bed for a moment before getting up, being mindful of his sleeping wife. She propped herself up on an elbow, "Is everything okay?"

He stood up and stretched his body before finding his clothes. "It's probably nothing. An abandoned car was found on the side of the road."

She asked, "Would you like me to fix you some coffee?"

He bent down and kissed her, "No, you get some sleep. I am sure that the little princess will be awake soon enough."

Not listening to him, he watched as she shuffled off to the kitchen. By the time he was finished with his shower and dressed, the aroma of coffee filled the air. He hated that she was awake with him this early since the little one kept her busy.

When he entered the kitchen, he found that she had prepared him a breakfast sandwich and a thermos of coffee. She was sitting at the kitchen table eating a bowl of oatmeal and playing on her laptop.

He bent down and kissed her mouth, "Thanks, hon."

When he stepped outside, he saw Detective Comeaux pull up, "Do you have any idea why we are being called to an abandoned car?"

Boutin shook his head, "No, but I guess we will find out soon enough."

It did not take them long to arrive at the scene. The morning sun was just starting to peek through the fog that rolled in from the bayou. It was already humid outside, which meant it would be a scorcher of a day.

Sheriff Anslum walked over to greet them, "Morning."

They replied in unison, "Morning sir."

Sheriff Anslum informed them, "I have a bad feeling about this one. Come daybreak, I plan on having search and rescue scour the area for her."

Detective Comeaux ran his hands through his hair, "It could be that another woman pulled up behind her, and they went to find some help you know."

"That could be. I plan on having someone stay here, so you two look around, and see if anything stands out."

Detective Boutin looked around into the darkness. They would not be able to do anything until daybreak. While waiting for dawn, the mosquitoes made a meal out of them. It had taken an hour before the sun began to filter through the trees that lined the road.

It took another thirty minutes for the K-9 unit to get to the scene. A petite woman made her way out of the van along with the bloodhound. Her partner was a well-muscled man who appeared to have woken up on the wrong side of the bed.

The bloodhound immediately started sniffing around the car and walking in circles around the trunk. The young woman walked up to the two detectives, "Hi. I am Officer Amy Landry, and this is my partner Officer Joshua Thompson."

After Detective Benoit had made the appropriate introductions, he informed the K-9 unit of what was going on, "We have an abandoned vehicle with a flat tire. The owner is nowhere to be found."

"Do you have an article of clothing or something belonging to the owner?"

He nodded his head, "There is a suitcase in the trunk that no one has touched. No one has touched the car except to pop the trunk and make sure her body was not in there. After you are done, we will have a tow truck bring it back to the garage to be properly processed."

Officer Landry asked, "What makes you suspicious that something has happened to the woman?"

"Nothing really, we are just being extremely cautious. Four women have gone missing this year with no bodies found."

"Okay then. Let's see what Old Blue here can find." She opened the door to allow him to get a good sniff of the inside and the victim's purse. Next, she carefully pulled some articles of clothing from the trunk and let him smell that as well. He caught a scent right away at the trunk and just circled the area near the tire tracks. Officer Thompson informed them, "It looks as if she did get in the vehicle that pulled in behind her."

Detective Comeaux got on the phone with forensics. "We need to tow this car to the garage ASAP and have it processed. I also need someone on scene to take casts of tire tracks."

Chapter 38

Bill and Misty Freeman had been planning this trip to Rexma, Louisiana for months. Marquette Plantation was now open and allowing guests to stay there. The Freemans adored staying at new places and preferred to be one of the first to post a review. So far, they had stayed at numerous bed and breakfast inns, hoping to find a haunted one, but had no luck.

It was a long trip, over fifteen hours, from San Antonio, Texas to Rexma, but they finally arrived. They stopped over in New Orleans for a Muffaletta sandwich and hit the road once again, wanting to be there before dusk. The drive was mesmerizing, especially with the sun setting.

As they drove up, they noticed the deserted parking lot. As they stepped out of their car, the steamy heat of the day hit them full force. The house stood in front of them, the dusty shadows of twilight danced across the property. Misty could not wait to explore it and the land. She could already picture herself sitting on a rocker out front while reading one of her paranormal books. She was into everything haunted; the scarier, the better.

Bridgette saw her guests drive up and waited patiently for them. She watched in fascination as the piano keys rose and fell as it played by itself. Her ghost was playing a lovely concerto piece tonight. Having grown up with the nuances of the house, the piano playing by itself never bothered her, but she feared what it might do to her guests. She hoped with the arrival of new guests that they would remain quiet. So far, that had not happened. The piano could be easily explained.

Bridgette waited to greet her guests, "Welcome to Marquette Plantation."

Bill walked up to Bridgette, "Mr. and Mrs. Freeman from San Antonio. We made our reservations online."

Bridgette smiled up at the young man, "Yes sir. Everything is ready for you. Please, make yourself at home. I hope you enjoy your stay. Dinner is served at seven o'clock, breakfast starts at six o'clock and the dining room will remain open with various treats until checkout at one o'clock. You are more than welcome to explore the main grounds, but please do not venture into the cane fields and swamp land. A person can get lost out there quite easily if they don't know their way around the grounds."

Bill took his room key from her, "Thank you so much for opening your house to us. My wife is hoping this place is haunted."

"Well, hopefully, no ghosts will keep you up tonight. The house is very old though, and you never know what you may see. Pierre and Genevieve Marquette built the house in 1757 and the Marquette family have owned it ever since."

Bridgette pointed to the entryway mirror, "You will notice that the mirror in the entryway is cloaked with a black cloth. It is done in remembrance of my deceased ancestors. Years ago, my mother started this tradition and I keep it alive today. Over the years, some tragic deaths have occurred here. It has been a tradition, since the house was built, to cover every painting and looking glass, what we call mirrors today. Several family members swear that they have seen a face in the mirror, but I am not sure how true that is. My mother did not like the ghost stories and was always paranoid about looking in the mirror, thus she started the tradition to keep it cloaked."

Bridgette pointed over to the doors that opened to the front parlor, "If you notice on the front parlor doors, the keyholes are upside down. That is because Genevieve Marquette was also a very superstitious woman. She believed that if the keyholes weren't set in just so, then evil spirits would find their way into that room."

Misty came up behind Bill and happily exclaimed, "Oh, this is so exciting. This is exactly what I wanted. I have stayed at various plantations since I was a teenager and have yet to find one that is really haunted."

Bridgette smiled at her, not wanting to scare away other guests with talk about a haunted plantation. That could scare business right off. "Well, I hope you aren't too disappointed when nothing shows up tonight."

Misty could barely contain her excitement. The very thought of seeing a ghost sent goosebumps up and down her arms. "It will be okay. This is a lovely place."

Bridgette agreed, "Yes, it is. There is an old blacksmith shop out back, which you can explore as well as various other buildings. In your room is a brochure with the layout of the plantation and the areas you are welcome to explore."

"Thank you so much for your hospitality."

"You are in Room Four upstairs and to your left. If you need anything, please don't hesitate to ask."

Misty was so excited about spending the night here, she could hardly contain herself. It was almost midnight before they climbed into bed. As she fell asleep, Bill informed her that he was going outside for one more smoke. She despised him smoking, but she could not complain in front of him since she had her own vices.

Somewhere between REM sleep and dozing, a rush of cold air blew across her. She grabbed a blanket to warm herself and felt Bill's side of the bed push down as he climbed in bed. She moved closer to him to warm up. Reaching for him, she found that he was not there.

Suddenly, the whole room was freezing. A sensation washed over her, as if there was someone else in the room with her. She bolted upright in bed. A chill swept over her when she saw the silhouette of someone sitting at the corner of the bed just watching her.

She tried not to panic. Could she make contact with this ghost? Did she want to? As the ghost looked at her for a moment, Misty thought it would actually speak to her. Something in the ghost's eyes resonated with her. This ghost seemed to be either scared or angry about something. Misty could not wait to ask the owner in the morning if someone died in this very room.

She believed the ghost was asking for help, but for what? For some reason, she could pick up on its emotions. If only she could help it find peace, but how? Then, as quickly as it had appeared, it disappeared.

Misty hoped that the ghost was not upset that they were spending the night here. She would hate that she upset someone, even if it was just a ghost. She had been obsessed with seeing one for years now and she could barely contain her excitement. It's a shame Bill was not here to see it. She should have picked up her camera and taken a quick picture. That would have been perfect.

Chapter 39

Bridgette walked into the dining room and grinned as she surveyed the guests enjoying their breakfast. The young family that stayed last night looked well rested and the children's laughter was music to her ears. She had worried about allowing children to stay the night, but then she realized that this old home had survived for many years with the squeal of laughter and pitter patter of little feet.

Looking outside, the place was starting to take shape. She had hired a local landscaper to help her with the maintenance, so the grounds looked magnificent. They worked out a fair trade; he was in desperate need of a place to stay, and the grounds were more than she could handle. When Father Bill Rabelais, from Mary Immaculate Catholic Church, approached her several months ago about Tim Doucette looking for work, she jumped on the opportunity. After talking with Tim, they came up with a proposal that helped both of them. He would stay in the old caretaker's cottage, which was still in good shape and had electricity and running water, and would come to the house for his meals. Bridgette could not explain it, but she had not been as jumpy since having Tim stay on the property. He helped put her mind at ease.

She greeted Tim as he walked in from the kitchen, "Good morning Tim. Where are you off to today?"

"I have a new client I am meeting with in town. The developer, Marcus DuPont, is looking to hire someone to landscape some of his properties. I sure hope that is okay with you Ms. Marquette.”

She gave him a look of utter surprise, “Of course it is. Why wouldn’t it be?”

“I know that he has pressured you an awful lot lately to purchase this place.”

She shook her head, “Don’t let that bother you none. He isn’t the only one interested in buying the plantation. I have nothing against the man.”

“I don’t want to make you mad. You have been so kind to me.”

“Think nothing of it. Did you sleep well last night?”

Tim looked at her sheepishly, “The ghosts seemed to be upset last night. I just locked my doors tight and prayed for morning light.”

“What do you mean the ghosts were upset last night? I hope you don’t think they are trying to scare you off?”

“I swear I saw lights off the bayou last night and heard some kind of scream cut through the night. You did not hear anything?”

She told him honestly, “I have grown comfortable with their haunts over the years, I guess. I sure hope they don’t scare you or any of the guests away with their mischievousness.”

“Since this is an old Louisiana plantation home, I knew that ghosts would roam the grounds. I am sure I will get accustomed to it. With regards to your guests, I suspect that most are hoping for the haunted experience, even if they do not want to come out and admit it. There is no hiding the fact that something roams around here at night.”

Bridgette hoped it was only the old ghosts roaming the grounds. There had been no recent deaths around here, yet there seemed to be more ghosts than she remembered. Still, she wondered what might be going on. She did not want to believe that it might be her parents.

As she stepped outside for a breath of fresh air, an uneasy feeling swept over her. She shrugged it off. She was just being silly.

She walked down to the bayou to enjoy the brief solitude. When her ancestors built the plantation, they took full advantage of not only the bayou, but the breezes that rolled off of it. She looked around as she absorbed the history. Over the years, her family made sure not to change the plantation, even when modernizing the old home. Even though a central air conditioning unit with heat was added, on mornings like this, all the French doors could still be opened to allow the breeze to blow in.

She was pleased with her decision to open Marquette Plantation Bed & Breakfast. She never expected it would be this popular right off. So far, it had been a tremendous success. The historical society had helped her with the tiny details and word of mouth kept the rooms full.

As she walked back to the house, a darkness seemed to fall over the area. She looked up to see that a dark cloud blocked the sun. As she looked at the plantation, it appeared to be covered in a fine mist. She stopped for a moment, unsure of what she was seeing. For a moment, she thought she saw a figure surface in the mist.

As a breeze blew in off the bayou, an odd feeling came over her that something was askew here. She shook off the feeling. She was reading too much into what Tim told her earlier was all. The ghosts here were not restless. Nothing was amiss.

Vidrine's, Bridgette's grand-mere, haunting words echoed in her mind once more. The world was filled with ghosts. Some were trapped on this earth by events that were cataclysmic, either tragic or sometimes joyous. It could be that these spirits could not, or refused to, leave because of what happened to them or they must do something before moving on.

Vidrine lived in New Orleans and was a big believer in voodoo and its mysterious powers. She believed that there was not any difference between her believing in voodoo and her parents believing in their Catholic religion. Bridgette's mom grew up with strong beliefs from both grand-meres and kept those same beliefs. When Bridgette's mom met her dad, she fell madly in love and converted to Catholicism for him. Her mom kept her strong Catholic beliefs, but voodoo also held a place in her heart from her childhood, so she passed those beliefs on to Bridgette.

Where in the Catholic religion they believed in the devil, in voodoo they had a spirit that controlled the malevolent spirits of the night. That spirit was known as Kalfu.

Voodoo had been given a bad name by some who had evil intents. That was not voodoo, but those who wished to practice black magic. Voodoo was intended to be a positive teaching of life and nature. In the voodoo belief, you could call the spirits, like saints, who would come and help with your problems.

Bridgette closed her eyes and saw her grand-mere standing in front of her. There was always something special about her appearance. She had one of the kindest faces Bridgette ever saw. Her hair was gray and had been since an early age, but she never once considered coloring it. She said she was proud of each and every strand.

Growing up, Bridgette could remember walking into her grand-mere's house and seeing all the exquisite artwork and fascinating trinkets. There were Gris Gris bags, potions, and oils that she used. She had several statues, mainly of saints, as well as a skull mask and a few African tribal pieces. There was even a voodoo altar set up in her house. She was well known for her handmade voodoo dolls.

Lately, she had contemplated finding someone to perform a banishing spell on the house for any evil spirits that may be lurking about. She did not want to banish the spirits of her ancestors, but she was fairly certain that a new presence lurked about; one that was evil. If performed correctly, the banishing spell would help the ghosts she wanted to move on and find some peace so that they would leave. Her grand-mere always warned of the importance of doing the spell right because it could be very dangerous if done incorrectly.

As she walked back inside the house, the buzz of chatter from her guests filled the entryway. Several more of her guests were in the dining room and front parlor, ready to begin their day. Delores outdid herself this morning on the buffet; a variety of muffins were available as well as scrambled eggs, grits, and her homemade biscuits. Bridgette chose a blueberry streusel muffin and a cup of coffee. This may be her only chance to eat a quick bite before tending to her guests and offering tours.

A young woman was coming to interview for a front desk position in the afternoons so that Bridgette could have a little time to herself. If Marquette Plantation Bed & Breakfast stayed booked, she might also look into hiring a chef. So far, she and Delores had done well at keeping up with the demand, but she detested imposing on Delores.

After her bath, Bridgette slipped on a pair of yoga pants and a T-shirt. A chill had settled in the room and she wanted something warm to wear.

She plopped down in the overstuffed chair that she had arranged in the corner of the room and sighed. Doubts about making the B&B a success plagued her mind. The ghosts were more restless of late. She could not explain why there were so many new ghosts.

She could not explain it, but there seemed to be a strange energy in the house now. Almost as if there was an eerie presence nearby. From the corner of her room, a movement caught her attention. A shadowy figure stepped from the corner, gliding in her direction. From the shape, it appeared to be a woman. It appeared cloudy, but definitely a woman. Her features were not completely distinguishable, but she had a shape. The wall was visible through her.

A glowing aura surrounded her. "It's so cold... So, so cold."

Bridgette's mouth opened, but she remained speechless. She stared at the form in silence. *What did she want?*

The woman slowly lifted her arm and pointed towards the bayou.

Silence enveloped the room; the only noise heard was the thump of Bridgette's excited heart. She panted, trying to catch her breath. She sat there, transfixed.

The image once again spoke. "Please, please help me. I am so cold."

Bridgette asked, "How? How can I help you?"

Instead of answering, the ghostly woman let out a loud wail and dissipated.

Chapter 40

Bridgette had to run into town to pick up a few things before the gala. The local multiple sclerosis chapter was having their annual gala here. Bridgette promised them the rental free of charge and all she asked for in return was their thanks. This was free advertisement for her. Some very prominent people would be attending tonight. A ticket ranged from $150 to $200, plus Bridgette offered a discount rate to any guests who wished to stay overnight.

For the price of the ticket, guests would enjoy an evening of music, dancing, and dining; complete with wine, champagne, and various other beverages. Several of the local restaurants donated a sampling of food, which helped cut the cost even more for the charity.

Since it was so close to lunch time, she stopped by Lagniappe for a quick bite. As she stepped out of her car, an eerie sensation crept over her, as if she was being watched. She shook off the feeling and headed inside. The place was busy today, even at this early hour. The tables were jammed with talkative guests, and even the bar seemed to be full of people. Everyone in town must have had the same idea as her.

Lately, she had become comfortable eating out alone in the small town, but today it was glaringly apparent she was dining alone. It seemed as if everyone here had a companion. She finally found a seat at the bar, toward the back. As she made herself comfortable, she still could not shake the feeling that someone was watching her. She took a quick look around to see if she noticed anyone. Not seeing anyone, she brought her attention back to the young woman who was busy hopping from table to table, writing down orders.

Bridgette did not see how she could walk in those high heels all day. Her feet must kill her by the end of the day. She wore several bangles on her wrist that jangled every time she wrote or made any movement.

The bartender saw her sitting down and asked if she would like anything, "A coke and today's special, please."

He smiled at her, "Coming right up."

As she sipped her drink, she checked her emails. There were a few from clients, reminding her she needed to get busy reading manuscripts, getting those edited and out the door, especially if she wanted to keep her clients.

"Good afternoon Ms. Marquette."

Bridgette looked up to see Marcus DuPont standing in front of her. She extended her hand, "Mr. DuPont." She waved her hand to the empty seat next to her, "Would you care to sit?"

He pulled out the chair next to her, "How is Marquette Plantation Bed & Breakfast going?"

"It's doing well. Thank you for asking."

"I am glad to hear it. I won't keep you from your lunch. I saw you walking in and just wanted to say hi."

Perplexed by his visit, she asked, "Would you care to join me?"

He shook his head, "No, I was curious how the new business was going. If you are ever interested in selling, please don't forget about me."

She should have known why he stopped by, "I can't part with the plantation. It's in my blood and part of my heritage."

He nodded, "I understand. Your dad had the same love for it. He was never interested in selling the property either."

As he sauntered off, the bartender delivered the shrimp stew. "Can I get you anything else?"

Bridgette shook her head, still taken aback by the sudden appearance of Mr. DuPont. Could he be the one she felt watching her?

To add to her unease, when she walked into the grocery store, on the bulletin board at the main doors was a white flyer among the dozens of business cards tacked to the corkboard. The flyer caught Bridgette's attention.

Missing: Amy Daigle, age 20, last seen leaving 223 Maple Street

In the color picture, the young girl looked somehow older than the tender age of twenty. Perhaps it was the sad eyes. Bridgette wondered if the person who created the flyer was a concerned relative, a friend, or perhaps a boyfriend.

Bridgette wondered if she perhaps disappeared on purpose, or had something happened to the young girl.

Chapter 41

Bridgette was anxious about the gala tonight. Her mouth watered at the thought of some of the more popular dishes. Chez Maurice, out of New Orleans, would serve samples of their famous bread pudding with amaretto sauce. The Cheesecake Bistro, here in Rexma, would serve samples of their bananas foster. Also on the menu was crawfish etouffee, turtle sauce piquante, fried alligator, jambalaya, and a duck and Andouille gumbo.

Everybody who was anybody would be attending this event. They would be dressed to the hilt so she made sure everything looked elegant. Fresh flowers adorned the plantation and candlelight helped set the mood. It had been a long time since such an elegant affair had been held in these walls. She anxiously waited to see the men in their tuxedos and the women in their cocktail dresses.

Once Bridgette was confident with the progression of everything, she rushed to her room to get dressed.

He watched as she mingled with the guests. So far, she had turned down all of his offers to purchase the plantation. Tonight may be his chance to charm her. One way or another, he would get this plantation.

He walked up to the buffet where she was talking to people and feigned interest in the various appetizers, uninterested in any of the tempting morsels. Choosing a few of the smaller appetizers, he loitered about waiting for his moment to move in and talk to her. Through veiled eyes, he observed her. She was a very attractive woman, and even though she was older than most of the women he chose, she did not show her age at all. She would be one of those lucky women who grew old gracefully. He could not help but admire her clean and well-toned skin. Her skin was perfectly kissed by the sun, which meant she took great care in protecting it from the sun's harmful rays, but enjoyed being outside as much as inside. She was also a little shorter than he liked; with his build, he preferred women closer to 5'10" and she was maybe 5'5". Her body, though, was sheer perfection. Another guest interrupted his eavesdropping. Damn, it would be just when she started talking about how business was going. "This is a lovely event, isn't it?" The woman looked at him with hunger in her eyes. Oh, what he would love to do to her if he did not have ulterior motives tonight.

He smiled down at her, "Yes, it is very lovely. The hostess did an excellent job."

Just then, Bridgette must have overheard his conversation because she looked over at him and grinned. He watched as she blushed and tucked a strand of hair behind her ear. That's when he realized it might be easier than he thought to charm her.

She continued speaking to her guests and glanced his way now and then with a smile on her lips. He loved being able to "play" women. They were so easy to manipulate. She would be putty in his hands by the end of the night.

The evening was going better than she anticipated. She stepped out to the courtyard for a breath of fresh air. The weather was eerily calm tonight, almost as if a thunderstorm was brewing. Tonight was not the night for a thunderstorm. A downpour of rain would run the gala guests away.

Marcus DuPont watched Bridgette step outside and followed her. He had watched her all evening. He admired the way she handled herself. Even in business dealings, she looked at you level and direct, never avoiding eye contact. The way she carried herself gave her the impression of height. She was a very attractive woman with a narrow waist, and a face that most models would kill for. She had high cheekbones that she accentuated with a soft touch of blush, and full lips on a mouth that just begged to be kissed. He wondered if her hazel eyes changed colors in the throes of passion.

"Business must be doing well."

Bridgette jumped, "You startled me. I did not know anyone else was out here."

Marcus let out a deep laugh, "I saw you come out here and couldn't help but follow you."

She looked at him with speculation on her face, "You won't be able to get me to change my mind. I have no intentions of selling this place."

"Perhaps I came out here to enjoy a beautiful night

with a beautiful lady."

Bridgette blushed from the compliment. There was no denying the true exotic beauty of her Cajun heritage. "I guess I should apologize. Here, I thought you had an ulterior motive for following me out here."

Despite himself, Marcus moved in closer to her. Animal magnetism coursed through him, the chemistry between the two sizzled in the air. "Maybe I do have an ulterior motive. It's just not what you are thinking."

He found himself caught in her gaze. This woman was completely alluring. He knew he should not kiss her, but something must be in the air. She was here and he was here, and suddenly kissing her seemed to be so right.

His lips met hers and he felt her arms wrapped around his neck, pulling him closer. His arms encircled her waist as the kiss intensified. She tasted of ripe peaches and he could not seem to get enough.

Her lips parted in a soft moan as she melted into his body. Desire heated her blood as he drew her flush against him.

She kept telling herself this was crazy; she should not be kissing this man. As he pulled away, he looked into her eyes and saw the desire building inside of her. She pulled him back to her mouth and kissed him with sweet provocation. Their mouths connected with hot, passionate urgency.

In the distance, he heard the door open and someone laugh. They quickly broke away reluctantly. "This is so unlike me."

"Do you want me to leave you alone?"

His nearness made her breath catch. If standing next to him fully clothed could make her body do such crazy things, what would it be like to be intimate with this man? She shook her head, "No, please stay. I need to show the guests to their rooms first though." She could not believe she was even contemplating this.
"I am in no hurry to go anywhere."

"I have private quarters away from the guests." She headed to the French doors that led to her room, "If you want, you can wait for me in here. I will try to not keep you waiting."

He kissed her one more time, "You can change your mind you know?"

She kissed him back, "I can't promise you this will lead to anything more than tonight."

"Go tend to your guests. I will be waiting."

It took her a little over an hour to bid farewell to those who were not staying. Delores offered to make sure the guests made it to their rooms if she wanted to call it a night so she slipped into her room, fearing that her guest had slipped out without her noticing. She let out a sigh of relief when she saw him lying on the bed.

She hurried towards the bed and as soon as their lips made contact, a desperate need to feel close to someone took over. They tumbled onto the bed. The room was lit only by the soft glow of the moonlight finding its way in through a small slit in the curtains.

Even in the dark of the night, he saw the desire in her

eyes. His calloused hands wandered over the silkiness of her body. His kisses trailed down her body, pausing a moment at the curve of her neck.

Her hands massaged and kneaded his shoulders before exploring the rest of his well-defined body. The mindlessness of need washed over her body as he teased her with his tongue. She savored every torturous moment.

She loved the feel of his heart beating against hers As his hands wandered further down her body, she felt as if her body would burst into flames at any moment. She was not sure how much longer she could take this sensual torment.

Later that night, they made love again. Neither was sure who initiated it, but both needed each other once again. Once done, they fell into a deep slumber.

Bridgette woke slowly the next morning. Was last night a dream? She rolled over to find him staring down at her.

She could not remember the last time she slept so deeply. The ghosts did not wake her last night and she hoped they left her guests alone as well.

She looked up at him and smiled languidly. Last night she did not realize how broad and tanned his shoulders were. His hair was mussed slightly and he had a shadow of a beard along his jawline. He bent down and kissed her, "Good morning."

"Good morning. I wish I did not have a house full of guests to take care of." Bridgette heard Delores in the kitchen already getting breakfast ready. They had a full house today and it would be busy until after lunch when they all checked out.

"I have to get back as well. I have a meeting shortly." As he got out of bed, Bridgette watched him. He had a gorgeous, well-defined body. She followed him into the shower, "We may as well conserve water."

He pulled her close to him, "My thoughts exactly."

Chapter 42

Adriana Thompson was so excited about her trip to Louisiana. She saved the money she earned tutoring just to afford this trip. This summer, instead of teaching summer school, she would enjoy herself. This was the biggest and most expensive vacation she had ever taken and it would be worth every dime it was costing her.

Adriana had taught American History for ten years now, but for some unknown reason, Louisiana history had always drawn her in. She made plans to go to New Orleans for a week and absorb as much history as she could. New Orleans was known to be the land of vampires, ghosts and, of course, voodoo. This was a fantasy come true for her. She found an inexpensive hotel to stay in while there, and then she would rent a car and drive to Rexma, Louisiana. Part of her vacation would be spent at an actual plantation home.

She was giddy with excitement. She had not decided yet if she wanted to see an actual ghost at Marquette Plantation or just experience the ambiance of staying there.

As Adriana arrived at Marquette Plantation Bed & Breakfast, she bubbled over with excitement. New Orleans had been more than she expected. She had not been bored once while there. She ate more than she should have, but the food was to die for. Most days she explored The French Quarter, enjoying all the jazz musicians that played for entertainment there and visited Bourbon Street with its grand nightlife.

Adriana was ready to relax a bit though and enjoy her stay at the bed & breakfast. As she drove up to the house, she was in complete awe. This place was truly historic and fantastic. It was something straight out of the movies.

When she entered Marquette Plantation Bed & Breakfast, she looked around and just absorbed everything. If she were to close her eyes, she could envision an elegant tea being served in one of the front parlors or the ballroom in use. She could see the elegant Southern belles swirling around in their gowns being led around the dance floor by handsome gentlemen in their dress attire. She could imagine someone sitting at the grand piano playing a musical piece while a fire burned in the enormous hearth.

The staircase in the foyer was the grandest she had ever seen. Even the furniture proudly displayed around the house had been chosen with tender, loving care. The owners of this plantation took great pride in keeping it well-preserved.

After checking in, she walked upstairs to inspect her room. She turned the light on and was taken aback by its beauty. A beautiful, four-poster canopy bed sat on an antique Persian rug, allowing the natural beauty of the hardwood floors to shine through. As with most houses this age, there was no closet, but an antique wardrobe was available for her use. She was, however, glad that the owner did renovate the upstairs to where each room had its own private bath. She was not sure how she would feel about sharing a bathroom with other guests. Large French doors opened to the balcony that wrapped around the house. She looked out and noticed her room overlooked the courtyard and the bayou that ran along the back of the property. She could not wait to get a book and curl up on the chaise lounge that was available for her use on the balcony.

The courtyard out back was breathtaking. It was paved with red brick and in the center sat a fountain surrounded by red roses. Out on the bayou, a white egret came in for a landing. This place was more than she had ever hoped for.

By the time Adriana returned to her bedroom, it was almost midnight. She had stayed up with several of the other guests in the front parlor and talked to Ms. Marquette about her family history and living here. Even if she did not see any ghosts, this place was magical. A chill went down her spine as she thought of all the history these walls held.

Before crawling into bed, she stepped outside on the balcony. Off in the distance, near the bayou, a flickering light caught her attention. She swore the light was moving. She tried to peer into the darkness to make out what she may be seeing. A movement in the courtyard drew her eyes, and a ghostly image seemed to be walking around. It must have sensed that it was being watched because Adriana swore it turned around and looked at her. Suddenly, the image lifted its arm and pointed toward the flickering light.

A feeling of uneasiness washed over her. The moon

shifted and the image disappeared.

She wondered about the flickering light. Could it be another ghost? If only she had a better look. She was certain that she saw a ghost in the courtyard, it had a nearly translucent look to it.

As she drifted off to sleep, a vision of an elegant lady flitting around the courtyard filled her mind. She paced back and forth, mumbling something, but Adriana could not make out what she was saying. It sounded as if she was speaking in French, but she did not understand the dialect. She kept pointing to the bayou. The picture was so clear in Adriana's head, she wondered if she was dreaming. The room became chilled and she reached for another blanket at the foot of the bed. The ghost seemed to pace faster and faster, as if agitated.

When Adriana awakened the next morning, the dream was still fresh in her mind. She would have to ask Bridgette about the woman who visited her.

Chapter 43

She woke up dazed and confused; her mind cloudy. She was unsure where she was, but she knew it was not her bed.

She lay on a bed, her wrists and ankles were restrained to its frame. She pulled as hard as she could to loosen the restraints, but the rope was too tight. The duct tape across her mouth pulled at the corners. She tried not to panic, but the blood in her veins turned ice cold from fear. The room smelled musty, old. It was dark and the moonlight filtering in through the small window created eerie shadows along the room. Something crawled along her body and she tried not to think about what it could be. She could just picture the spiders and bugs that were crawling along her skin.

Her head felt as if it would split open. A shuffling noise sounded behind her head and she became paralyzed with terror. She tried to move her head back and forth to see if she could catch a glimpse of what made the noise, unsure if she really wanted to know.

Closing her eyes, she attempted to remember how she ended up here. Who would do this to her? Her mind kept going over all the horrific things that could happen to her. A chill snaked down her spine at the horrors her captor would do to her body.

This had to be a nightmare. This could not be happening to her. She closed her eyes tight and opened them slowly, praying she would find herself in her room, in her own bed. She wanted to be any place but here.

The various missing person flyers, and the evening news ran through her mind, as she tried not to think about what may be in store for her. None of the missing women had been heard from. They were presumed dead, but no bodies had been found and, more than likely, would not be. Would she be a statistic, just a quick blurb on the evening news? Tears formed in her eyes and flowed down her cheeks.

As she started to wallow in self-pity, another noise brought her to her senses. Her breath caught in her throat as she listened to see exactly where the sound came from. The floorboards creaked on the side of her.

Her survival mode kicked in, and she desperately tried to free herself from the restraints. A rush of adrenaline ran through her when she felt the restraints loosen. That simple feat gave her hope. She jerked her arms harder, praying that her hands would slip free. The bristles on the rope cut into her sensitive skin, but she ignored the pain. She kept struggling to free herself; she tried to rotate her wrists to see if they would slip through. The ropes gave a little, renewing her efforts, she pushed through the pain. She could just imagine how red and bloody her wrists were, but she refused to give up.

Her hands started to slip through the small opening. She braced herself for one more attempt. This would be it. She must act quickly though, even if it meant she had to break the bones in her hand. Broken bones could heal. If her captor went through this much trouble to bind her, he did not plan on allowing her to escape.

She tried to keep the noise of her escape to a minimum. If that was him making noise, she did not want to alert him of her attempt to free herself. Perspiration covered her body. Fatigue took over, but she refused to give up. She could not if she wanted to survive.

She forced herself to relax. If she forced her hands to go limp, maybe she could pull them free. She took in a deep breath through her nose and quietly let it out. Somehow, she managed to force her body to relax.

If she could not escape, she would die. This was not how she planned on her life ending. She figured she would live to a ripe old age, just like her grandparents. This was so unfair, life was unfair. She did not want her face to end up on a missing person's flyer. She did not want her loved ones wondering what happened to her. She feared her soul would be trapped here, waiting for her body to be found.

Did anyone even know she was missing? Was anyone out there looking for her? How long had she been here? She had lost all track of time. From the moonlight filtering in from the window it was night, but that was all she could tell. For all she knew, she had been asleep for several days.

She had to accept her fate. She could not free herself from her restraints. Shock took over as the fight to live left her body. Hopefully, her death would be quick and painless.

She begged God to help her; prayed that a miracle would happen. Then her hand slipped through the knot. Acting quickly, she tried to work on the other knot. If she freed her hands, she could free her legs.

The sudden movement of rolling over to her side caused her to become dizzy. For a moment, she was disoriented. She forced herself to push through it. This was her one chance and she could not blow it.

His image appeared before her as if he materialized out of thin air. There was something dark and sinister about his presence. Her cry was muffled against the duct tape still across her mouth. She was in such a hurry to free herself from the ropes, she forgot about the tape.

Chapter 44

Bridgette walked out onto the pier to enjoy the scenery for a few moments. Right now, all of her guests were situated and enjoying themselves. She had set up a bar outside where they could enjoy a glass of wine, as well as some cheese and crackers before dinner.

She watched as a bec croche, which was what the Cajuns called a bird indigenous to this region, walked slowly on its delicate legs in the shallow waters of Bayou Renee. It was searching for a late afternoon snack as well. The bird craned its neck as it found a school of minnows to eat. They must have been unaware of the bird's presence.

The late afternoon sun moved toward the bottom of the azure sky, its fading rays disappearing into the trees that lined the backdrop of the bayou. A light breeze blew off of the water, bringing with it the dank smells.

Bridgette watched as a small boat made its way down. The noise from the engine broke the tranquil silence of the afternoon. The driver of the bateau was out for a casual drive and in no hurry to get to their destination. The bec croche sat unmoving, at ease with noise from boats that traveled the bayou. Most of the wildlife here was at ease with frequent intrusions, staying put and not scurrying off in fear.

Bridgette swore the view from this pier was one of the best in all of Louisiana. She and her dad had so many good times here fishing. Her favorite activity was catching redfish when they found their way into the brackish waters. They would bring the fish back to the house for her mom to stuff and bake. Her dad preferred to catch a mess of catfish to fry. Living on the bayou, they never went hungry.

Unfortunately, the tranquil scenery did little to soothe Bridgette's troubled nerves. She took her phone out of her jeans pocket and texted Haley.

"I am such a bad person. I am dating one man while sleeping with another man."

Haley replied back, "??? Are you sleeping with both men?"

"No, and I don't know if I should tell Greg that there is someone else now. But, in all honesty, Marcus and I just had that one night together, but it was an amazing night."

"Girl, you don't have to tell either man anything. Besides, you need to enjoy yourself."

"This is all just so confusing. And not something I normally do."

"Exactly. You need to break free from that shell you have built around yourself. Enjoy life."

Bridgette woke from a deep sleep. It took a minute for her eyes to adjust to the darkness of the room. She swore someone was calling her name. She had to blink several times before the shape standing in front of her took a form.

Genevieve must make contact with Bridgette; she must warn her of the danger. She had been patiently waiting for her to wake up, but she was growing weak. Just calling out her name had weakened her tremendously.

Genevieve waited for her to look directly at her and warned her, "There is evil here. A monster."

"What evil? Who is the monster?"

Genevieve looked solemnly at her, "I don't know who he is. I cannot see his face, but I can sense his presence. Even more tortured souls are here now and they wander the grounds as well."

"Do you know who they are? Where they came from?"

Genevieve replied, "No. I only catch glimpses of them. Their cries echo through the night. I cannot get too close to them; there is a darkness that surrounds them."

Bridgette was confused, "I don't understand."

"There is an evil that has broken the peace of this place. It has never been here before."

A shiver of fear ran down her spine. She had felt the same thing. "Do you know where this evil is?"

"No, it seems to move about the property, as if it knows this place. It has been here for some time now, but it is growing stronger. You must be careful. Something sinister haunts these grounds; it is filled with darkness and hatred."

She watched as Genevieve faded away. She could not help but fear what Genevieve was warning her about, though. She had been feeling the same presence lurking about.

Chapter 45

Bridgette helped Delores finish setting out the generous breakfast buffet. Along with the fresh blueberries, strawberries, and raspberries, there was also filled crepes. The fresh fruit would be the perfect accompaniment for the crepes. She also provided scrambled eggs, bacon, and sausage.

The smell of the chicken and sausage gumbo would also tantalize the guests as they ate their breakfast. Mamie's gumbo had become a favorite of the guests. Beignets were the preferred dessert for lunch.

Bridgette smiled at herself; Mamie Bouviere was too good to be true. When she first told Delores that she was considering hiring a chef, she never expected Delores to have someone already picked out for her. It turned out, Mamie recently moved back to be near her parents and had no luck finding a job nor a place she could afford.

They worked out an arrangement where she would stay in one of the old sharecropper's cabins as well as draw a salary. Mamie would be close enough to help her parents without having to live with them. Bridgette could relate to that feeling; she loved her parents dearly, but they all needed their own space at times. If they had lived together twenty-four seven, it would not have been a pretty sight. When Bridgette decided to take the job in South Carolina, she was ecstatic over the fact that she would finally live far away from this small town and away from her parents' ever watchful eyes. Her joy was short lived because a week after moving there, she became homesick. If it had not been for the fact that she truly loved her job, she may have moved right back home. Her mom was the one to make her see reason, explaining that this was the chance of a lifetime and they would see each other as often as possible. Her parents kept their word, too. Every chance they had, they would visit South Carolina and whenever Bridgette could, she returned home.

Now, she had returned, but missed her parents greatly. If only she knew they would not be around forever. Their deaths had been a lesson to her; life was truly short and needed to be cherished every single moment.

The sounds in the kitchen brought her back to reality. She looked over at Mamie, "Are you sure there isn't something I can help you with?"

She shooed Bridgette out of the kitchen, "Mais non. Go tend to your guests and let me finish up in here."

Bridgette still felt lost not being in the kitchen cooking breakfast, but Mamie had everything under control. She loved walking into the kitchen and smelling the spices and aromas of the food. Delores was not kidding when she said the young woman's skills were truly something special.

When Bridgette met Mamie, she felt a sudden surge of kinship with the woman and vowed to herself that she would get to know her better. After all, Bridgette had few friends here in town. It would be nice to have an-other person to talk to and visit with.

Only, Mamie was a very closed person and Bridgette had found it difficult to get the woman to open up. But, Bridgette was hopeful that one day she would break through that hard shell Mamie had built around herself.

Lost in thought, Bridgette did not hear Tim come inside. "Excuse me, Miss Marquette." He spoke softly as if he were trying not to startle her. "I am done mowing the grounds. However, I have an errand to do in town. I'll be back this afternoon to finish weedeating and planting some more flowers."

"No hurry," she assured him. "Do it when you can. I probably stated this many times, but I love what you have done with the landscaping. The guests compliment me all the time, especially about the new waterfall and Koi pond."

His bright smile was a dazzling contrast to his dark skin. "It's an honor and privilege to help keep this place beautiful. And I cannot thank you enough for allowing me to stay here. You have been so nice to me."

While Bridgette was sitting on the back patio reviewing a manuscript, the sound of a woman crying broke her concentration. Worried that perhaps it was a guest, Bridgette went in search of the sad woman.

As Bridgette neared the water, a shadowy figure stood at the edge of the woods and stared out toward the bayou. Afraid that if she moved quickly, the ghost would disappear Bridgette walked slowly toward the figure.

"Hello. Is there something I can help you with?"

Startled, the ghostly figure turned away from Bridgette. "No, please don't go! I want to help you."

Deep sobbing wracked the young woman's body. "The pain, the pain is too much. I cannot... I cannot take the pain." Sobbing more, "I am still very, very afraid of him."

"How... How can I help you? Tell me who you are afraid of, perhaps I can help you move on."

"No, no. It is too dangerous. He is pure evil. No, it is better if you just stay away."

Before Bridgette could ask her any more questions, the ghost dissipated.

After returning home, Bridgette was still unsettled from the conversation she had with the ghost. Bridgette sent Haley a text. "I finally had a conversation with one of the new ghosts. She seemed consumed with grief and pain. She was terrified of someone, but I don't know who."

After a few minutes, Bridgette received a reply text. "Do you think something happened to her there?"

Bridgette replied back, "No, I don't see how that would be possible. Perhaps because of the other ghosts, this place has become a portal for all lost souls."

Bridgette laughed to herself as she read Haley's reply, "Girl, I would be freaked out. I don't think I could have talked to any ghost."

Replying back, "LOL. I needed a laugh. Good night, girly."

A few days later, Haley texted Bridgette, "Has your mystery guest returned?"

Bridgette replied, "No, I haven't seen her. Actually, I haven't seen any ghosts."

"Perhaps talking to you, she found the peace she needed to move on."

Bridgette thought about that comment before replying, "Maybe so. Either way, it has been nice with the ghosts quiet."

Haley's comment had Bridgette curious now. As night fell, Bridgette walked towards the woods and called out, "Hello... Hello is anyone out there? I would love to talk to you again, if you would like."

Bridgette waited several minutes to see if anyone replied. After no movement came from the woods, Bridgette went back inside. Perhaps Haley had been correct, and the young woman had found peace finally.

Chapter 46

Chris Ingram slowly shook his wife, "We are here."

Amanda woke up from her nap; it had been a long trip. They left Santa Fe early this morning and drove practically nonstop. They stopped to get a bite for lunch and then hit the road again. Both wanted to get here by dusk and it appeared they would make it just in time.

By the time they arrived, the side parking lot was full. As soon as she stepped out of the car, the Louisiana heat hit her. She thought Santa Fe was hot, but Santa Fe's heat had nothing on the heat here. The humidity was also much higher. Her clothes were already sticking to her; she dreaded seeing what it would be like during the day.

She could not wait to explore the plantation home and grounds. She read several reviews online and they were all good. Very few mentioned anything about a haunting, but some hinted at it.

Adam looked at the plantation, "I don't know why, but I thought it would look creepier."

She shook her head, "It's absolutely gorgeous. Can you imagine living in a place like this?"

"I wouldn't want to pay the electricity bill for a place like this."

She laughed at him, "Oh, you. You are always harping on how much something costs instead of living in the moment."

"All I am saying is this place must be expensive as hell to keep up. In the winter, it is probably cold as can be. These old places tend to get really drafty."

"I don't care about that. I would love to own a place such as this, just for the history."

He scoffed at her, "You say that now, but wait until you get that first electricity bill. I can see you closing doors and turning off lights."

"I am glad the owner decided to turn the place into a bed and breakfast. There are so few open anymore in this area within our price range."

"Give it some time; the owner will discover that she has to raise the prices."

She ruefully shook her head, "Why must you be such a cynic?"

"Hey, I am just stating the facts, babe. If she keeps her prices reasonable, she won't be able to stay open with the economy the way it is. Right now, small businesses are finding it difficult to stay afloat."

After checking in, they made their way up to their bedroom, which Amanda immediately fell in love with. She was afraid that the room had been renovated too much and would have lost its old world charm, but it had not. The owner managed to add bathrooms to the bedrooms, but kept the room just the way it should be. She sat down on the bed and sighed in relief. The room looked vintage, but the mattress was far from it. "I need to find out the brand of this mattress set. We need one for the house, it is divine."

She looked outside to see the view. It was gorgeous. Their room overlooked the courtyard as well as the bayou. She watched as a mist slowly moved in from the bayou and made its way to the courtyard. She could just imagine this place in the spring when the flowers started to bloom. It must be a magical experience.

Before going to eat their dinner, they decided to walk around outside a bit. Being stuck in the car for so long, they both wanted to stretch their legs and get some fresh air. Flower beds were everywhere and the most beautiful rose bushes. You could even smell the spearmint that grew along the brick walkways. Along one section of the grounds, a large bunch of banana trees hid an old work shed. Along the bayou were several cypress trees as well as some ancient oak trees that dripped with Spanish moss. This was the experience she hoped for. Now if they saw a ghost or two, it would be perfect.

Chapter 47

When Bridgette's phone rang in her pocket, she flinched. Once she saw who was calling, though, she became excited, "Hi Barbara."

"Hi, sweetie. How are you doing today?"

"Busy, but good. How are you doing?"

She sighed, "Hal left the other day to go back to work. So, I am missing him something fierce right now. I thought I would call you to cheer myself up."

Bridgette chuckled, "I am glad you did. You can call me anytime. How are the kids?"

She sounded almost flabbergasted, "The first few days when Hal leaves are always hard on them. They miss their dad, but otherwise, they are fine. Thankfully, they have school to help keep their mind off him being gone."

The sound of breaking glass caught Bridgette's attention. "Barbara, I am going to have to call you back. It sounds like someone is here."

"No problem. We will talk later. Bye."

Dolores rushed into the room, "Did you hear that? It sounded like glass breaking?"

Mamie rushed into the room, "It sounded like it came from outside."

The three women walked outside and gasped. The sounds around Bridgette muted. The only sound she heard was her beating heart. Her car window had been smashed. She moved closer and examined the broken glass. What the heck? A large rock rested on the front seat - the source of the damage.

Mamie stated, "I am going to call the police."

Bridgette moved toward her car when Dolores stopped her. "No, don't touch anything. Let the police take everything into evidence."

Bridgette stopped herself. Of course, Dolores was right. She should not touch the evidence. This was no accident. Someone meant to damage her car.

Perhaps Sheriff Anslum was right, and she should have a glass shop on the premises.

Mamie informed the women, "The police are on their way. Who would want to do this?"

Bridgette's stomach was in knots. Her hands were shaking.

Several minutes later Sheriff Anslum himself showed up. He parked his cruiser behind her car and climbed out of the car.

After studying the damage, he sauntered over to the women. "Officer Richard is on his way. He will bag the evidence and take pictures. But I was closer and wanted to come check on things, and make sure you all are safe."

"Do you think you can get fingerprints from the rock?" asked Bridgette.

Sheriff Anslum shook his head and informed Bridgette, "If it was the same person as last time, there probably won't be any fingerprints. I think this time, however, we need to increase patrols out this way. I've already called Dwayne to come fix your windshield."

Chapter 48

Bridgette walked into the dining room and the aroma of fresh muffins, oven-hot biscuits, and freshly brewed coffee filled her senses. The room was starting to fill up with guests, the hum of their voices made the perfect background music. Out on the patio, a guest sat at a table, admiring the gorgeous ferns that were a recent addition.

Delores was also outside, preparing more tables for the guests. Bridgette stepped out on the patio and greeted Delores, "Good morning."

Delores unfolded a black and gold fleur-de-lis print tablecloth, shook it, and then spread it evenly across one of the tables, smoothing out the wrinkles. "I thought I would liven the tables up a little bit out here. I hope you don't mind."

Bridgette shook her head, "No, not at all. I forgot mom had bought these."

"I found these the other day when I was putting away some freshly washed sheets. They had a musty smell, so I washed them and realized they were too pretty to sit in a closet."

Bridgette agreed, "Yes, they are very pretty and unique."

"Don't worry if someone spills something on them. I am a master at stain removal; I haven't met a stain I couldn't get out."

Bridgette laughed, "What would I do without you."

Bridgette walked outside with her laptop. It was too pretty of a night to sit inside. While everything was quiet, she planned to review several pages of a manuscript that was due soon.

"No, no don't you do it. Don't you dare do it!" Bridgette hit on the keys of her laptop. "Come on, come on!" She muttered between clenched teeth. Aggravated, she closed the laptop.

That did it! Tomorrow she would go computer shopping. Her bank account may not want her to, but she needed a new laptop.

That was the price of working from home, she told herself callously.

As Bridgette got up to go inside, her cell phone rang. When she did not recognize the number, she cautiously answered, "This is Bridgette."

"Bridgette, this is Marcus DuPont. I did not catch you at a bad time did I?"

Her heart raced at the sound of his voice. "No, of course not."

Marcus had not been able to get Bridgette out of his mind. After the other night, he thought of her nonstop. "Are you busy tomorrow night?"

"I only have a few guests staying here tomorrow night. After dinner service is over, I plan on retiring to my room and catching up on some manuscripts. Why?"

"Would you like to go out to supper?"

She was stunned for a moment, "I would love to go out with you, but I don't have anyone to watch the bed & breakfast."

"Well, what kind of food do you like?"

"Oh, I don't know. I like all kinds of food, grilled steak, seafood, chicken, pretty much anything but pasta, and Mexican food."

"So, you won't be in your room during dinner service?"

She could not hide the skepticism in her voice, "No, but why?"

"Let's just say since you can't go out, supper will come to you."

"Oh."

"Is that okay with you?"

Desire stirred deep inside of her, "That's fine with me."

Thinking about seeing Marcus again set her body on fire. It's a good thing her laptop was in a foul mood because she doubted she would be able to concentrate on work.

The sound of piano music drifted through the downstairs. She wondered which of her guests were up at this hour playing the piano. The sight as she rounded the corner caused her to gasp. Her favorite ghost was back and she hoped he did not wake up the others.

She watched in glee as the piano keys rose and fell effortlessly to the old tune. She listened to him play for a little while longer and then sat on the piano bench beside him. Whispering near where his ear should be, "You know we do have guests sleeping right now."

She was disappointed that the music stopped playing, but she doubted her guests wanted to be woken up at one o'clock in the morning to the tune of a piano piece, no matter how lovely it was.

As she went back to her room, the sound of a flushing toilet from her room caught her attention. She wondered which ghost was being this mischievous tonight.

Bridgette was anxious for dinner service to be over with. After her last guest retired to their room, she rushed back to her room. It was already going on nine o'clock. She hoped Marcus had not given up on her and left. The sight astounded her. Not only had he set up a small intimate table in front of the French doors, but candles were lit all over the place and flowers were everywhere. The smell of Asiatic lilies and gardenia filled the room. A soft jazz piece played in the background.

She informed him, "This beats eating out anytime."

He walked over to her, shutting the door behind her. He pulled her close to him, molding her to his body. She moaned as his lips claimed hers and wrapped her arms around his neck. A fire ignited deep inside of her. Passion soared through her as his kiss deepened.

Her hands wandered over his perfectly chiseled and sculpted chest. She broke off the kiss and let her lips wander over his massive chest.

His hands framed her face and his lips took hers greedily one more time. His tongue plundered her mouth, demanding more. She shivered with desire.

"Your body feels as if it is on fire." He told her.

She loved the way his hands felt on her body. His thumbs traced her jaw before his fingers entwined in her wavy hair. "You drive me crazy," she whispered in his ear.

This man was the only thing on her mind right now. The very smell of him intoxicated her.

He picked her up and carried her to the bed. He looked deep into her eyes, causing more heat to pulse through her body.

Marcus nuzzled her neck and whispered in her ear, "The food is probably cold by now."

Bridgette kissed him, "That's why they invented microwaves."

He let out a laugh and kissed her on the nose, "Well, then let's go check out this microwave contraption that you are talking about."

She laughed and swatted at him with a pillow, "Come on then."

She slipped on a robe and peeked under the silver domes to see what he chose for supper. Under each dome was trout almandine with rice pilaf and green beans. "This looks fantastic."

He grabbed the plates so that they could go to the kitchen to warm up the cold food, "Thanks, but I can't take the credit. I had Lagniappe prepare everything."

After the food was warmed, they returned to her room where Marcus opened the bottle of champagne and poured them a glass. Bridgette took a tentative sip, normally not a fan of the tart tasting champagnes. This one, however, was very good, it had a peach aftertaste. As they ate, she studied Marcus from across the table. What was she thinking, getting involved with this man? Why did she let her guard down with him and not Greg Dawson? This was the first time she had been in this predicament, two men chasing after her. She hoped that she did not let her heart take over her mind.

Marcus watched as Bridgette's fingers fidgeted over the stem of the champagne flute. She was extremely sexy with her hair all tousled and an afterglow to her skin after making love. As she ate her food, he wondered what she was thinking about.

"You must have something weighing heavy on your mind."

She looked up at him in surprise, "I am just not used to all this attention is all."

"I find that hard to believe. You are an incredibly sexy woman. When you walked into the room earlier, you took my breath away."

She shook her head and smiled at him, "Don't get me

wrong, I've had dates, but I've never had a man shower me with this much attention. A girl could get spoiled being around you."

He smirked as he listened to her ramble on, slowly revealing more about herself. As she began to let her guard down, he realized that his plan to charm her was working better than he thought it would. Just watching her play with the champagne flute while she ate gave him such lascivious ideas. The more excited she became when she talked the more animated her hands waved through the air. Right now, she was talking about her future plans for the bed & breakfast and how she hoped she could pull it off. That caught his attention. He had wondered if she would bring up Marquette Plantation tonight.

Yes, this was all working out wonderfully. He was glad he brought the food here instead of going to a restaurant. Plus, a part of him was completely selfish. He preferred having her all to himself. This was indeed turning out to be a very romantic evening.

He asked, "Have you managed to check out that little cabin in the back?"

She shook her head, "No, I have been so busy with other things that I haven't had a chance."

"You have plenty of time. It's not like it is going to go anywhere."

She let out a soft laugh, "No and it may be safer to go in the winter when there won't be as many snakes and alligators lurking about." She shuddered at the mere thought of running into one of those reptiles. "Besides in the winter, the underbrush won't be as thick and I may see it better."

"Have you thought about looking for it from the bayou?"

She shook her head, "I have a confession – I am not a big fan of boats. I have always been deathly afraid of riding in a boat on the bayou. My dad would laugh at me, but I just could not do it. Whenever I try to get in a boat, I freeze up. I could just picture an alligator making his way into the boat or a snake dropping into it."

She saw the amusement in his eyes, "So no romantic boat excursions for you then."

"No way, no how. I am pretty sure Dad has an old bateau somewhere around here, but I haven't even looked for it."

As she talked about her dad, he saw a sadness come over her face, "Do you still miss them?"

"Yes, I miss them very much. They will always be a part of me though. I no longer feel bitterness toward the person who took them away from me, but I do regret that they are not here with me. All I can do is hope that they have found peace."

"Do you think this is what your parents had in mind when they left you the plantation?"

Marcus loved finding more information about her. At least he did not have to worry about her taking any little trips down the bayou trying to find that old cabin. Now, if he could keep her from venturing into the woods, he would breathe a little better.

Bridgette was surprised to see that it was well after

midnight when she looked at the alarm clock on the nightstand. Time seemed to have flown by while they talked.

She could not remember the last time she felt so at ease with another person. He did not seem to care that she talked nonstop. He was completely at ease in her room, with the candlelight flickering around them and just talking.

A wickedly sexy grin formed on his face, "Would you care to dance?"

She took the hand he extended as he pulled her up from the chair. "I would love to dance."

"I prefer another type of dance, but you look so irresistible that I want to feel your body swaying to the music."

She laughed at his remark as they swayed gently back and forth to the jazz music that filled the room.

He held onto one of her small hands and placed his other hand at the small of her back. She leaned into him, resting her head on his chest. "Do you wish we had gone out tonight?"

She muffled a reply against his skin, "No, this is perfect." She looked up at him and smiled. He saw the desire building in her eyes once again.

Tonight had been wonderful. He had not expected her to be so guarded when he first met her and had hoped to learn more about her and he was happy that he discovered so much.

With the curtains to the French doors open, they could see the moonlight and stars reflected across the bayou waters. She sighed, "It is beautiful out tonight."

"I prefer the sight in here."

He felt her smile against his chest. When the next song came on, they stayed just as they were. Who could ask for anything more? Holding her this close, he realized just how tiny she was when her head fit perfectly under his chin. She stood on her tippy toes to kiss him on the lips. Her lips were soft and warm and he could still taste the champagne she had earlier. The kiss was purely intoxicating. He tangled his hands in her thick, curly tresses, reveling in its silkiness. He could not even imagine her with short hair, ever.

Pressing this close against him, her womanly curves teased him. He whispered in her ear, "I want you."

He picked her up and carried her back to the bed. She pulled his head down to hers, kissing him passionately. His blood heated up. She gently broke the kiss, trailing kisses down his jawline and neck.

His hands skimmed her body, leaving goosebumps in their wake. She felt soft as silk beneath his calloused hands.

Bridgette became lost in the feelings that overtook her body. She took in the very sight of him in the candlelight. His chest was wide and sculpted and his tan body shimmered in the soft light. She marveled at the feel of his rippling muscles underneath her exploring fingertips. She reveled in the way his fingers teased and taunted her body. His dark skin was such a stark contrast to her barely sun-kissed skin.

His touch was such sweet torture. Kisses followed his hands, leaving no part of her body untouched by his hot mouth.

Bridgette stretched languidly in bed, reaching out for Marcus. She was exhausted from last night, but exhilarated as well. She heard the shower running and stepped into the bathroom. The steam from the hot water welcomed her.

She stepped into the shower just as he lathered his hair. "I was wondering where you had run off to."

He pulled her close to him and kissed her, "I have an early meeting; I knew you woke up early for your guests."

His arms wrapped around her tighter to bring her closer to him. His lips skimmed along her neck. Shivers of desire moved down her body. She turned toward him and watched as the water ran over his perfectly sculpted body. Desire burned deep in his eyes. He held up the bottle of soap, "Would you like to wash my back?"

As she lathered his back, her hands continued to explore his body with a slow touch. He whispered in her ear, "That's not my back."

She smiled up at him wickedly.

Chapter 49

Exhaustion consumed him and as soon as his head hit the pillow, he would be dead to the world. The dream came to him as soon as he closed his eyes. He was standing by the bayou near the old cabin while a thick fog rolled in. The murky water started to churn as a cold wind began to blow around him. A mist reached out to him with long, icy fingers as voices whispered all around him, but he could not make out exactly what they were saying.

Suddenly, a long, jagged streak of lightning flashed across the black sky. Thunder rumbled in the distance. The air was charged with thick and palpable tension as a cold rain began to fall from the sky.

A cry close to him echoed through the night air. The voices grew louder when the fingers in the mist began to pull at him, dragging him closer to the water. Shapes slowly appeared in the mist. Lightning flashed all around him. The bayou water began to boil.

The darkness and fog were impenetrable, but pulsed with life. When he attempted to run from the water's edge, arms reached out from it and grabbed at his ankles. A large clap of thunder shook the air surrounding him. Blackness enveloped him as the heavy fog began to swirl around him. Moaning reverberated through the air, and a coldness swept through him. Haunting faces were luring him back to the water's edge.

He bolted upright in bed. It took him a moment to

catch his breath. He looked around in the darkness, trying to place where he was. He was back at the plantation. It was just a dream; he let the ghost stories get to him was all.

He closed his eyes and tried to banish the dream from his mind. The plan involving Bridgette was going well. She was starting to trust him and open up. Soon he would have her madly in love with him.

He drifted back to sleep with Bridgette on his mind once more. He did not want to analyze the dream right now. The faces floating in his dream were just memories. They were all dead and could not hurt him. Why, suddenly, did they have to enter his dreams? Was it because he spent the night so close to where they were killed and disposed of? They could not possibly be trying to haunt him from their graves.

He needed to purchase this property to ensure that his work went undiscovered. He made sure that nothing was left of the bodies. He, however, was not ready to give up his perfect playhouse. Destiny led him to it and he would not give it up.

The hunger built deep inside of him once again. The monster was ready to strike.

Chapter 50

He watched her in the shadows. The darkness of the night enveloped him, swallowing him whole. She would not know what hit her when the time came.

He patiently waited until she moved closer to him before he struck. Anticipation rushed through his body, making him feel excited, expectant. The monster was hungry and must be fed. His appetite had grown insatiable lately. He could not wait anymore.

The beating of his heart thudded loudly in his ears. She took her time walking toward him tonight. He wished she would hurry before someone came along. He did not want anyone to come along and mess up his plans. As she neared him, he looked around one more time to make sure no lights shone in the darkness. Finally, she was in his sights. A sinister smile formed on his face as he quietly approached her from behind.

Chapter 51

Bridgette was too restless to sleep and her mind was too preoccupied to work on editing any manuscripts. She thought the fresh air would do her good; a walk may help clear her mind, so she pulled on her tennis shoes and a nylon windbreaker.

Once outside, she turned her head up to the sky; the rain was barely a mist. In all her life, she had never had two men vying for her attention. Marcus made her forget the world around her just by a simple touch. She loved being around him and could not get enough of his touch. Something about him made her feel complete.

Then there was Greg Dawson, who showered her with compliments. A simple touch from him sent shock waves through her body. The way he looked at her made her feel as if she were the only woman on the planet. While she had given herself completely to Marcus, she and Greg had simply kissed. She had never been one to sleep around and she had no plans on starting now. When Marcus kissed her, nothing else mattered. Greg never stayed long enough to pursue a relationship. However, when he was here he did devote all his attention to charming her.

Bridgette had never been truly in love and both men seemed to make her knees go weak. If only she had someone to talk to; she wished her mother was here so she could talk to her. She missed her friends from South Carolina. Maybe she should plan a trip up there to visit with everyone.

She shook her head as the various thoughts ran through her head. She was sleeping with one man, and thinking about another man at the same time. What happened to being a one man woman? She kept telling herself that she and Marcus were not in a monogamous relationship; they were not even really dating. It just happened to be that both times she saw him she fell right into bed with him. Yet, truthfully, she had not given Greg the opportunity.

The rain may not be heavy, but it was making the ground muddy. Her feet sluiced through the mud as she ventured back further into the property, maneuvering around some water puddles. She walked over to the edge of the bayou and shone her flashlight out onto the water. Throwing a rock into the bayou, she watched as it caused tiny ripples along the water. She found the water calming. There was something going on between her and Marcus, but what about Greg? Could she possibly have feelings for him as well? What about Marcus? Did he have feelings for her or was he just toying with her? Why must life be so complicated at times or was she possibly the one making it complicated?

As a breeze blew off of the bayou, the fog rolling in reminded her of her latest dreams. It was actually somewhat creepy. She shook her head; she was just being silly. Nothing out there was going to hurt her.

If she wanted to find the old cabin, she needed to get a move on. For a moment, she thought she heard a noise and stopped to listen. Not hearing anything out of the ordinary, she continued on. Not paying any attention to where she was going, she ran right into Greg Dawson. Greg had checked in this morning before his afternoon meetings. Surprised that he was out here, she asked, "Are you okay?"

"Yeah. I was not expecting anyone else to be out in this weather." He sighed, "I came out to see if I could find any of your ghosts lurking about. I am guessing the weather has driven them away, though."

She laughed, "I don't think the weather bothers them, but unless you are familiar with the terrain, I wouldn't venture out this far without a flashlight."

"I did not want to scare off the ghosts. Besides, I have excellent night vision. What are you doing out in this weather?"

She replied, "I needed to clear my head and was too restless to sleep. I thought a walk would help."

He asked, "In this weather?"

She looked up at him, "The weather doesn't seem to bother you."

He snickered, "No, I guess not. Would you like me to walk you back to the house?"

She found herself not wanting the night to end just yet. She was not ready to go back, but wanted to spend a little more time talking to Greg so she accepted his offer, "That would be nice."

From here, you could barely make out the plantation. What was she doing? She really did like Marcus, yet here she was spending time with Greg. It's not as if she planned this, though. He was already outside and offered to escort her back to the house. Besides, it was nice talking to him.

Suddenly, a cold wind blew right past her. In the

distance, lightning flashed across the night sky. Greg pointed in the direction of the lightning, "It looks like a storm is moving in."

She shook her head, "We should be back in time before it hits. I guess it's a good thing I did not venture out deeper into the woods."

True to her word, they made it inside as the rain started coming down. "So much for a walk before bed," Bridgette told Greg. "I guess this is my cue to get some work done."

"Goodnight Bridgette. Sweet dreams."

"Goodnight, Greg."

Bridgette waited to see if Greg was going to kiss her goodnight, but instead, he walked up the stairs and to his room.

Sighing, she went to her room as well. As she prepared for bed, Bridgette's phone dinged, and it was a text message from Haley. "Just seeing how the man situation is going."

Bridgette thought about it for a moment before replying, "When I am with Marcus, the world around me ceases to exist. All I hear is the beat of my heart. But is this love?" Sighing, she texted, "But, I think Gregory just sees me as a friend. I don't know what to do? Is it even infidelity if you have dinner with one man while you are sleeping with another man?"

Haley texted back, "Live in the moment girl. Enjoy yourself. You've been through a lot, and need this."

"Perhaps you're right. But I feel guilty, seeing two men."

"Nothing to feel guilty about. It's not as if you are cheating on Marcus. You, yourself just said that you and Gregory are basically just friends."

"How is it you always know what to say? Mwah. Love you to pieces."

As he walked back to the cabin, he made sure to stay deep in the shadows. Why was she walking around at this hour of the night? He was lucky she did not see him with his date. That would not do at all. For a moment, he considered having two women tonight, but that would complicate matters. If Bridgette went missing, questions would be asked. The sheriff's department would tear the property apart looking for her and they would find his playroom. He doubted they would find the cisterns, but he could not take that chance. He had to convince her to sell it to him; she needed to leave this place.

The intoxicating aroma of Bridgette's scent still lingered on him just from being close to her. He loved the way she smelled, it was completely intriguing. He could see himself settling down with her, but he knew the monster that lived inside of him would not be satisfied with just her. No, he had an insatiable appetite that must be fed, but what about him, he needed someone to come home to. He needed someone to love him. Bridgette could be that person. Besides, if he made her his and moved out here, he would be able to keep her or anyone else from discovering his secret life.

Chapter 52

As Bridgette walked into the house, her phone rang. It was one of her close friends from South Carolina, Aimee Hathaway, "I am so happy you called. I have missed you so much."

Sounding heart broken, "You know you can also call."

"I know. I am an awful friend."

"You know I am just giving you a hard time. It's not like you have not had anything going on. What with your parents' death and then trying to open a bed and breakfast."

"But still, I should have called. I have missed you so much."

"I miss our lunch dates. This office isn't the same with you gone."

"I bet I miss our lunch dates more than you. I have to eat lunch alone lately."

"Ha, I figured you were spending all your time remodeling and did not have time to eat."

"No, there is always time for food. But you are right, the house has kept me busy lately. And we have stayed busy, especially on weekends. I think I made the right decision in opening the house as a bed and breakfast."

"It is a charming plantation. People would be crazy if they did not want to stay there." Letting out a wry laugh, "If it wouldn't be haunted, I could see myself living there."

Scoffing, "The plantation isn't haunted. It just creaks a lot."

"Mm-hmm. Sure, it isn't haunted. It's just a plumbing issue that causes the toilets to flush in the middle of the night."

Laughing, "I love this house and its little idiosyncrasies."

Giggling, "Enough talk about the house. Let's talk about your love life now – or more specifically, do you have a love life?"

"Oh my goodness, you have no idea. I have quite a dilemma going on here."

"Oh really. Well, girl, you have to tell me all the dirty little details. Don't you dare hold anything back."

"I don't know what has gotten into me lately I am sleeping with one man, and I have another man vying for my attention whenever he is in town."

"Wow! Maybe I need to move there, ghosts or no ghosts. You go girl."

"But this is so not like me."

"It's about time you let your hair down and have some fun. Every woman needs some really good sex in her life."

"Oh, this isn't good sex; it is mind-blowing sex. I have never had an orgasm like those with Marcus. Girl, I tell you there are fireworks. Sometimes I think the fire department will have to be called to put out the flames."

"Oh, I definitely need to find me a man like that. If sex with him is that good, then I say forget the other man."

"I know, I should. But when I am with Greg, he makes me feel so special, like no other woman matters."

Trying to sound serious, "But has he made any moves to take the relationship to the next level? And is Marcus only interested in a friends with benefits relationship? Does he want something more? Or is it too soon to tell?"

"I don't know. Marcus and I seem to make love more than date. Greg and I actually do things together, except have sex."

Sighing, "I wish I could give you some advice, but I have never had that problem. And let me tell you I am jealous."

After talking for several more minutes, Bridgette and Aimee said their goodbyes. Bridgette reinforced, "I promise I will call more often. I really do miss you."

Bridgette sat in her favorite chair on the patio, glad that the last of her guests had retired happily to their rooms. She finally had a moment to let go of the day's tension. She inhaled the aroma of the dank water as it mingled with the trees and allowed it to calm her nerves.

The full moon shone brightly, hiding the stars and exposing a layer of fine white haze that hovered ghostlike above the cane fields.

An owl hooted from somewhere nearby and she mimicked its sounds, enjoying the back and forth banter her and the creature seemed to have. Was it possible it was really responding to her? A rustling noise interrupted her thoughts, and she thought she saw a whitetail vanish into the woods. Perhaps it was a deer.

She mindlessly threw some of the bread out on the grass. She wondered how many raccoons, opossums, or other woodland creatures would help themselves to the treats. Tim had even started feeding the woodland creatures. After each meal he gathered the scraps and started a feeding area for the animals in the woods near the water, he did not like to see the food go to waste, and Bridgette agreed. Besides, Tim had suggested feeding the animals might keep them out of the flower beds and scavenging in the trash. So far, his assumptions had been correct. Plus, feeding the animals what the guests did not eat, had kept the trash from overflowing.

Tim had even convinced Mamie into helping him start a compost pile, which he assured everyone would be beneficial to the plants. Mamie's only request was that he allow her to plant an herb garden, which he happily did. Bridgette was beginning to suspect that perhaps the two are starting to grow fond of each other. Could it be they have a romance blooming between the two?

A raccoon scurried to where Bridgette had dropped the bread pieces. She sat quietly and watched him eat. She loved it out here. The woods teemed with wildlife, hidden by the shroud of night. From here, she could watch raccoons, opossums, rabbits, and the occasional deer. And then, how could she forget, the owl friend that liked to talk to her.

Chapter 53

He should be spent from the night he had, but he had an overwhelming urge to see Bridgette again. For others, it may be too early to call, but he knew Bridgette would be waking up shortly to prepare breakfast for her guests.

Bridgette rolled over in bed to answer her phone. Who could be calling at this hour? A smile formed on her face when she saw his number on the caller id, "Good morning."

He asked, "I did not wake you, did I?"

"I love being awakened by you."

"Do you feel like having company right now? Is it too early?"

She replied, "Come around to my room. I don't want to wake any guests at this hour."

Marcus's body tensed with anticipation. It took him only a few minutes to get to her house. As he walked up to the back porch, his breath caught as he saw her in the French doors. This woman was a seductress.

She opened the door for him and greeted him with a kiss. This morning would be better than he imagined. She asked, "Did you want me to make you a cup of coffee?"

He shook his head. "I had to see you. You are a drug that I can't get enough of."

She let out a soft laugh and pushed him onto the bed.

"I can't get enough of you either."

Her long, silky hair tangled between his fingers as he kissed her passionately. His body became electrified with desire. He came here to seduce her and somehow the tides had turned and now she was seducing him. This woman was showing him pleasure beyond compare. As she moved up his body, her hair brushed across his thighs and stomach. It tickled and caressed at the same time. Her teasing tongue tantalized his burning flesh. He closed his eyes in pure bliss.

All around him was the intoxicating fragrance of this seductive woman. He was in heaven as he felt the heat radiating from her skin. His body throbbed with need; he was unsure how much of this sensual torture he could take.

Afterward, she snuggled up to him before she had to get out of bed and help with the breakfast preparations. After they showered, she gazed outside. Marcus grabbed her from behind and pulled her close. "I wish you could stay in bed longer."

She turned to him, "So do I, but I have a full house today and several tours coming in as well."

"One of these days, I will take you out on an actual date."

She kissed him on the lips, "I am easy to please. I am just as happy having a picnic out here rather than in a fancy restaurant. All that matters to me is that I am with you."

Chapter 54

From their room, they could hear the rain fall from the sky. Adam Jenkins was not sure exactly what woke him in the early morning hours. He looked at his sleeping wife and he felt the desire building up inside of him. As he leaned over and kissed Grace, she wrapped her arms around him and brought him closer to her. They made sweet, slow love.

Grace had planned this vacation for months. She hoped by staying in a plantation home, she would see a ghost and also relax enough to be able to conceive. They both desired a child and it had not happened. Grace's doctor suggested that it might be their daily stress that kept her from conceiving. Medically, they were unable to find any causes.

This vacation had been relaxing. Adam could not remember the last time they had so much fun. As they snuggled up in bed, an image appeared before them. Adam felt Grace stiffen under him. She whispered, "Please tell me you see that too."

Barely audible, he replied, "Yes."

They watched, partially in awe and fear, as the ghost pointed outside the window. Both looked at each other, unsure of what the ghostly image was attempting to tell them. Grace could not wait to see Ms. Marquette in the morning at breakfast to tell her about their experience. This was just what she wanted.

Chapter 55

A loud crash boomed from somewhere in the house causing both her and Mamie to jump. Bridgette, even after all these years, still was not used to the unexpected noises.

Mamie asked, "What was that?"

Bridgette shrugged her shoulders, "I am not sure, but I better go find out."

Bridgette walked into the entryway to find the vase of flowers that welcomed guests knocked over and broken. Roses were scattered all over the floor.

Dolores walked into the room, "Oh my goodness, what happened here?"

Bridgette gave her a puzzled look, "I think someone wants us to know that they are here." Bridgette looked at Mamie, wondering if she was going to run from here kicking and screaming.

The air in the room turned thicker. Negative energy filled the house, now more than before. Another loud crash reverberated from somewhere in the house.

Bridgette cringed, expecting the worst. Her worst fear was that a chandelier had fallen. She rushed into the dining room to check in there.

Thankfully, there was no damage in the room. Dolores asked, "Now where on earth did that noise come from?"

Mamie stated, "I am not sure, and I am not sure I want to find out."

Bridgette informed them, "I am going to check the house to see if anything is broken. We don't have any guests, they are all out and about on excursions, I am not sure who – or what - made the noise."

Mamie looked at her skeptically, "Oh, we know who made the noise, and I just don't like knowing that a ghost can actually break a vase."

Dolores said, "Mais, I don't think the ghost broke the vase. You're letting your imagination run wild child."

Mamie raised her eyebrows, "As if. Something broke that vase - something not of this world."

Bridgette informed the two women, "Well, I have to find out where the noise came from. Did you want to separate and search the house?"

Mamie shook her head, "I am not going anywhere in here by myself. I'll follow you."

Dolores informed them, "I'll take down here. You'll go check upstairs."

As Bridgette and Mamie searched the upstairs, she swore someone was watching her. Although she did not see anyone, she felt eyes watching her every movement. She searched for shadowy figures in the corners, but found none. Nor did she find the source of the noise. After a thorough search yielded nothing, she was left scratching her head.

Bridgette found Dolores in the entryway, "Find anything?"

"Nope. Not a thing."

As the women stood there, staring at each other, a coffee cup flew across the room, striking and breaking the mirror that hung on the wall by the front door.

Where it had come from, Bridgette had no idea. Mamie stated, "Someone must've made a ghost angry."

Bridgette could not deny that fact. The spirit activity was definitely increasing.

Dolores stated, "I think you need to get a priest out here with some holy water. Something's going on for sure, nothing like this has ever happened before."

Bridgette wondered if a priest would even come here to try and cast out any spirits.

Mamie looked at Dolores and stated, "Well, now I think it's safe to say this place is haunted." Mamie looked at Bridgette, and informed her, "I don't mind working here, but I don't think I am going to stay here by myself anymore."

Bridgette smirked, "I don't think they meant to hurt anyone. I think someone is trying to get our attention. I just need to try and figure out what they want to say."

Bridgette swiped her hands together, and told the ladies, "Okay, I think we need to take our minds off of this. Let's go get some coffee and beignets, and talk for a little while."

Dolores smiled, "That sounds like a fabulous idea."

Mamie agreed, "I need to take my mind off of what just happened."

In the kitchen, Dolores poured them each a cup of coffee while Mamie arranged the beignets on a platter. Bridgette set the little table in the kitchen for them to eat at.

Once they were seated, Bridgette popped a beignet in her mouth and thought about everything that had just happened. She watched as Mamie picked at the edge of the tablecloth.

Mamie looked up and asked Bridgette, "What was it like growing up here?"

Bridgette grinned, "It was fun. I definitely did not get bored living here."

Dolores scoffed, "No, you were never bored. You kept your mom on her toes for sure."

Mamie asked Bridgette, "Did you ever get lonely being an only child?"

Bridgette shook her head, "No, occasionally I had cousins that came for a visit, and they made me realize that I was better off without any siblings."

Dolores smirked, "I don't think your mom could've handled another child like you. You were a little terror when your cousins were here."

Mamie's eyebrows rose, "I can't see Bridgette getting in trouble. I would've thought she was a quiet child."

Both women laughed at the same time. Dolores said, "Oh no, not this child. She definitely stayed in trouble when her cousins were here."

Bridgette shrugged her shoulders, "Justin was just a plain old bully. I had to fight back with him. He would keep picking on me."

"Oh, so because he was a bully that's why you fed him a mud pie?" Dolores looked over at Mamie and told her, "One time when her cousins were over here, Bridgette told her cousin Justin that she had made a chocolate pie just for him. Only Bridgette did not tell Justin that she had used bayou mud for the chocolate. That poor child was so sick."

Mamie could not help but laugh, "Now, why on earth would you want to do that?"

Bridgette looked at them seriously, "He put a garden snake down my shirt, and I had to get even."

Dolores looked at Bridgette and asked, "And why did you have to terrorize your Aunt Colette?"

Bridgette chuckled, "I completely forgot about Aunt Colette. Now, perhaps I did go too far with that practical joke."

Mamie looked at the women and informed them, "Okay, you have to let me in on this little secret."

Dolores started to tell the story, "Well, Bridgette's Aunt Colette came to visit one Sunday and was suggesting to Judy that Bridgette needed some more girly things to do or she would always be a tomboy. And, all we could assume was that Bridgette did not take too well to that suggestion."

Bridgette shook her head, "No, I did not want to do girly things, and Aunt Collette should have minded her own business," Bridgette looked at Mamie and grinned, "So, anyway, while she was visiting with Mom one Sunday I went and caught a bucket of frogs."

Mamie giggled, "I am not sure I want to know what you did with the bucket of frogs."

Bridgette continued her story, "Aunt Colette always left her purse at the entryway. And she always had this big straw purse that had a clasp closure. This thing was huge. So, I decided that Aunt Colette needed some company on her drive home."

Mamie interrupted, "Oh no, you did not, did you?"

Bridgette continued, "Yes, I placed all of the frogs that I had caught, around 8 to 10 frogs, in her purse."

This time Dolores interrupted, "In Bridgette's defense, at least the child left them in the burlap sack."

Bridgette chuckled, "Well, of course, I had to leave them in the burlap sack. I did not want to take the chance that the frogs would find their way out before Aunt Colette left."

Dolores rolled her eyes, "I'll never forget when Colette called Judy. That was an extremely upset woman. It seems Colette did not find the frogs until she had made it home and her dog kept barking at Colette's purse. By that time she opened her purse, the smell was quite strong."

Mamie burst into laughter, "I can only imagine the mess they made in her purse."

Bridgette replied, "The burlap sack had become quite wet since the frogs had been in there for a while. I thought Aunt Colette would hear them croaking when she was in her car. I guess that did not happen. I was grounded for a few days after that."

Dolores shook her head, "Of course, it did not teach Bridgette a lesson. She was always up to some kind of mischief. One time she hid a fish in her cousin Justin's backpack. It was several days later before his mom finally figured out where the odor was coming from."

Mamie could not stop laughing, "You better hope you don't have a child like you."

Bridgette giggled, "I was not that bad. Besides, I know what to look for when they're quiet."

Dolores said, "Yes, we all knew when Bridgette was quiet, she was up to no good."

Mamie giggled, "I wish I could've known you when you were younger. You must've been quite a character."

Chapter 56

Bridgette was grateful that business had been this good. Although most of the guests were ghost hunters, some were hoping to prove that ghosts really did exist and others wanted to disprove the myth about ghosts. She was just thankful that the ghosts had not run anyone off screaming into the night.

Growing up, you only saw the ghosts when they wanted to make their presence known, but lately, they made their images visible to guests as well as herself.

Genevieve watched as guests came and went into the plantation. She could not remember the last time the place had seen this much activity. Pierre would be proud of Bridgette; she had a head for business like he did.

She enjoyed seeing the school children come in for the tours. It had been a very long time since children's laughter echoed down the halls. The other day, a little girl reminded her of her own daughter, causing trouble for some of the boys. Her daughter was always a breath away from trouble as well.

Some guests, she could pass in front of and they paid no attention to her, and then there were other guests who noticed her right away. She had tried to get Bridgette's attention, but she was too busy to listen to her right now. Genevieve must warn Bridgette that the evil which lurked about on the property had made its way inside the house. When the monster appeared to Genevieve, it was a ghastly image with glowing red eyes. She could only see his dark soul and not his human form. If only she could tell Bridgette which person she should be wary of. Charles Marquette had also tried to warn Bridgette. Charles was Pierre and Genevieve's grandson who died in a tragic hunting accident. He wandered these halls with her. He could not see the monster's face either, but he felt his presence just as strong as Genevieve.

Whereas Genevieve liked to wander the property, Charles would rather stay inside. After his hunting accident, he preferred not to venture outside. There were too many bad memories outside. Charles, regrettably, saw his son born through a thin mist and never had a chance to hold him in his hands.

Most nights, Charles sat at the piano and played haunting tunes. Even as a young child, Bridgette shared her love for piano music. She would sit down at the piano and play alongside Charles as he pounded out a few notes. Genevieve loved to watch Bridgette sit at that piano; she played like a dream with her hands arched so dainty. Her fingers just glided over the keys, rarely hitting a wrong note. Whenever those two played at the piano, even now, the sorrowful and poignantly sweet music filled the air.

Tragedy struck Marquette Plantation once again in the late 1940s. A deadly tuberculosis outbreak plagued the area; Etienne Marquette died here in his bed. Genevieve shuddered at the thought of what those poor people endured during that harsh year. Not only did several of her beloved family members become ill, but the doctor ordered the house be boarded shut and quarantined until the members either died or miraculously healed themselves. They were forced to endure their sickness with no fresh air or sunshine. Genevieve would sit at the foot of her loved ones' beds and try to help calm them. If death was their fate, she attempted to help them see the light so they would not be left here to wander these halls. All but Jean Paul survived tuberculosis, and he had been too bitter to go into the light. Now, he walked these halls with her and Charles.

The only good thing from the late 1900s was a new-fangled thing called electricity. The first time her family members could turn lights off and on without the need of candles, Genevieve was in awe. She was also thrilled to see the indoor plumbing added to the house. For the longest time, Charles would play with the things they called toilets, constantly pulling the lever to make the water go down.

Genevieve's mind went back to when Bridgette's dad married her mom. They were such a happy couple, but when Mrs. Vidrine visited, there always would be trouble afoot. She would come out here and spin all kinds of voodoo spells on the property and would bring a Gris Gris bag for little Bridgette. That woman could do too many bad spells, and Genevieve had never liked that she taught Bridgette her wicked ways.

Chapter 57

After the last guest checked out, Bridgette stepped outside for a walk. It had been a busy weekend with all of the rooms filled. Thankfully, tonight she only had a few guests and could relax some.

Bridgette walked towards the water thinking about how fortunate she had been with the bed-and-breakfast. Walking past the area where the lady had been a glimmer of something on the ground caught her eye. Kneeling on the ground, Bridgette carefully brushed the leaves away and gasped in wonder. It was a locket, but not an antique locket. No, this locket appeared to be newer.

She would keep it at the front desk. Perhaps a guest had lost it. Putting the locket carefully inside her jeans pocket, Bridgette finished her walk. Once back home, Bridgette secured the necklace in the front desk drawer.

As Bridgette went into the kitchen, there was a knock on the door. When she looked through the window at the side of the door, she could barely contain her excitement. She opened the door and gave Haley a warm hug, "Oh my goodness. What are you doing here?"

Haley smiled, "Rick is paying for this trip, he just doesn't know it."

Laughing, Bridgette asked, "What do you mean?"

Haley explained, "I have to meet with an author in New Orleans. This author prefers to talk face-to-face, instead of email. And since you live so close, I told Rick I would be happy to take him on as a client. Only Rick doesn't know that I had an ulterior motive - to visit with you."

"I don't care the reason, I am just ecstatic that I get to see my best friend more often." Shaking her head, Bridgette explained, "However, you don't need to bring gifts."

Giggling, "Oh, but, wait until you see what I found. We can have some fun tonight, and I will leave in the morning to meet with my new client." Haley handed Bridgette the gift and told her, "Now open it."

Bridgette asked in wonder at the gift, "Where in the world did you find this?" Laughing.

Haley replied, "At a flea market I went to over the weekend. As soon as I saw the Ouija board I knew I had to buy it."

Bridgette was a little apprehensive about trying the Ouija board, but also did not want to disappoint her friend. "Well, if you want to, we can play with it for a little while. We have a few hours before tonight's guests arrive." Setting the gift on the kitchen bar, Bridgette asked, "Have you had lunch? I can prepare a quick bite to eat before we try the Ouija board."

"You don't have to cook for me. We can go out to eat if you would rather."

"Nonsense, girl. I am sure Delores left me something to eat in the refrigerator before she went home for the day."

Sure enough, in the refrigerator was some of Delores's famous gumbo, "You are in for a treat too. We have gumbo to eat while we catch up on things."

While Bridgette warmed up the gumbo, Haley set the dinnerware on the bar. After the gumbo was warm, Bridgette served them each a heaping portion. As they ate, they talked about everything that had been going on in their lives.

After lunch, they cleaned the dishes and Haley asked, "Where do you want to use the Ouija board?"

Bridgette considered that for a moment before responding, "Perhaps we should try where I saw her."

Before going outside, Bridgette went to the linen closet for a blanket. When she walked into the kitchen, Bridgette burst into laughter. Standing by the back door was Haley with the Ouija board, a carton of salt, a bottle of wine, and wine glasses. "Okay, I understand the wine and the wine glasses, but what on earth is the salt for?"

Shaking the carton of salt in front of her back and forth, Haley responded, "Don't you know anything?

We need a protective circle around us before we start talking."

Bridgette began laughing so hard it gave her a stomach ache, "And where did you learn about a protective circle with salt?"

Haley shrugged her shoulders, "I don't know, a book or something. I just remember reading something about a protective circle of salt protecting against demons, ghosts, old boyfriends - you know anything evil."

As they were heading to the backyard Bridgette stopped, "Hold on. I remember my Grandma Vidrene saying something about it helps to contact a ghost if you have something that belongs to them."

Haley looked at her puzzled, "If you don't know who she was, how do you know if you have anything that belongs to her?"

Bridgette shrugged her shoulders, "It probably doesn't belong to her, but it never hurts to try."

Bridgette walked over to the desk and removed the locket. She held it up for Haley to see. "I found this where I saw the ghost the other night. It could be that it belongs to a guest who possibly lost it while walking. But, perhaps, it does belong to our mystery ghost. Besides, this is just for fun, and it never hurts to try something."

However, Bridgette secretly hoped the locket did belong to the ghost and it helped summon her.

When they arrived at the area where Bridgette had seen the ghost, she laid out the blanket, placed the Ouija board in the center of the blanket, and the locket next to the Ouija board. While Bridgette had been busy arranging the area, Haley had poured them each a glass of wine. They each found a comfortable spot to sit and took a sip of wine. Bridgette stated, "Well, if nothing else, we get to enjoy a nice glass of wine and have some fun before my guests arrive."

Haley nodded her head, "Absolutely. But, to be honest, I am paranoid. Hopefully, we don't conjure up any ghosts."

Bridgette laughed, "No, we probably won't. Besides, the ghosts usually only make an appearance at night."

Haley read the instructions printed on the back of the box, and stated, "Okay, it says that we need to both place our hands on the message indicator."

Bridgette shook her hands and exhaled, "Okay. Are we ready for this?"

Haley replied, "As ready as I will ever be."

Bridgette exclaimed, "Hold on a minute. I remember Grandma Vidrene saying something else. When she did séances, she would keep a lighted candle on the table, so that she would know if there was a ghostly presence nearby."

Haley looked to her friend suspiciously, "If we are just doing this for fun, why would we need a candle?"

"If we do this, we should at least try to do it right."

Bridgette rushed back inside and found a candle and lighter. Once back outside, she placed the candle near the Ouija board and lit it.

Bridgette asked Haley, "Okay, are you ready to try again?"

Shuddering, "As ready as I will ever be, I guess."

The women placed their hands on the message indicator, and Bridgette began talking to no one in particular, "We wish to commune with any spirits that are nearby. If the lady is here that I spoke with the other night, I would like to know what happened to you. Why were you in so much pain?"

Haley giggled, "I have to admit, I do feel kind of silly. We are actually trying to commune with an unknown spirit."

Bridgette stifled a laugh, "Yeah, I do feel kind of foolish. But, after all, we are just doing this for fun."

As the women laughed, Bridgette noticed that the candle flame started flickering and then getting brighter. She looked over at Haley, "Do you see that?"

Haley stammered, "Yeah, but it might just be a breeze."

Bridgette told Haley, "Let's try this one more time, just to see what happens."

Haley confessed, "The flickering candle does kind of freak me out, but we started this, so let's see what happens."

Bridgette tried to talk to the spirits again, "We wish to communicate with any spirit that may be nearby."

A cool breeze blew through the area, lifting her hair. Haley took a sip of her wine, "We have to be insane."

Bridgette burst into laughter, "I have to know - why did you buy a Ouija board, especially being scared of ghosts."

Before Haley could respond, the message indicator started spinning. Haley took a large gulp of her wine, "Please tell me that is the wind turning the pointy thing."

Bridgette looked at her friend, "No, I don't think the wind is strong enough to move the pointy thing."

Haley grimaced, "Okay, okay – pointy thing may not be accurate. But I am a little too freaked out to think clearly."

Bridgette burst into laughter again, "Girl, I am so glad you came. I haven't laughed this much in a long time."

Acting hurt, "I am glad my misery is bringing you so much happiness."

Suddenly, the candle began flickering again. The flame would increase in size and then almost blow out, and then increase in size again. Without warning, the message indicator flew off the board.

Haley jumped to her feet, "Okay, I think we've had enough fun for one afternoon."

Bridgette agreed, "Me too. We sure don't want to anger any ghosts." As she picked up the candle, indicator, and the Ouija board, she stated, "Besides, I need to get ready for this afternoon's guests."

As they were walking back inside, Haley's phone rang. She let out a long sigh when she noticed the number, "It's the author from New Orleans. I am going to have to take this." She handed the wine bottle and glasses to Bridgette.

"Of course. I completely understand."

Haley answered the phone, "Yes sir, how can I help you?"

After Haley's conversation with her client was over, Haley told Bridgette, "Something came up, and he needs to meet with me tonight." Sighing, "So, I guess I won't be able to stay the night after all." Letting out a small laugh, "And I won't be able to find out how great of a medium we were today."

Bridgette chuckled, "I don't think we were very good mediums today. But, we had fun." They dropped the items on the kitchen counter.

Bridgette walked her friend out to her car, "It was great seeing you, however, I am going to miss you. Have a safe trip to New Orleans."

The two women gave each other hugs goodbye and Haley got into her car.

Chapter 58

She woke with a start. Something woke her up, but what? She looked around to see what it was, but her surroundings were unfamiliar. Where was she?

The moonlight filtering into the room cast eerie shadows along the walls and floor. It was too dark to make out where she was. She tried to sit up and terror exploded inside of her. Her arms and legs were restrained to a bed frame.

She yanked as hard as she could to free herself from the restraints, but the rope was too tight. The duct tape was pulled tightly against her mouth, causing her to itch. As she moved her head back and forth to see if she was alone, an eerie silence surrounded her. Her captor could be hiding in the shadows preparing to strike at any moment. This had to be a horrible nightmare. Any moment now, she would wake up and find herself back home, in her own bed.

Random, horrifying thoughts ran through her mind of all the things that could happen to her. The police had warned women to be aware of their surroundings, do not go out alone at night. But she did not take any heed to the warnings. She figured the missing girls decided to start a new life somewhere away from here. Besides, nothing bad ever happened here, right? She never thought anything bad would happen to her, she was cautious and knew self-defense. How could she have been so wrong?

Tears built in her eyes as she took in her dire situation.

She did not want to die this way. She would not shed a tear; she would figure a way out of this. She took a deep breath and concentrated on freeing her hands from their bonds. She paused for a moment, was that a floorboard creaking? She listened intently to see if there was someone there. Not hearing any more noises, she went back to work on freeing herself.

This may be her only chance to escape and instinct kicked in. She slowly tried to work her wrist free from the ropes, hoping that it may be better to work on one wrist at a time. The rope brutally cut into her wrist as she tried to maneuver her hand through the small opening. If she could squeeze them free. She felt the rope give some, and hope bloomed inside of her. She continued maneuvering her wrist in small semicircles.

She ignored the pain as the rope burned into her raw and bleeding skin. The blood helped ease her hands out of the tight bindings. She refused to give up and gritted her teeth against the excruciating pain. Her hand slipped free.

Being quiet as to not alert her captor, she slowly stretched her arm to begin working on the rope binding her other arm. It took some stretching and maneuvering, but she finally had both arms free.

Before moving to free her feet, she listened intently to make sure all was still quiet. Freeing her feet was faster with both hands free. A chance of surviving this experience helped speed the process.

She slowly dropped her feet to the ground, trying to regain the feeling back in her legs. She must have been out for longer than originally suspected. As she became accustomed to the darkness that enveloped her, she assessed her situation. Her captor could be right outside the door so that means of escape was out. The window was a fairly good size; it may be her best means of escaping undetected - if it would open. Before making her move, she scanned the room to ensure that no one was hiding in the shadows.

Moving quickly, she tried the window. It took a bit of effort, but it eventually opened enough to allow her to escape. A light breeze whispered against her skin as the smell of damp earth and pine trees filled her nostrils. She squinted through the darkness, trying to make out any defining shapes. It was oppressively dark. If only the moonlight could filter through the thick canopy of trees.

The pine straw and underbrush scraped against her bare feet. She looked around, unsure of which way she should run. She heard a noise behind her; someone was opening the door to the cabin. She had to hurry, her captor would soon discover she escaped and come after her.

The incessant buzzing of insects surrounded her. Not knowing which way she would find help, she began running, uncaring as to her state of dress. She prayed that help was close by. She heard movement behind her and picked up her pace. She broke free of the dense woods and found herself at the edge of a sugar cane field. Her spirits picked up. Someone must live close by, but where? She began running in between two sugarcane rows unsure of what would be at the end. The sharp leaves cut into her tender flesh. She pushed on, ignoring the pain.

Run! The voice was almost audible. *Keep going. Do not stop!*

Do not let him catch me. She could do this. She had to do this. She attempted to protect her face by shielding her face with her hands as she ran through the sharp leaves that whipped and scratched her skin - hopefully farther and farther from the madman.

She stopped briefly for a moment, her hands on her knees, and struggled to catch her breath. She could hear her captor behind her. He was coming after her. If he caught her, she was dead.

Would she find help? Or would she die in this field? Then it fell quiet. Eerily quiet except for the sound of her panting and the buzzing of insects. Her captor had stopped shouting. She listened for the swishing sound of someone moving through the stalks and heard nothing. Where was he?

She stood in a jungle of sugar cane stalks that were considerably taller than she, swatting at the mosquitoes that were feeding off of her. She was soaked with perspiration, including her hair. Her exposed skin had been whipped and slashed by the sharp sugar cane plants.

The stifling heat and heavy air made it hard to breathe. She took a few more steps, pushing aside the unforgiving leaves of the sugar cane plants. She heard a swishing sound behind her and froze, listening intently. There it was again. He was close. Her heart hammered inside of her chest.

She tried not to lose her sense of direction in the dark. The wind had picked up.

She felt a tickle on her wrist and locked gazes with a hairy spider the size of a quarter. Instinctively she shook her arm. She had to find help. It was her only chance of survival.

She pushed forward, her arms folded in front of her face, shielding her as much as possible from the sharp leaves. She would either make it, or die trying.

How deep was she into this field? How much further to the other side? What if she couldn't find her way out? What if she was trapped in here?

Trapped? She took a shallow breath. And then another. And another. Why did it feel as if her throat was closing? Why couldn't she breathe? Her pulse raced. She could not afford a panic attack. Not here. Not now!

You can do this. You have to do this. Do not give up. Think about where you are going - not where you are.

She kept moving, her hands in front of her, attempting to keep the leaves from cutting into her face. She tried not to think about the mosquitoes feasting on her. But, then again, mosquito bites were more pleasant than what could be happening to her. What would the man have done to her? What would he have forced her to endure?

She picked up her pace and emptied her mind of how miserable she was, attempting to stay focused on escape.

She could feel the blood dripping from her arms and legs. Had she been able to protect her face? How much further could it be until she came out on the other side? A noise caught her attention. What was that? She crouched down and listened intently. Had she imagined it? Was it her kidnapper or possibly a wild animal? There it was again - a mumbled curse. Had it come from behind her, or ahead of her - to the right or to the left? Was it her captor?

She could not move. Or breathe. She heard another sound. It was getting louder. Finally, she recognized the sound - it was someone moving through the cane stalks. He was close. She had to hurry.

She began running again. All of a sudden, her foot caught in a tangle of vines. She toppled forward, her elbows landing hard on the ground. A silent scream caught in her throat as pain shot through her.

She lay on the ground in agony, surrounded by weeds and towering cane stalks. Fear consumed her. She took a slow, deep breath and exhaled. She tried to imagine herself in a wide open field.

She forced herself to get up and pushed forward. How much time had she lost when she fell - one minute, two? Where was her captor? Was he staying out of sight, waiting for the right time to strike?

It felt as if she had been running for miles. Where was the road? Had the field angled in a different direction without her realizing? Or did the road not come this far? Was there even a road?

She could hear someone catching up to her. She kept running through the rows of sugar cane, hoping to lose him in the process. She tried to keep her frenzied thoughts at bay. She had no idea how long she had been running. She prayed she had lost him.

Relief washed over her when she saw a light near the end. That may be her only chance of survival. She hoped someone there could help her. Ignoring the leaves of the sugar cane, she pushed on.

Then she was free from those sugarcane stalks.

Run! The voice resounded in her head. Was it just her fear talking?

Go!

She hesitated for only a second, then sprang out into the open, running with abandon toward the house. The searing pain in her body ignored, but determination given her legs the energy to move forward.

She pushed herself harder than she thought possible. What if she was running to his house?

She did not stop and rushed toward the house. She tried to catch her breath. Her body shook, her feet throbbed. As she neared the house, she listened. She struggled to hear if her abductor was close by. Hopefully, this house did not belong to him. She slowly eased her head from her hiding spot, peering into the night and feared her abductor would be in front of her. She did not see anyone nearby so she made her move. A sliver of light from the porch light helped outline her way. She made sure to stay out of the light, hoping to blend into the darkness. She dashed across the backyard.

He still could not believe she had escaped. The ropes had been tight; the bindings had no slack in them.

This one had spirit. At first, the chase gave him a new exhilaration, but he quickly grew tired of the new-found game. He hoped she had not found the house yet. He had been closely watching, making sure the new owner did not discover his current playhouse and disposal ground. If she did, then he would have to take drastic measures.

He slowly made his way through the sugar cane field, listening and looking intently for his escaped captive.

For the first time, he truly began to feel fear. His prey made her way up on the porch screaming and banging on the door. Lights began to turn on all over the plantation. He knew he should have pushed harder for Bridgette to sell him the place. There were too many guests tonight for him to make a move.

He moved back to the cabin quickly. He must act fast before the police arrived. He had not been careful there and his fingerprints were all over the place. At least the woman never saw his face.

Just holding the lit match caused him to tremble in anticipation. Knowing that he was once again back in control rushed adrenaline through his veins.

He watched in fascination as the place went up in flames. He had found some old moonshine in a corner that would be the perfect accelerant. As he made his way quickly back to the bayou, he could hear the sizzle of the fire. White smoke began to fill the air as the smell of sulfur tickled his nose. For some reason, the smell energized him. The fire roared to life and devoured any evidence in its rampage.

He doubted the police would ever put the clues together. The missing women, the one who escaped, and the burning cabin were all connected. He had abducted women for years without getting caught. He had honed his skills and expanded his talents all right under their noses. Unfortunately, now he had to find a new playground, which would take time.

That was unless he convinced Bridgette to sell. Perhaps since this happened she would want out of here fast.

As he pushed the bateau in the bayou, flames shot up from the cabin. He heard the sirens in the distance. He must move quickly. The night air was filled with the sounds of crackling, popping and sizzling as his playground burnt to the ground.

Chapter 59

Bridgette thought she was dreaming at first when she heard a woman screaming. Lately, the ghosts had made a lot of noise at night and she was too tired when her head hit the pillow to worry about them. Yesterday, two schools booked tours of the grounds and all of her rooms were booked solid for the rest of the week. Business was better than she ever expected. On top of that, the restaurant and the new chef were a huge success. She wished she had hired Mamie Bouviere earlier. Every table had been full tonight and people came from miles away to eat her cooking. If Bridgette did not watch it, she would gain more weight than she cared to. Mamie may not be a people person, but she was magnificent in the kitchen.

The incessant screaming grew louder, but when the banging on the door began, she bolted out of bed. Grabbing her robe, she rushed out of the bed. In such a hurry, she tripped over the bed covers, tangling them in her feet. Who could that be at this hour? She prayed something did not happen to one of her guests.

When Bridgette opened the door, what she saw caught her by complete surprise. She quickly ushered the nearly naked girl inside, looking around before closing the door.

She cried out, "Please, you have to help me. He isn't far behind me."

"Who is after you? Are you okay?"

The young woman shook her head and said through

her tears, "I never saw his face, but I did hear him following me. I don't even know where I came from."

Bridgette took off her robe and wrapped it around the young girl, "Here let's put this on you. You sit right here while I call the police!"

She nodded her head and pulled the robe tight around her. Bridgette heard her guests making their way downstairs. Bridgette picked up the kitchen phone and called 911, "I have a young woman who just appeared at my back door that is almost naked, and she is scared. She says she was abducted and held hostage somewhere in the woods nearby."

The dispatcher asked, "Does it appear that she is hurt?"

Bridgette replied, "No, not that I can tell, but she is shaken up."

A guest shouted, "It looks like there is a fire somewhere in the back!"

Bridgette looked out the window. Muttering a string of obscenities under her breath, she informed him, "You better send a fire truck as well. It appears he may have held her prisoner in one of the sheds in the back of the plantation and is burning the evidence."

The dispatcher made all the necessary calls while keeping Bridgette on the line, "I am sending the fire department, ambulances, and police officers. Please keep everyone inside and the doors locked until we know you are all safe."

Bridgette looked at her guests and hoped one of them was not the one that did this. Bridgette told the young girl, "The police are on their way."

She looked over at her guests, "I will put us on a pot of coffee. I am sure that the police will want to talk to all of us and see if we noticed anything out of the ordinary tonight."

They all nodded their heads. Bridgette hoped that this did not hurt her business. As far as tonight, she planned to rectify that matter right now, "Tonight's stay is on the house."

The pungent smell of smoke reached the plantation rather quickly. Realization soon hit her that someone had burned down part of her plantation and if the fire department did not arrive soon, the fire would spread.

She looked out back and watched as deep orange flames filled the night air. How long had the fire been burning? A surge of raw fear pulsated through her body. Thankfully, she heard the sirens' wailing fast approach the property. She rushed to the front door to explain that the fire was near the bayou.

Thick smoke continued to fill the air. The bayou was all but a gray haze from the smoke, causing her eyes to burn. Hopefully, the fire department would extinguish the fire before it spread.

She watched as the fire truck strobe lights and the siren wailed right past the plantation. The young officer must have gotten word to them on where the fire was. The EMT unit stopped in front of the house and she informed them where their patient was.

Chapter 60

Sheriff Anslum heard his phone ringing, but it took a minute to clear the sleep from his mind. It was the dispatcher calling, "Sheriff, a 911 call just came in from Bridgette Marquette. She has a scantily clothed woman in her home claiming to be abducted and held against her will. Right after she arrived, a fire was reported near the bayou on her property. It appears one of the old sheds in the back is on fire."

Sheriff Anslum let out a deep sigh. So much for it being a quiet day. "Have you dispatched anyone?"

"Yes, sir. Officer Graham Richard is there right now. He thinks Detectives Ryan Boutin and Todd Comeaux should be called in as well. Turns out the lady was on her way back to her car from Jackson Square when she was abducted. Everything is still rather vague in her mind."

Damn! This did not sound good at all, especially when they had missing young women whose bodies had not been found. His gut told him this was not a coincidence. "I am on my way. Go ahead and call Detectives Boutin and Comeaux. Have them head out there too."

As he headed out to Marquette Plantation, he noticed how devoid of life Rexma was at this hour. He loved this town; his parents moved here when he was a teenager and still lived in their small two bedroom house where they raised three boys. His parents worked hard to keep them clothed and fed. His mom cleaned houses and ironed to help make ends meet. His dad worked hard farming other people's land, but still they managed to put all three of their sons through college, all the while remaining happily married. Sheriff Anslum worked hard to get where he was. He somehow managed to earn his degree in criminal justice and made rank. He still strove to earn the respect of the people in this town. Even after he was elected the town Sheriff, some here still considered him an outsider since he was not born here.

When he arrived at the Marquette Plantation, chaos was all around him. Another fire truck made its way past him to the fire in the back. The night sky was illuminated by the red and blue strobe lights of the police cruisers. Even from here, he could hear the firefighters shouting out orders in an attempt to desperately contain the fire.

Sheriff Anslum headed inside to talk to the young lady. Detective Boutin was already there and speaking to her, "Miss, we need to get your statement."

She stared at him blankly.

"I understand tonight has been an ordeal for you. I promise this won't take too much longer. The paramedics want to take you to the hospital so they can check you out."

She continued to gaze at him blankly. Sheriff Anslum could tell that shock was starting to affect the young woman's system. Tears fell from her eyes, leaving more trails of mascara down her cheeks.

Detective Boutin desperately tried to put the young woman at ease, "I am truly sorry that we have to put you through this." He gripped his pen tighter. He despised having to push victims further when they were traumatized, but it had to be done. Her abductor may already be searching for a replacement. "Can you tell me your name?"

She whispered, "Justine. Justine Rachel."

Detective Comeaux wrote down her name. "I know these are questions you don't feel like answering right now, but please understand we want to catch the person who did this."

She looked up at him with tearful eyes and nodded. "Did you see the man who abducted you?"

She shook her head, "No."

"Did you notice anything about him?"

Again, she shook her head, "No. I am so sorry."

"You have nothing to be sorry for. Your bravery and quick thinking are what helped you escape."

Every time she closed her eyes, she pictured herself restrained to that bed. "I had to get out of there. I heard a noise and knew he could come back at any moment."

He pushed down the empathy he felt for this victim. He must remain professional, especially in front of the sheriff. "Is there anyone I can call to meet you at the hospital?"

She did not know who to call. She was so embarrassed that this happened to her. "My brother. Would you please call my brother?" John would come to her rescue without worrying her parents just yet.

As the ambulance took Justine to the hospital, Detective Boutin needed to ask Ms. Marquette some more questions, "Miss, we need to make sure that all of your guests are still here and accounted for."

Bridgette looked up at him dazed, "What? Oh, yes, of course. Most of the guests are all gathered in the front parlor. They were curious as to what happened and couldn't go back to bed."

Bridgette stepped into the parlor and looked at all of her guests. A chill swept through her when she did not see Greg Dawson anywhere among the guests. "Greg Dawson isn't here, but, I just saw him a few hours ago. He was out walking around and escorted me back inside. I am certain that he went back to his room when we got back."

"Are you sure he is in his room?"

"He has to be. Maybe he is a sound sleeper and slept through all the commotion."

Even as she said the comment, she had a hard time believing it. The sirens alone could wake the dead.

Detective Comeaux looked at her, "Which room is he in? I need to make sure he is there."

"I can go check for you."

He placed a hand on her shoulder to stop her, "Miss, it would be best if you let me do it."

Startled by the statement, she let out a whisper, "Oh. Oh! Of course. He is staying in room five. It is the third door on the right."

Detective Comeaux asked, "Are there any other guests who seem to be unaccounted for?"

Bridgette shook her head. "No, he is the only guest I don't see. I sure hope nothing happened to him. You don't think he went back out and stumbled into the abductor do you?"

"I am not sure. Right now, I need to make sure he is indeed up there."

She handed him a key to Greg's room and watched as Detective Comeaux walked up the stairs. She heard him knock and announce himself. It seemed to be an eternity before Detective Comeaux made his way back downstairs. "I am sorry miss, but Mr. Dawson isn't in his room."

She looked at him with disbelief on her face, "I sure hope he is okay. I just don't understand where he could be."

Detective Comeaux believed they found their suspect for the abduction, but there was still the chance that Ms. Marquette was right, maybe he ran into the abductor while out walking around and came to an unfortunate end.

Detective Comeaux walked over to Sheriff Anslum, "A guest is missing. Ms. Marquette confirms his presence here earlier this afternoon. They were both walking outside. She thought he retired to his room, but she isn't sure of it."

"Let's get some extra hands out here and search this property. With the fire trucks busy trying to put the fire out, we don't have much of a crime scene, but we need to make sure he isn't out there somewhere, hurt or worse."

"Yes, sir. I will have Detective Boutin start organizing a

search and rescue team. Dawn is fast approaching so at least we will have some daylight to contend with."

Sheriff Anslum informed him, "We can also have the fire trucks turn around to allow their lights to illuminate the surrounding area in case he is somewhere out there. I already have a few officers combing the area in case our abductor is still around, but he probably hightailed it after torching the small cabin."

Sheriff Anslum walked over to Bridgette and cleared his throat to avoid startling her. "Ms. Marquette, I understand Tim works for you?"

Looking at him curiously, "Yes, sir, he does the lawn maintenance here. Father Rabelais asked if I would be interested in hiring him as the groundskeeper."

"Does he live here on the property?"

Bridgette nodded her head, "Yes sir. He lives in one of the caretaker cabins out back. Both him and Mamie live here on the grounds."

"Have you seen him tonight?"

Bridgette thought about this question from before responding, "No, sir, I have not seen him tonight." Bridgette thought about how Tim worked with the delicate plants around the plantation. He created beautiful gardens here. Planted pansies, jasmine, gardenia, roses, daisies, daylilies, irises, and others she could not

even remember now. How could someone who handled such beautiful, delicate flowers, possibly be a suspect in the destruction that happened? Could he kid-
nap a woman, then he set fire to a place he claimed to
love so much?

No, he could not do this. He was a good and decent
man. He created beautiful things. He was a man who
liked to work with his hands, and did not mind getting
dirty.
"But I don't see him having anything to do with this
either. He has done an amazing job on landscaping
here, and he is so kind-hearted."

Sheriff Anslum pursed his lips and linked his fingers together. "To me, if I heard all this commotion, I would
want to know what's going on."

Bridgette shook her head, "No, no... Tim could not
have done this. There's just no way."

"Well, if you see Tim before I do, would you let him
know that I need to talk with him?"

"I will, but I am telling you he did not do this."

"I am not accusing him, but I would like to talk to him."

Walking outside, Sheriff Anslum put on his dark glasses
as the sun cleared the top of the tree line. It was going
to be another scorcher of a day. He turned to Deputy
Boutin and caught him in the middle of a yawn.

"Sorry, sir," Deputy Boutin said. "It's been a long night."

"May as well go get some coffee. We are just getting started. Tell your people to search the woods again. The sun is out enough now that they should have enough sufficient light."

By the time John arrived at the emergency room, Justine felt like a pin cushion. She scowled at the nurse drawing blood and watched as the young nurse placed a cotton ball over the site and applied a piece of tape. As John appeared in the small exam room, the nurse explained, "The doctor will be here shortly."

The sounds of the emergency room chilled her to the bone. From her small room, she could hear the phones ringing and muffled voices. She never imagined anything like this would happen to her.

She tried to make herself comfortable on the exam table. Now that the fear left her body, her feet began to throb. The nurse cleaned her feet and wrists and applied a layer of gauze over them until the doctor could inspect the damage. Several deep lacerations may need stitches. She did not even remember cutting her feet.

The young triage nurse explained that there was a chance of infection in several of the lacerations because dirt had made its way into the sites. Justine shuddered when she thought of how much worse the outcome could have been. Would he have just raped her or did he have something far worse in mind?

She could not seem to get warm and asked John for another blanket. She was just grateful to be alive. She finally stopped crying; she had shed enough tears the last few hours to last a lifetime. Would she ever be able to close her eyes and not picture herself waking up in that small cabin? Could she live a normal life after this?

The detective who asked her a lot of questions at the plantation entered the small room, "Ms. Rachel, I wanted to see how you were doing."

John introduced himself, "I am her brother, John."

The detective shook John's outstretched hand, "It's nice to meet you, sir. You have one brave sister here."

Detective Boutin looked at Justine, "I just want to let you know that the cabin where your abductor held you burned down tonight."

As she listened to what the detective said, another chill rushed through her body. She pulled the blankets around her tighter. She looked into the detective's eyes and noticed they were filled with compassion, or maybe pity. He was only doing his job, but she just did not know if she could answer any more questions.

Chapter 61

Now that the guests were gone and the B&B was quiet, Bridgette started a task she dreaded. She went into Greg's room and started packing the items he left behind.

Bridgette ruefully shook her head. Packing his belongings reminded her of when she packed her parents' belongings after their death. She hoped this was not the same case. Perhaps Greg had an emergency meeting and meant to come back later.

As she packed his belongings, she noticed a mist coming from underneath the bathroom door and rising along the wall. Curious, she slowly opened the door. The mist appeared to be coming from the bathtub. She slowly walked to the bathtub. The tub was full of water.

How strange, she thought to herself. She reached into the tub to drain the water and was shocked to find it so cold. Numerous scenarios ran through her head. Had something happened to Greg while he was preparing a tub of water?

As the water drained, an image formed. It was the reflection of a woman, but her skin was sallow looking. Pasty almost. When the woman reached for her Bridgette jumped back in fear. Then just as quickly, the vision disappeared.

Bridgette was worried about Greg. What could have happened to him? She thought he would return by morning, but he never showed up. What if something terrible happened to him? Had he gone back outside after they said good night? Did he meet the killer unexpectedly in the woods?

Once his belongings were packed, Bridgette called his cell phone. "Greg, this is Bridgette at the Marquette Bed-and-Breakfast. I have your belongings safely packed. Please give me a call. I hope everything is okay with you."

Another horrifying thought occurred to Bridgette. What if he was out in the woods, unconscious?

But no, he would not be unconscious in the woods. His car is missing. But why leave his belongings behind?

Needing a meaningless task to keep her mind occupied, Bridgette packed the newspapers to be brought to the recycle bin in town. As she carried one stack to the car, the wind came and took several of the newspapers with it. Cursing under her breath, she chased after the newspapers. Bending down to pick up one of the newspapers an article, or better yet - a picture, caught her attention. More specifically, It was a group of pictures showing the missing girls. More importantly, one of the missing girls had around her neck the locket Bridgette had found. A shudder of unease ran through Bridgette.

Especially after learning a cabin on this very property had been used for a killer's sadistic pleasures. And now Greg Dawson was missing.

Needing someone to talk to, but not wanting to worry Haley with what happened Bridgette sent Marcus a text, "I've been thinking about you. So much has been happening here. Was wanting someone to talk to."

Later that night curiosity took over. Bridgette retrieved the locket, brought a candle into her room, and opened the book that Haley had recently given her. On her makeshift table in the room, she placed the locket, the book, and the candle. Bridgette opened the book to a particular page that had caught her attention earlier. It was similar to a spell, one that explained how to communicate to a specific spirit.

Bridgette lit the candle and read over the instructions. She picked up the locket and placed it in the palm of her hand and grasped it firmly.

Unfortunately, before she could try the incantation, there was a knock at the front door. The guests that had called earlier to state they would arrive later than expected tonight must be here.

Chapter 62

Bridgette walked onto the front porch for a moment of fresh air before preparing the dining room for the lunch guests. The breeze carried with it a heavy layer of humidity and the musty aroma of the bayou.

One of her local customers pulled into one of the available parking spots and stepped out of her car.

Bridgette glanced at her watch. Perhaps lunch would be starting early today. It was only ten thirty in the morning and lunch guests were arriving. She went inside and waited to greet her customers.

Delores had already picked up the breakfast items, cleared the tables, and set out the new dishes. The center of each table held a bud vase with a pretty yellow rose that had been handpicked from her garden.

The enticing aroma of warm bread and rich chicken and sausage gumbo emanated from the kitchen, where Mamie was busy preparing something delicious for today's luncheon special.

Bridgette was fairly certain that the activities from the previous day were what brought most locals for lunch today.

As the lunch crowd started to gather, Bridgette greeted each customer. "Good morning Mrs. Gros. How are you doing today?"

"Mon dieu, I should be the one asking how you are doing today, my child. You've had an exciting couple of
days recently."

"I am fine. I am just glad the young lady was able to
escape before something worse could happen to her."

"Mais, no one is saying who the young girl was, or even
saying what really happened. But I still can't believe
that something could've been happening here, of all
places."

"Sheriff Anslum is still investigating the matter. And
for the lady's safety, it is best for her identity to remain
a secret."

"Oh, oh my, of course, the poor girl must be petrified
after all. But who would think something like that
could happen here in Rexma, of all places."

"I feel the same way as you Mrs. Gros. That poor girl
has gone through a horrific ordeal. I am certain she
will want to keep her identity hidden forever."

"But does she have any idea who could have done this
to her?"

"No, not that I know of."

After Bridgette seated Mrs. Gros and her lunch guests
at a table, Bridgette went to greet the next guest.

"Mr. and Mrs. Duval, it is nice to see you today."

Mrs. Beverly took Bridgette's hand in hers, "What a rough night you had the other night. I am so sorry that something like that happened here, and not too long after your parents' deaths. What kind of person would do that to someone else, and of all places out here?"

Bridgette ruefully shook her head, "It takes a truly evil person to do something like that to another person, in my opinion."

Mr. Duval hooped his thumb in his red suspenders while he rocked back and forth and contemplated what the women were talking about. "I don't see anyone from Rexma capable of doing something that cruel."

Mrs. Beverly agreed, "Oh no, of course not. It has to be someone from another town. We never have any crime here in Rexma."

Bridgette wondered about their statement. Could they perhaps suspect that a guest of the B&B had committed this crime? Bridgette thought to herself, *"No, she had met all of her guests, and none of them would be capable of committing such an atrocity."*

Bridgette showed Mr. and Mrs. Duval to a table near Mrs. Gros and her lunch guests. After they were seated, Bridgette went to greet the next guests.

"Mr. Hebert and Mr. Daigle, it is good to see you all today."

Mr. Hebert's mousy gray curls peeked through the rim of his hat. The ridges of his leathery skin appeared deeper by the intensity of his gaze, "My dear, we weren't sure you would be open today."

Mr. Daigle looked perplexed, "Mais, why wouldn't she? She got a busy restaurant to run, and she got to keep the lights on in dis place. No, she got to keep busy."

Mr. Hebert looked at Bridgette and stated, "Pay no attention to this old fool. He has ice water in his veins."

Mr. Daigle looked at his friend, "You crazy old coot. I am not trying to be mean, I just know that life goes on. This girl can't let what happened stop her."

While the two men continued their bickering, Bridgette led them to their table. Bridgette wished she knew what the two men were bickering about. But, they were speaking in rapid Cajun French. While Bridgette could speak some of the language, when they were speaking this fast, she could not understand what they were saying. Bridgette wished she had learned the language from her grandparents, or even her parents. But instead, she had just learned French in school, which was a completely different dialect.

"Delores will be with you shortly. Our luncheon special today is gumbo."

"Oou eee, gumbo sounds good," stated Mr. Daigle.

Bridgette smiled at the elderly man and excused herself. Today would be a trying but entertaining day.

An hour later, every table was occupied with customers. The hum of their voices made the perfect background noise.

After the last lunch guest left, Bridgette walked out onto the porch. She was surprised to see Mr. Hebert and Mr. Daigle at the end of the porch playing checkers. It was obvious Mr. Hebert was shamelessly gloating after beating his friend. She watched as Father Rabelais stepped out of his car. She walked over to Father Rabelais, "We've already picked up for lunch, but I am certain Mamie wouldn't mind fixing you a bowl of gumbo."

Father Rabelais gave her a smile, "That's very kind of you, and a bowl of gumbo sounds great. However, I did not come here for food. I wanted to see how you were doing and how Tim was doing."

Mr. Daigle glanced up from his spot, and asked, "Something wrong?"

Father Rabelais smiled at the elderly man, "Nothing at all. I just came to talk to Bridgette."

Mr. Daigle shrugged his shoulders, "I thought it had something to do with Sheriff Anslum suspecting Tim of having something to do with what happened out here the other night."

Bridgette groaned, "No, Sheriff Anslum was just doing his job. Nothing to worry about. He said it was just routine to talk to everyone who has access to the property."

Mr. Daigle sat back in his chair, folded his arms across his bony rib cage, "If you ask me, dat young man needs to be talked to."

Mr. Hebert looked at his friend, "You old codger. You really tink Tim would have done that. If so, you crazier than I thought."

"Nah, I don't tink he did it. But why is Sheriff Anslum so persistent on talking to the man over and over again. And besides, it makes sense. The man is the groundskeeper and knows every inch of this property. Might of seen something and not even realized it."

Mr. Hebert rolled his eyes, "Nah, I am telling you- whoever did tis ain't from Rexma."

Bridgette told both men, "Sheriff Anslum is just covering all of his bases. He's just doing his job. But Tim did not do this."

Mr. Daigle snorted, "Huh, no one really knows the man. He just showed up in town one day. But if the man has nothing to hide, the authorities will realize it. Let the Anslum boy do his job. He ain't no cooyon. He got him an edumacation. We got to let the Anslum boy do his job."

Mr. Daigle groaned, sat back in his chair, and changed the subject, "Father Rabelais, I don't know how he does it, but I can't beat them. Why don't you give it a try?"

Mr. Hebert snickered, "That's all you got, you old coot?"

A grin tugged at the corner of Bridgette's mouth. Mr. Daigle began resetting the checkers. "Come on, Father Rabelais, show dis old man what you got?"

Mr. Hebert laughed, "I ain't gonna let you win. You gotta earn it." Taking off his glasses, and wiping the lenses with his shirt, "Besides, all this talk about what happened here makes me motie fou."

Father Rabelais grinned, "It makes us all half crazy. And the uncertainty of who did this, has everyone uneasy."

Chapter 63

Justine Rachel sat in the sparse office of Sheriff Anslum. Her brother, John, stood behind her as they waited patiently for one of the officers to speak.

Justine had been released from the hospital two days ago. Her feet were mending and the bruises were finally starting to fade, but she was still afraid to close her eyes. She watched as Sheriff Anslum shuffled through the papers on his desk. Detectives Boutin and Comeaux were sitting in chairs on either side of her. Sheriff Anslum finally spoke, "I really wish we had more to give you, but so far we don't have much to go on. Whatever evidence the small cabin had in it burned. We are combing the area for clues, but, unfortunately, the guy was smart. He left no evidence behind."

She let out a sigh, "I really wish I could remember something more. I never did get a good look at his face."

Sheriff Anslum informed her, "I want to try a different approach to this. Go back to what you were doing that day. Let's see if that helps jar your memory some. Sometimes it takes just stepping back from the moment to remember some small insignificant detail."

She let out a sigh, "I guess we can try it, but I just don't see how it will help."

"Will you humor me for a little bit? I know it is tiring when we keep going over the same things, but maybe it will help you remember something you forgot. To be honest with you, any information you can give us is greatly appreciated."

Sheriff Anslum omitted to inform her that this person had something far worse than raping her in his plans, the acid filled cisterns were a dead giveaway. With that discovery, he wondered about the missing girls and their fate. There was no way to determine how many bodies had been placed in there. On top of that, he had been smart enough to burn down the place. They had no way of knowing who did this or where he may be. With the cabin burnt down to the ground and his disposal site having been found, there was no telling where he would move to next. He may not even be in the area and moved on to parts unknown. If that were the case, then they may never know who was responsible.

The unknown drove her crazy. She would give anything to remember what happened. "I was leaving Lagniappe to go home. It was later than normal because I stayed late to talk to a friend and we were cutting up."

Detective Boutin asked, "Which friend?"

She looked at the younger detective. She doubted he was even six feet tall. He was not a bad looking man, though. He was almost rugged looking. She wondered if he was from here. He did not have an accent and there was something sexy about his dirty blond hair and deep gray eyes. "Marcus DuPont stopped in for a drink and asked if I was still there. He is getting ready to open another hotel here and wanted to know if I was happy working there or if I would be interested in coming to work for him."

When Detective Comeaux heard her mention Marcus

DuPont's name, his ears perked up. Bridgette Marquette mentioned in passing that she was seeing Marcus DuPont. He had been over there a few nights before, but not that night.

Detective Comeaux asked, "Did Mr. DuPont leave before or after you?"

She thought about it for a moment. "He left before me. After he left, I went to get my purse and keys so I could go home."

"Did you happen to accept his job offer?"

She shook her head, "No, I did not. Mr. Marcel has been too nice to me. I could not leave him to go and work for someone else. Mr. Marcel gave me a chance when no one else would. Besides, I really do love working there. I have been the Chef there for three years. Now that I have made a name for myself and shown everyone my talents, they are interested in me." A look of worry came over her face, "You don't think it could have been Mr. DuPont do you? Was it because I did not accept his job offer?" She shook her head, "But no, that wouldn't make any sense. He did not come on to me. He asked if I was interested in a job with his new business. From what I understood from the conversation, he is in the midst of buying a plantation home around here and turning it into some luxury spa."

Now, Detective Comeaux definitely wanted to talk to Mr. DuPont, "Do you happen to know if he mentioned which plantation he was purchasing?"

She shook her head, "No, he did not say where the spa would be. He just mentioned that the plans were in the works and that he would like to offer me the job before anyone else. Mr. DuPont is a regular here and he did state that he thought I would make a good fit with what he was planning."

She could not believe that Mr. DuPont did this to her. Besides, she had seen him and Ms. Marquette in the restaurant. There were rumors floating around that they may even be an item. No, she could not imagine that he did this to her.

Detective Comeaux needed to talk to Ms. Marquette and see if she planned to sell the plantation to Mr. DuPont. He had not heard any rumors as to that fact, but if the rumors were true about them being a hot item maybe they planned to open something together.

As they were wrapping up the interview, an image flashed in front of Justine's eyes. She stopped dead in her tracks, "Wait. I remember something. I am not sure if what I saw is real or not, but when he put me over his shoulder, I came to for a moment, I believe. His shirt was wet from either the rain or his sweat. I swear I saw an image of a tattoo under the white of his shirt." She took in a deep breath, "Oh no. It could not be though. Marcus DuPont wore a suit, as usual, that night. He had on a white button shirt. It had to be a coincidence though. I don't see him as the type to have a tattoo."

Detective Comeaux needed to find Marcus DuPont and fast. He also needed to find out if Gregory Dawson had been located.

He walked out of Sheriff Anslum's office to call Ms. Marquette, "Ms. Marquette this is Detective Comeaux. Have you heard from Mr. Dawson?"

She informed him, "No, sir. I sure haven't. I packed up his belongings in case he does come back. I am starting to worry that something happened to him."

"We are dragging the bayou again. Search and rescue went over the property several times and haven't found any signs of him."

Bridgette was still disturbed about the fact that they found the cisterns full of acid. She could not accept the fact that someone did this awful thing on her family's plantation. What kind of person even thought like that? The Haz-mat team was still out there emptying the cisterns, as a matter of fact. After they were done with the cleanup, she was having the damn things cemented in. That way, no one would ever be able to use them again.

Detective Comeaux went on to ask, "Ms. Marquette, are you and Mr. DuPont in the middle of negotiations? It has been brought to our attention that he is opening a luxury spa here in the area. He is in the process of purchasing a plantation."

Bridgette felt as if the floor dropped from underneath her, "What? No. He did ask a while back if I would be interested in selling him the plantation, but I said no. As a matter of fact, Mr. Dawson was also interested in buying the plantation."

"Do you know why Mr. Dawson was interested in buying the plantation?"

"He swore it was for personal use, but I honestly don't know. He said that he was interested in finally having a place that he could call home and found the place very relaxing. Whenever he came into town for business, I think he only stayed here."

Detective Comeaux asked, "Do you know what business he did?"

"I think he found oil leases for companies, but I am not sure?"

"It isn't the same oil company that has pressured you to sell is it?"

"No, I don't think so. I will look and see though."

Bridgette did not believe Greg worked for the same company that was pressuring her to sell. That would have stayed with her when he mentioned the company he worked for. The company that had pressured her was out of Dallas, Texas, she believed.

While Bridgette was worried about where Greg Dawson was, she also wondered what Marcus DuPont was up to. He had not mentioned anything about opening up a luxury spa. She had not heard of one around here for sale. Which plantation did he plan on purchasing?

Chapter 64

Justine was having trouble sleeping. She kept going over that night in her mind. Everything was more like smoke and mirrors instead of one clear image. Did she see the outline of a tattoo under his shirt or was it just her imagination? She was in and out of unconsciousness on the trip there. She briefly recalled a boat, but she just could not be sure.

She was grateful the sleeping pills finally started to kick in. Lately, that had been the only way she could sleep. She was in a deep slumber when the images began flashing through her mind. She was running blindly in the dark. She could hear his heavy breathing from behind her. Hands reached out from all over trying to grab her.

She bolted upright in bed. Terror choked her and fear ran like ice water through her veins. Even though she was partially awake, the images still flashed in her mind.

She took in deep, steady breaths in an attempt to calm her nerves. What she would not give for one full night's sleep. The dream was worse tonight than it had been in the past. Maybe she was starting to remember more.

She reached for her robe to snuggle up in. The dream left her feeling cold. She tried to conjure up the image from her dream one more time. She had a feeling it was something important, but it disappeared so quickly. Something nagged at the back of her mind, though. The more she thought about the dream and its ghostly images, the more fear pulled at her mind. Cold seeped deep into her body.

She hated this feeling of the unknown. She was nothing more than an inconsolable child. She had been deathly afraid of the dark since that night. Even in the safety of her house, she was afraid monsters were hiding in the dark, waiting to finish what he started.

After her latest dream, she was afraid to go to sleep. As it tried to take over her body once more, she went into the kitchen to make herself a pot of coffee. Awake she could keep her guard up, but once asleep, the images began their brutal attack on her subconscious.

As the smell of the coffee filled the kitchen, her eyelids grew heavy. She shook her head and poured a cup of coffee. Right now, her life was in limbo. In order for her to keep her sanity, she needed to find a way to move on. Currently, she was lost, confused, and afraid to fall asleep. She hoped the sleeping pills would knock her out so hard that she would be unable to dream. So far, that had not been the case.

Sleep was a nightmare. The images waited for her to fall asleep so they could devour her in fear. She had been a strong woman once, but now she was weak.

She heard her brother walk into the kitchen, "What's wrong?"

Shaking her head, "Nothing. I couldn't sleep."

"You can always come stay with me for a while, I can ask for more time off."

Letting out a sigh, she replied, "No. I need to get on

with my life, and so do you. I should be thankful that I escaped with my life. I just hate the unknown. It's like he still has control over me, even though I escaped."

"What about the dream? Did you remember more?"

"I vaguely remember the dream. The images come and go. Something keeps nagging at the back of my head. I just wish I could remember more."

He reminded her, "The doctors did say that he had used ether to knock you out. You may never remember anything, he wanted you unconscious."

"I know, but I swear I remember him bringing me to the cabin in a boat. I distinctively remember a boat and the water. I remember the rain hitting my face."

"Maybe you should call Detective Boutin and see if there is a chance you were brought to the cabin by a boat."

"I'll do that first thing in the morning. There is no sense waking him up right now. Maybe by then, I can remember what else is bothering me. I don't know what it is, but something tells me it is an important piece of the puzzle."

John came over and gave her a big, brotherly hug. She would miss him when he left today, but they needed to get on with their own lives. She did not like that she let this monster turn her into a quivering mass of tears. It was crushing to be brought this low. She did not like being this vulnerable.

She looked out the kitchen window and stared out into the predawn darkness. Daybreak would soon be here to chase the shadows away. She had enjoyed watching the sunrise, now the darkness scared her. He could be out there, waiting. She was afraid to go out at night. She had been turned into something she always feared, a coward.

She rubbed her hands up and down her arms, trying to warm her chilled body. John was behind her pouring himself a cup of coffee. She felt guilty that he was up so early because of her. With him leaving, she considered having an alarm system installed at her house. It may help bring her some peace of mind.

She could not go through the rest of her life living in fear. She jumped at every little noise, any slight movement in the shadows. She was waiting for him to strike again. She had to snap out of this. She could not let him drive her crazy.

The night was still and quiet. The darkness swallowed him whole. Even the moon and stars must fear him because they hid behind the dark ominous clouds looming overhead.

He patiently watched the house, waiting to make his move. The cops here were imbeciles. They did not even have someone watching over her. All he needed was for her to step outside and he would make his move. If it weren't for the fact that her brother was still with her, he would have made his move already.

How dare she think she could escape from his clutches! After he was done with her, he would deal with Bridgette. She fell for his charm and now it was time to swoop down and save her from the deadly monster that lurked about her property.

Anticipation rushed through his blood when the kitchen light went on. He made his way closer to the house in hopes that she would step outside. This may be his only chance to attack. The darkness hid his movements. Now, he must wait to see if she did indeed step outside.

Chapter 65

Bridgette crossed another name off the guest list and picked up the ringing phone.

"Marquette Plantation.   This is Bridgette speaking. How may I help you?"

"Bridgette, this is Victoria Jackson. Some weeks ago, I made a reservation for Friday night. But after seeing the news, my husband and I have decided to postpone our trip. I hope that's okay."

"I completely understand, Mrs. Jackson."

"Thank you so much."

Before the customer could continue, Bridgette informed her, "I will refund your deposit, in light of everything that has happened. You are more than welcome to reschedule when you feel comfortable. Is that okay?"

"Oh, thank you so much. Are things really as bad as the media makes it sound?"

"It's not as bad as the media is making it out. But, they have no suspects. So, I can understand someone's wariness about staying here."

"When I researched the town, and your plantation, it just seemed such a peaceful place."

"It is very peaceful here, and it is a tragedy that something like that had to happen here. But I am confident that the police will find who did this."

"I sure hope so, more for your safety than anything else. I can't imagine something like that happening in my own backyard."

"It has been a trying past few days, but we will persevere."

"Well, good luck with business. We look forward to staying there eventually."

"Thank you, Mrs. Jackson. We look forward to having you stay with us."

Bridgette hung up the phone, and let out a deep sigh. She hoped guests did not continue to cancel.

The phone rang again. Bridgette took a deep breath and answered. "Marquette Bed-and-Breakfast. This is Bridgette. How may I help you?"

"This is Jessica Landry. My husband and I have been watching the news and noticed what has been happening there. We would like to cancel our reservation for now. Wait until things settle down there."

Bridgette groaned inwardly, "I will refund your deposit. Please know that you can renew your reservation whenever you feel more comfortable. I do understand your worries, and completely understand."

"Thank you so much, I was worried that we may lose the deposit."

"No, I completely understand. I can't fault a customer for not wanting to stay where a tragedy occurred."

"Do they have any suspects yet as to who may have caused the destruction there?"

"The police are only releasing what information they feel is necessary to keep the public safe. It is an ongoing investigation, so, unfortunately, they cannot divulge too much. However, this is a peaceful community, and once the suspect is caught, it will be a great place to visit again."

After Bridgette hung up the landline, her cell phone rang. While she dreaded speaking to another person, perhaps talking to Barbara would help lift her mood. "Hey, Barbie girl, how are you doing today?"

With a high-pitched voice, "How am I doing? How am I doing? Girl, I would be freaking out right now. I had to call as soon as I heard the news, and see how you were doing."

"Oh, I am definitely shaken. But also furious. I cannot believe this is happening here of all places."

"I am scared to death. And, of course, Hal had to leave early. Something about one of his captains needing to take off a week early. I don't know how you can stay out there by yourself, when I am beyond scared to stay here. I don't want the children going outside to play right now."

"Oh, that bites that Hal had to leave early. I can understand you wanting someone there with you at night. It's just so unsettling after all this happened."

Before Bridgette could continue the conversation a blustery wind rushed through the room and started spinning all the papers and items she had on the front desk. It reminded her of a mini tornado, except inside. "Barbara, something came up, I need to go."

"If you need anything, anything at all, give me a call. You are more than welcome to spend the night here. Besides, there is safety in numbers."

"Thank you for the offer, I appreciate it. I'll talk to you later."

Once Bridgette hung up with Barbara, the items spinning in the air came crashing down with a loud clatter. Bridgette was puzzled. What caused the ghosts to get so upset? It was almost as if the mention of Hal's name infuriated them. Which was crazy, wasn't it?

After cleaning up the mess that the ghosts caused, Bridgette went into her bathroom to grab an aspirin. She hoped that the ghosts calmed down and that guests did not continue to cancel their reservations.

From her bedroom window, Bridgette peered outside and took in the peacefulness of the area. She could not let what happened recently defile her feelings for this place.

Bridgette could not sleep once again. She still had not heard from Greg Dawson or even Marcus and she desperately needed Marcus right now. She tried calling him the other night when she found out about the spa he planned to open, but he did not answer nor bother to return her call. Could he be involved? She shook her head. No, she could not picture him doing something this horrible.

She sat on the settee in her room and watched as the stars danced across the night sky. Sleep eluded her once again. She could only imagine what the poor girl must be going through.

She opened her laptop and looked at the monitor. Maybe work would help ease her mind, it would give her something else to think about. As she worked, her eyelids became heavy. She tried to fight the sleep, but her eyelids closed and she drifted off to sleep. In her mind, she was back down by the bayou. All around, there was a heavy mist. Screams mixed with cries of pain. In the darkness of the night, someone called her name. She turned in circles, searching for whoever was calling out to her. A gust of wind blew, sending a chill through her. The warm air around her turned ice cold. The cries and moans became more anguished. All around her were young women, their pale skin almost translucent in the moonlight. They all were pleading and begging for help. She did not know what to do.

The whispers grew quiet and the mist began to

dissolve. What were they trying to tell her? Was there still danger lurking about?   A dark, menacing face appeared before her.   Red eyes glowed through the darkness.

A scream woke her up. She was surprised when she realized that it was her own screaming that pierced the night air. She clamped a hand over her mouth, praying she did not wake any of the other guests. Her eyes darted around the room to make sure there was no one lurking in the shadows.

It was just another nightmare. She stared out into the night. How could something so peaceful hide such evil? Suddenly, the hair rose on the back of her neck as a slight creak was outside the French doors.   Her breath caught in her throat. Was someone really out there? She stepped closer to the door to peer outside. She heard another creak, almost as if it was a footstep on the deck. Someone was definitely out there. She shook her head. It was more than likely the wind blowing one of the rockers.

There was someone out there. A shadow fell across the light glowing outside. It was the silhouette of a man.   She froze in fear when she saw there was something in his hand. She slowly backed away from the door. What should she do? Terror took over her body. She had trouble thinking. Her eyes never left the door as she waited for him to make his move. If she screamed, how long would it be before someone came running? Would they save her?

She hid deeper in the shadows of her room and watched in horror as he stared in. Sheer terror moved through her body. She tried to recognize the silhouette of the man. Who was he? She watched as he grabbed the doorknob and slowly turned it. She tried to move out of the room, but her legs were shaking too badly. She let out a shrill scream. Suddenly footsteps sounded overhead. The shadow by her door disappeared. Whoever had been there was now gone. She picked up the phone and called Detective Boutin to let him know what happened.

She watched in trepidation as once again police walked the perimeter of her property. Damn it, this was her house. Rage coursed through her body. It was barely three o'clock in the morning and she had guests being woken up from their peaceful slumber once again.

As she did previously, she offered those staying at Marquette Plantation Bed & Breakfast a free night. If this kept up, she would have no choice but to close the bed and breakfast part of the plantation. People may want to stay at a haunted inn, but they sure in the hell did not want to stay at an inn that was being stalked by a killer.

Detective Boutin watched her actions closely. Right now, she was sitting on a couch in the parlor and from the way she rubbed her forehead, she probably had one doozy of a headache.

He informed her, "We are fingerprinting the deck out back. Did you get a good look at the intruder?"

She shook her head, "No. I just saw his outline."

"Did you recognize the outline? Did it remind you of someone you may know?"

"No. It was too dark and I was too scared to think clearly."

"The young woman who was abducted remembered seeing a tattoo on her abductor. She believed it was a fairly large tattoo. If she is correct, she believed it started at his shoulder and possibly wrapped down his arm some."

He watched as the color drained from her face. It was a good thing she was sitting down or she would have fallen flat on her face. "I think I know who you are looking for. But it can't be. He would not do anything like that. No, it just isn't him." She kept telling herself repeatedly in her mind that it was not him. The woman was mistaken. She had just dreamed that she saw a tattoo.

Detective Boutin took her hands in his and asked her softly, "Ms. Marquette, who do you believe is the killer?"

Tears streamed down her face. She answered in a barely audible whisper, "Marcus. Marcus DuPont. He has a tattoo of a dragon on his back that wraps around to his biceps. He keeps it covered up. He said that it was a mistake he had made in his youth, but instead of having it removed, he kept it to remind himself of his troubled past and what he has overcome. He said growing up in a family of privilege had its own share of problems. He had problems with drugs when he was younger and became involved with the wrong crowd."

"Ms. Marquette, do you happen to know where Mr. DuPont is?"

She shook her head, "I've been trying to reach him

since all this happened. He has not returned my calls. This whole time I suspected maybe Greg Dawson had something to do with this and now it looks like it could be Marcus."

Bridgette felt as if her whole world was crumbling before her. She slept with the man and was falling in love with him. How could she be such a fool? Where was Greg Dawson? Why had he not come to collect his things? What if Marcus hurt him as well?

She could not stop the tears from flowing. How could this be happening? Would she ever be able to bounce back from this?

Detective Boutin asked her, "Maybe you should consider taking an impromptu vacation until we can arrest Mr. DuPont. Right now, all we have is circumstantial evidence. We just don't have enough to bring him in. Since he has been here in the past, he can easily explain how his fingerprints were outside."

"I refuse to be scared away. I will not run like a coward. What about setting a trap for him?"

Detective Boutin ran his hands through his hair, "That can be very dangerous for those involved."

"Well, if he is after me, then what's to say he won't go after Justine Rachel as well?"

"We have nightly patrols watching over her house, but after tonight's scare, I think it would be safe to say we need to place an officer at each of your houses."

"What if I offer Justine a room and you post an officer here? I will even give up my room for whoever you assign to stay here. That way you can dangle both of us right in front of him."

"I don't know. This will be a very dangerous trap. Besides, how will you inform Mr.   DuPont of your plans?"

"Right now, he doesn't know that I suspect him as the abductor. I can call him all upset and tell him I felt guilty about what happened to Justine. I can let him know that I am going to help her overcome her fears by offering her a room here for a few nights."

She watched as Detective Boutin stared at her intently, "That may work. We have a few female officers that are about your height. I can ask for one of them to volunteer to spend the night in your room and another in a room upstairs. However, if we do this, the two of you have to stay away from the windows. I would prefer if you stay out of sight."

"I have guests to tend to.   But, with all that has happened, there aren't too many." It broke Bridgette's heart that Marcus might be the one guilty of the abduction of Justine and that he possibly burned down the cabin in the back. If it was him, she wanted him stopped. Either way, she needed to put this all behind her and move forward.   She was sure that Justine wanted the same thing.

Detective Boutin asked her one more time, "Are you certain you want to do this? Would you like a few days to think this through?"

"No, I refuse to go into hiding because of this monster. I want him caught before he can do this to someone else. You already believe he may have killed in the past and what if he has? I could not live with the fact that a killer was running loose. Besides, you and I both know he will go after Justine. She is a loose end that he needs to take care of."

Over the next couple of hours, they made plans. Detective Boutin called Justine to let her know about the trap they were laying for the suspect. She was ready to put this behind her and was more than cooperative.

Chapter 66

The monster living inside of him was once again in turmoil. He paced back and forth unsure of what to do next. Neither woman seemed to ever be alone right now. He had hoped people would stay away from Marquette Plantation once Justine Rachel escaped from his clutches. However, instead, business was once again picking up. He tried to scare Bridgette the other night, but that plan failed as well.

It was time to visit Marquette Plantation to see if the rumors were true and they were busier than ever. With Justine staying there, this may be his chance to rid the world of both women once and for all.

Once inside the plantation, he watched from a distance, all the while waiting for the right moment to make his move. He must find out how much Bridgette knew before handling her. The other one he would deal with later, when she least expected it. He glanced into the dining room and noticed how busy it was tonight. Most of the faces, though, seemed to be locals. Perhaps there were not many overnight guests.

He watched as Bridgette flitted around the room, almost nervously. She did not stand still for long at all. Did she suspect what fate had in store for her tonight? What fate was in store for either woman tonight? The two women's destinies were intertwined.

Bridgette would be first. She was the easiest to get alone. Once that happened, he would have to act fast in finishing off the other. The monster raging inside of him must be appeased. It was too bad that Bridgette would have to die though. He had such hopes for the two of them, but she knew too much.

A sigh of contentment moved through him. The time was finally drawing near; the monster inside of him roared to life when he saw her. Soon, he would be sated, but first, he must wait. The smell of her still lingered in his memory. He smirked as he thought of what was about to happen.

He watched as she stopped dead in her tracks and just stared at him. He saw the recognition in her eyes. She remembered completely the power he had over her and what he was capable of.

Chapter 67

The dining room was buzzing with activity. Guests were downstairs eating, but so was half of the town. This was the busiest it had been in a while. Bridgette hoped that this meant business was picking up once again.

Mamie outdid herself tonight; the food was superb and everyone seemed to be enjoying themselves. They even had some soft jazz music playing in the background. Several bottles of wine had already been opened and the atmosphere was relaxing. She wished her nerves were as calm. She could not remember the last time she was so nervous. All they could do was wait to see if Marcus took the bait. It caught her by surprise this afternoon when Greg Dawson checked back into Marquette Plantation Bed & Breakfast. She had been so worried about him and relief washed over her when he walked up to the front desk. He looked extremely handsome in his suit. Where Marcus was more distinguished in his looks, Greg was more rugged, but both men were very good looking. She shook her head. She should not compare Greg to Marcus; each man was their own person. If only things with Marcus had turned out different.

It turned out Greg had an emergency call regarding a business deal and had to rush out. He just now had a chance to return for his items. When he heard about the excitement the other night, he wanted to check on her. Bridgette was so relieved to see him, she immediately gave him a huge kiss.

Glancing over at the bar, she smiled at Greg and waved. She watched as Justine walked into the room. Bridgette knew that the poor woman was nervous as hell about coming back here and was very proud of her. She had shown a lot of bravery in her decision to put this plan in motion. Both women were even wired just in case he made contact with them. So far, Marcus had not shown up or bothered to contact Bridgette. Since he was not answering his cell phone she had to leave a message with his secretary.

She was such a fool. She honestly thought the two of them had something special. Never again would she fall for someone. It would take a while for her broken heart to mend.

The hair on the back of her neck rose as a chill swept over her. Without showing her fear, she looked over the dining room. She did not see anything out of the ordinary, but she could not shake the feeling that someone was watching her intently. She was just being silly. It's most probably her overactive imagination and the fact that her nerves were strung tight tonight.

A movement from the back of the room caught her attention. As Marcus DuPont walked into the dining room from the parlor, she felt the world shift underneath her. She never thought he would just walk into the room.

As soon as Justine walked into the dining room, she felt the floor underneath her shift as her world crumbled. It all came back to her at once. She was walking down the street when she heard someone approach her from behind. She turned around to see who it was when he made his move. It took her by complete surprise.

Whatever he had on the rag took effect fast. The world around her went black. On the trip to the cabin, she was in and out of consciousness. Her world was a blur. She remembered waking up cold and barely clothed, not seeing him anywhere around and managed to escape. She never once thought she would live through the ordeal, but she refused to surrender to that fate and pushed through it. When she saw the plantation house, she knew she was safe. Now, he was in front of her.

The dining room seemed to be frozen in time. Silence was all around her. She tried to open her mouth to warn Bridgette, but she just stood there trembling.

Bridgette watched the scene unfold before her in horror. Justine was completely petrified. Her hands were shaking at her sides. From this distance, she did not look as if she was breathing.

Justine felt the shaking start deep within her and struggled to stay calm. Her stomach started to churn. Tears blurred her vision. Standing right next to Bridgette was the monster. Everything fell seamlessly into place. His image was clear in her mind now. She remembered him placing the rag over her mouth, throwing her on the bed and chasing her. She remembered that night vividly now. She remembered the terror she felt when she woke up restrained to that bed. Reality hit her, this had happened to her and not someone else.

Her mind raced back to that moment when he approached her on the street. He must have thought he was being quiet, but she did hear him. She remembered looking into his eyes and seeing the anger, the pure hatred, he had for her. Now, she had a face to the monster and Bridgette was in extreme danger. She tried to find her voice. She must warn her.

Suddenly, a scream pierced the room. It took her a few moments to realize the sound had come from her. She looked at Bridgette, "Run, you must run. He's right there."

For a moment, Bridgette looked confused and saw Marcus had just stepped into the room. As she looked at him with fear in her eyes, he advanced. She backed right into Greg. When she turned to look at him, her blood turned to ice. Looking into his eyes, she could see pure hatred. His features were contorted into a malicious creature. She heard him talking, but it sounded as if he was far away. What was going on? They knew who the suspect was, it was Marcus. Had she been wrong about him? Was it really Greg Dawson behind it all?

She heard Justine call out to her one more time, "Bridgette you must run. Get away from him." Bridgette watched as Marcus advanced closer. Greg had a tight grip on her and would not let her free. She struggled from his grasp.

Marcus watched in horror as Greg started advancing towards the door, dragging Bridgette with him. He had been out of town handling problems with one of their other properties and was unable to take care of his missing cell phone until he returned. As soon as he heard what happened, he had come to check on Bridgette.

Rage burned through him as the fear registered on Bridgette's face. The thought of what this man had planned nearly stopped his heart. A range of emotions washed over him as he tried to think of a plan to free Bridgette. A movement near the exit caught his eye. Marcus kept his eyes focused on Bridgette, not wanting to give the man a hint of what was about to come.

Greg held the knife at Bridgette's throat. She could feel the tip of the sharp blade sink into her tender flesh. Greg leered at Justine, "You bitch. You ruined everything. Why did you have to escape? I should have killed you and your brother the other night."

Before anyone could react, Greg dragged a kicking and screaming Bridgette outside. As she desperately struggled to free herself from his grasp, she still could not believe he was the one responsible for the deaths of all those poor women.

As the realization that Bridgette was abducted by a maniacal serial killer set in, Marcus became paralyzed with fear. He watched in horror as Bridgette was drug away from him. Until this very moment, he did not realize just how deeply he cared for her. He did not know what he would do without Bridgette. He loved to be around her, the smell of her hair, the feel of her body pressed against his.

Looking around, Detective Boutin pointed up ahead to a slow-moving dark figure. "There they are. I want officers coming in from every direction." The shadow appeared to be having difficulty carrying his hostage through the stalks of cane. He prayed that they made it to Bridgette in time.

Greg knew he had to hurry, it would not take long for the police to come after him. He could hear movement behind him and picked up his pace. His best chance was to lose them in the sugar cane field. He began running in between two sugarcane rows, ignoring the sharp leaves as they cut into his flesh.

He could hear someone catching up to them and continued running through the rows of sugar cane, hoping to lose them in the process. The bayou was not far from where they were at. If he could make it to the small bateau tied off to the pier, he may be able to escape.

Bridgette tried to shield her face from the long blades as they cut into her skin. This was her penance. Guilt consumed her very being for even suspecting that Marcus could somehow be responsible. How could she be so foolish?

"Why? Why are you doing this? Why did you kill those women?"

He glared at her with an intensity that chilled her to the very core. She could see the anger flaring through his eyes. His face contorted, becoming almost monster-like. It was terrifying to watch his temperament switch. Now she knew that pure evil lurked inside of him.

Her gut clenched as a fine mist rose from the water as they made their way to the boat. The dank smell of the bayou permeated her senses. Apprehension grew deep inside of her the closer they got to the water's edge. As much as she feared the water, she was even more terrified about what he may do to her.

Menace dripped from his tongue as he spoke to her, "No one can save you now." As he knelt beside her to restrain her feet, a wry smirk fell on his lips. When he leaned in closer to her, she saw a chance to possibly escape. She pulled her head back and slammed it forward with every ounce she could muster. Blood immediately poured from his nose and he yelped in pain. Even though her head hurt, she kicked him in the gut, and sent him crashing into the water.

Once in the water, skeletal corpses reached out to drag him under. No matter how hard he thrashed about, the corpses continued to dig their skeletal hands deep into his body. They tore into him as he prepared to escape. He was not willing to surrender just yet. He refused to die in this horrific way.

A noise near the bank of the bayou caught his attention. A bull alligator made a low, snorting sound as it glided sinuously down into the water. All that remained of the alligator was his glittering eyes and nostrils as it slowly floated towards the bateau.

A shiver of fear snaked through him. He despised alligators; they were too much like him as they killed without regret and without feeling.

His screams echoed through the night as the alligator started to do a death roll with his body. He could feel the creature sinking its massive teeth deep into his flesh. The alligator would not devour him just yet. Instead, it would wedge him underwater somewhere, such as between a pair of sunken cypress knees, to rot. Alligators preferred to eat their meals after the swamp water had allowed the corpse to bloat, tenderizing it before mealtime.

Bridgette tried to block out Greg's incessant screams as the alligator dragged his body down to the bayou's floor. A shudder racked through her body as the stress of the situation took over her body. Marcus wrapped his arms around her and whispered in her ear, "You are safe now."

Tears began to fall from her face as the guilt took over. She had believed he was guilty. How could she have doubted his innocence? She stuttered, "I-I-I I am so sorry. I should have known you did not do this. Can you ever forgive me?"

"What are you talking about?"

"I've been trying to call you. I've been so worried."

"Someone stole my cell phone right before I left town. I did not have a chance to get another one because I was so busy."

She looked up at him, "Can you ever forgive me?"

He cupped her face with his hands, brushing the tears away with his thumbs, "I am just as guilty as you. I should have called to tell you that I had to leave. I am so used to putting business before anything else. We have both made mistakes. But promise me that you will never, ever doubt my feelings for you again."

He tilted her face up and kissed her deeply. She wrapped her arms around him. As they walked hand in hand to the courtyard, Bridgette watched as Genevieve stepped out from the mist. Marcus squeezed her hand and pulled her back. She whispered to him, "It is okay."

Genevieve spoke, "The girls are at peace. The evil that loomed over the property is gone."

Marcus just stared at the mist. He had to blink several times and rubbed his hands over his eyes, trying to make sense of what he was seeing. He looked over at Bridgette. She had a smile on her face, "Please tell me that you see what I see."

She turned to him and then back to the ghost, "Grand-mere, I would like to introduce you to Marcus. This is the man that I love."

The ghostly image looked over at Marcus and smiled, "Cher, you best take good care of my sha babe."

He stuttered, unsure of what was happening before

him, "Yes ma'am."

As quickly as she appeared in front of them, she disappeared. "I warned you there were ghosts here. It's just up until recently they have been always peaceful. When Greg Dawson started lurking about, the ghosts here became restless. Their peaceful serenity was broken by evil."

He kissed her once more, "I guess I will need to learn how to live with ghosts. They don't just appear at any time do they?"

She shook her head, "I think they will give us our privacy."

She took his hand in hers, "I am so glad you showed up when you did. I've needed you so bad. I think I am falling in love with you."

He bent down and kissed her, "I know I am falling in love with you."

She smiled up at him, grateful that he did not hold it against her that she doubted his innocence.